CIRCLE
of
ASHES

WISH QUARTET BOOK TWO

CIRCLE
of
ASHES

WISH QUARTET BOOK TWO

ELISE KOVA & LYNN LARSH

Silver Wing Press

Published by Silver Wing Press

Cover Artwork by Elise Kova
Editing by Rebecca Faith Editorial

eISBN: 9781619849044
Print ISBN: 9781619849037

for those who pay the cost

CONTENTS

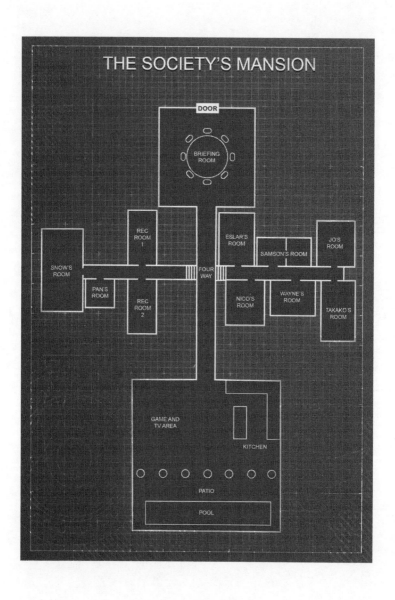

MAP OF NORTH AMERICA (circa 2057)

1. IN A BLINK

JOSEPHINA ESPINOSA THRIVED on chaos.
She had been an agent of anarchy for years, operating under various organized crime syndicates (whoever had the deepest pockets at any given moment) with little concern and even less remorse for her actions. She'd worked until her fingertips were calloused from typing, her eyes were bloodshot, and her throat was raw from energy drinks. Jo had given her life to her craft, quite literally when she'd been gunned down by the Rangers of the Lone Star Republic.

No, she'd watched her *friend* get gunned down by the Rangers. Jo had narrowly escaped thanks to a magical circle meant for casting wishes and the vague memory of her grandmother's stories. It was a circle that she had fully expected to die in, but instead it, and its master Snow, had woken the latent magic in her veins and brought Jo into the Society of Wishes—a place where Jo's life had only grown crazier, granting one wish after the next for four months straight.

Until now. . . when the world was quiet.

She stepped out of the recreation room, pulling her watch off the small shelf next to the door and freeing up the space for someone else in the process. Jo fitted the thin black band around her wrist, the device critical to her new world of magic. A world that was beginning to feel almost. . . mundane?

Jo rubbed her eyes with the heel of her hand and started down the hallway. The lights were dimmed and the windows in the central Four-Way were dark. According to her watch it was somewhere around three a.m. and it felt like there was not another living soul anywhere in the mansion.

Her feet stilled, stopping her in the center of the intersecting halls. Peering down the stretch that led into the common area, Jo caught a glint of movement. It was like a flash of light off a sequin, or ribbon of silken fabric. Curiosity got the better of her.

Tile became carpet down the long stretch of hall, muffling her footsteps. Couches, chairs, and small tables—more than could ever be occupied should every member of the Society decide to descend on them at once—absorbed every sound she made. It was so still that her ears were almost ringing, like the world was holding its breath.

She crossed the threshold into the common room, and looked around. There was no one in the kitchen, at the gaming table, or on the couches. The television was off and the patio was unoccupied.

"Huh," Jo murmured softly to herself, rubbing her eyes again. She must've been staring at the screen for too long.

When Jo lowered her hands, she was no longer alone.

Jo took a full step backward, her soul leaping from her skin and fleeing down the hall from where she'd come. Standing at the edge of the pool, staring at the purple-hazed mountains in the distance, was a petite woman. She wore a dress of rainbow ribbons, tied tightly around her chest and arms, bowed to synch the fabric of her skirt. Her hands were folded at the small of her back.

As if sensing Jo's presence, she turned with a smile. "Good evening."

"Hello Pan," Jo replied quietly. The surreal nature of the interaction had elevated to possess a dream-like quality. Pan was never seen outside of her room, other than for wishes.

"Can't sleep?" she asked.

"None of us can." She hadn't needed sleep since she was indoctrinated into the Society. It became a luxury, not a necessity, and even then usually elusive. "Just grabbing some coffee," Jo lied, suddenly compelled to have a reason to both explain her presence and escape after the task was performed.

"You've been sleeping for a long time, though." The woman-child's cat-like eyes seemed to flash in the darkness. "It's time to wake up."

"What?" Jo breathed.

Pan's smile widened, and she turned back to the mountain.

Without permission, Jo's feet crossed the threshold of the room, leading her out onto the patio by the pool. Pan must've heard her steps, but she didn't turn, or look, or say anything about Jo's sudden presence. She continued to stare forward into the landscape that was shades of darkness—the fake ether that the Society was nestled within.

"Do you feel it?" Pan whispered, ignoring or not hearing Jo's question.

"Feel what?"

"The pull."

"I have no idea what you're talking about." Jo went to turn away, leaving the cryptic (and likely messed up six ways to Sunday) woman-child behind.

"It's coming."

Her feet paused once more and as Jo mentally scolded them, she found herself turning at the same time.

The mountains Pan was staring at were suddenly ablaze, silhouetted by a now violently reddish sky. Jo blinked, and like someone clicking the remote on a channel, they were back to black. She took another step backward.

"Soon," Pan murmured. "It will end, soon."

Jo made the mistake of blinking again.

The woman had turned, grinning like a madman directly at her, an angry sky illuminating her shoulders from behind. Jo pressed her eyes closed, and everything was back to normal once more, Pan's back to her. There was not enough curiosity in the world to tempt her to ask what, exactly, was happening.

So Jo turned, wide-eyed and trembling. She did not blink all the way back to her room, coffee forgotten.

2. NOT A DRILL

WHEN DAWN CAME, it found Jo still staring out the window of her room, overlooking Paris.

When dawn came, it found Jo still staring out the window of her room, overlooking Paris.

She hadn't left for the rest of the night, willing herself to forget, to feel a little stronger and less afraid. That act became easier with the first light. A normal sunrise scared away the demons and bogeymen haunting her thoughts. It seared her eyes and her mind, giving the whole affair a hazy, dream-like quality.

Feeling safer (though she didn't know from what), or at the least much braver, Jo finally ventured from her room. She headed right for a door with a carefully painted bird and a name written in elegant script. Jo gave it a few solid knocks.

"You're early this morning." Nico opened the

door with a smile, wiping his hands on a grungy paint-stained apron.

"Yeah, I had a bit of a weird night."

"Come in and tell me about it? I'll only be a minute more." Nico stepped away from the door, leaving it open.

Jo did as asked, closing the door behind her and leaning against it. Nico paused his motions over by his easel, raising his eyebrows questioningly at her unorthodox behavior. "I ran into Pan."

Four words, and she suddenly felt very silly. Pan was a fellow member of the Society, an odd one certainly, but hardly an unknown quantity.

"That is odd," Nico agreed. "It's not like her to be out of her room without a wish."

"That's what I thought." Jo shrugged.

"Is that all?"

Jo paused, chewing on her tongue a moment. It wasn't all, *was it?* She'd spent all night willing the interaction to go away, and now it suddenly felt distant, like a dream she'd forgotten, remembered, and was already forgetting again.

"She said something weird, too."

"What?"

"I—" if her mind was a car, it would've just stalled out. Everything stopped, sputtering. Jo just shrugged, trying to play it off more casually than she felt. "Can't remember. I was up working and mentally spent at that point."

"Knowing Pan," Nico made for the door, "she was doing it with the intention of being strange." He clasped a hand over Jo's shoulder. It was a sturdy support that pushed her feet into the earth and reminded her she was on stable ground. "I wouldn't pay it any mind."

"You're right." Jo forced a laugh. "Not like I want to give her the satisfaction of taking me off my game."

"There's the Josephina I know."

They made their way directly to the common area to begin their morning ritual. From underneath the TV, Jo retrieved two tablets and, at the same time, Nico busied himself in the kitchen. She turned for the two chairs they had pulled together by the pool, and stalled.

There had been more, her mind insisted. Jo stared, transfixed by the mountains in the distance, as though she expected a monster to suddenly grasp their peaks with its giant claws and hoist itself over.

"Jo?" Nico's voice interrupted her thoughts.

Jo shook her head. "Sorry."

"Are you sure you're all right?" he asked as she approached.

"I'll be better with coffee. Nothing a hot cup can't fix." Jo smiled and handed him one of the two tablets. "For you."

"Thank you." He propped it against his knees as Jo sat on the chair next to his, placing hers on her own lap. The Italian man finished situated himself, taking a long sip of his espresso, eyes fluttering shut. "It is truly a delight to have someone to share the mornings with."

"Honestly, I still have a hard time believing you've converted me into any kind of morning person."

"What is morning? What is night?" It wasn't the first time he'd wondered as much, and Jo only hummed in response. When one existed beyond time, the hours ticking away on a clock became more guidelines than actual governances over life.

"Oh, look at this." Nico held up his tablet. A sketch glowed back at her in the dim sunrise. She squinted to make out the text below the picture:

Rare Da'Vinci Artwork Discovered. On exhibit, one week only.

"The man was a right loon." Nico pulled the tablet back. "But it's good to see his work still being appreciated so long after."

"You knew him?" Jo didn't know why the fact surprised her. Even though Nico was a ray of sunshine in the form of a forever-nineteen-year-old man, he was actually more than five-hundred and seventy years old. "Of course you knew him," she added hastily.

"Not 'of course'; he had a different patron than I and was already an old man when I was born."

The question of who exactly that patron was, or when exactly he was born, sat heavily on her tongue, until Jo washed it away with another sip of her latte. There were two rules, sort of, when it came to the Society:

One: Use your magic to help grant wishes.

Two: Ask no one about the wish that brought them there.

She looked up from the news sprawled out across her tablet, and out at the mountains in the distance. They reflected in the stillness of the pool water before her, perfectly mirror-like and undisturbed, not even a hint of wind to mar its surface. The temperature was comfortably cool as well, as it always was, and the sun peeked from behind scattered clouds, as it always did.

It was a paradise that sat just outside of reality, a utopia in which nothing changed. It was peaceful, quiet, and all the more maddening for it. She found herself liking those mountains and their perfection less and less.

"How're things in good old Britain?" Nico pulled Jo from her thoughts.

"All seems the same." Jo continued her welcome distraction of swiping through the morning's news— "research," as Nico had explained it. They never knew where a wish would come from, but keeping up with world news could give them a good indication. Additionally, it could sometimes help them think of creative ways to lessen the Severity of Exchange for the wishes that did come in by looking at things on the macro level. "Something to do with trade treaties."

"Still?" Nico leaned over, grabbing the side of the chaise closest to Jo. His eyes skimmed the article. "Well, at least we likely won't get another wish about it."

"Why not?"

"Because of the last wish."

Their last wish had involved taking down the CEO of a British competitor to the wisher. "Why would that have anything to do with it?"

"We never seem to get a wish too similar in scope or region back-to-back. Snow's choice? Chance? Something in the magic? Whatever the reason, it has always worked out that way." Nico shrugged and tossed some of his scraggly brown hair from his eyes. As if sensing her next question before she did, he added, "As to the actual *why* it's that way, none of us have the foggiest."

"I see. . ." Jo flicked away her frustrations by thumbing through news articles. She hated the reasoning: *because magic*. It was an underlying explanation to all things in her world now. As exciting as magic was, she wished she could understand it just a little more. Or she wished she could be like everyone else and just accept it for what it was and move on.

"The variety does help keep things interesting, at least," Nico offered.

"It does." Jo forced a smile. He was trying to cheer her up; she wouldn't make him feel bad for the fact.

A loud ringing sound disturbed what had become an otherwise peaceful morning.

"What's that?" Nico twisted, looking over the back of his chair and into the common area behind them.

Jo followed his gaze, squinting at the source of the sound. Their dark-haired elf now sat on the couch, glued to the television. He seemed not to notice the high-pitched alert the speakers were emitting.

"Can you kindly turn that down, Eslar?" Nico asked.

There was no reply.

"Wait, I know that noise. Well, sort of." Jo stood, leaving the tablet on her seat. "It's like the warning they'd play when there was a tornado in the area, or ran drills for one."

"A tornado?" Nico followed behind, now giving the anomaly his full attention.

She walked up the few steps and into the shade of the common area. The tile was cold under her feet, still almost icy with the chill from the night. But Jo barely recognized it. Her eyes were glued to the TV.

I've seen this before, she wanted to say. But what escaped her mouth was different entirely. "Wh-what movie is this?" She laughed, a sort of forced, strangled sound.

Eslar made no move to respond.

Jo watched as the TV continued to scroll the announcement across the bottom of the screen in Japanese, her eyes translating instantly by magic:

MT. FUJI ERUPTS. UNPRECEDENTED CATASTROPHE. DEATH TOLL UNKNOWN.

The screen filled with apocalyptic imagery alternating between news casters standing at a distance, smoke and darkness shrouding them, and social media videos posted by cell phones, most of which ending all too abruptly. Ash spewed from the earth and blacked out the sky, a stark contrast to the bright, peaceful morning where Jo currently stood.

It was worse than any horror movie she'd ever seen.

"Eslar." Nico walked over and placed a hand on the elf's shoulder, summoning him back to attention. "What is this?"

"The news."

3. SHATTERED

THE PHRASE "LIKE a train wreck" was one that Jo had heard used multiple times throughout her nineteen years of life, sometimes in all honesty, sometimes in hyperbole. Never before had she truly understood what that felt like, but it was undeniable now.

No matter how difficult the destruction was to watch, she couldn't seem to tear her eyes away from the screen.

"Is this live?" Jo asked, hardly above a whisper. Her voice sounded small and scared, barely even her own. Part of her already knew the answer. Eslar nodded, a single jerk of his head, as his brows furrowed.

"As of fifteen minutes ago."

"Shit. . ." Jo breathed, raising a shaking hand to cover her mouth, hiding her trembling lips. It didn't seem possible. Surely it couldn't be.

But there it was, right in front of her. A live broadcast interspersed with videos from hours ago, minutes ago, all highlighting the devastation.

Without really making the conscious decision to do so, Jo found herself dragging her feet around the edge of the couch, sitting down heavily to Eslar's right. Her hand never left her mouth, as if holding in the silent scream ringing in her ears.

"This isn't good," Nico said, mostly to himself it seemed, and when Jo managed to pry her eyes from the screen for a moment, she noticed his fingers digging hard into the back of the couch, knuckles stark white beneath his skin.

Of course it isn't, Jo wanted to say, wanted to *shout*, but she couldn't seem to formulate the outburst. Instead, she just turned back towards the broadcast and absorbed everything she could, hoping that eventually it would somehow stop being real.

". . .no way of anticipating the disaster," a reporter was in the process of saying. "Seismographs and supercomputers proved ineffective as the warning reached Prime Minister Tomo Nakamura barely two hours before the eruption. With no proper notice, and with transportation systems indefinitely grounded, evacuations are currently impossible and first responders are left waiting for the worst of the ash and lava flows to pass.

"Of the two million people within the surrounding cities of the Hakone region, already thirteen thousand have been proclaimed dead. The number is expected to rise as relief efforts are projected to begin in the outer, safest areas in two days."

Thirteen thousand dead, at least, in fifteen minutes.

With a jolt, Jo pulled the sleeve of her hoodie back and ran her finger along the fabric of her watch. Another ten minutes had passed since the three of them had started watching. How many more were already gone? How many more were waiting in hell for help that would never come and death that was taking far too long?

Jo looked from Nico to Eslar and back. Both men had their attention all but glued to the screen, Nico with noticeable tears in his eyes and Eslar with an expression on his face frozen somewhere between blank and tired. She wasn't looking for comfort. *She wasn't,* Jo insisted to herself. But suddenly, she couldn't help but feel cold and shaky, possibly even frightened. To call what she was witnessing "horrible" wasn't near potent enough. Jo was pretty sure that the more she watched, the more likely she was to throw up.

"You cats watching an action flick?" Wayne suddenly appeared in the entryway to the common room, Jo's back stiffening in surprise as she turned toward him. She caught the brief look of casual amusement on his face before he seemed to notice whatever emotion was betrayed by hers. "Everyone alright?" he asked, posture more on edge and voice more hesitant now. Before Jo could stop herself, she felt her expression crumple further, a hand reaching in his direction.

"Wayne?" she sniffed, and he was at her side in a second, grabbing her hand in a reassuring grip. His weight sank into the couch cushions next to her, a steady rock that she fell into willingly. It was physically closer than they'd been in months, but she needed him right now. He was the most familiar warmth in all of the Society.

"What's happening?" he asked the rest of the room, with a seriousness Jo would have scoffed at were it not for the situation. Instead, she just focused on the feel of his thumb tracing the length of her knuckles in a rhythm meant to be comforting—even if it wasn't quite. There was no comfort against something so inconceivably horrible.

"Mt. Fuji has erupted," Eslar replied without preamble, seemingly coming back to himself. "Thousands have already perished."

"Shit," Wayne cursed under his breath. Perhaps it was hysterics, but Jo felt a choked and bitter laugh crawl its way up her throat.

"That's what I said." She *thought* that was what she said, at least. Everything suddenly felt hazy and distant—like déjà vu, though she was certain she'd never witnessed something so terrible. In fact, Jo could've been blubbering this whole time and not realized it, and it wouldn't have surprised her.

Wayne squeezed her hand again and the room fell silent as they listened to the various reports, some of them recordings, some of them live. It wasn't until they'd seen the same report from earlier re-air that Wayne huffed a harsh breath through his nose, breaking the tension.

"So," he sighed, finally letting go of Jo's hand. He leaned back against the couch cushions, arms stretching along the back behind Jo's shoulders as if the furniture was the only thing propping him up. "Who's going to tell Takako?"

And, because even this alternate universe seemed just as willing to kick its immortal patrons in the ass as the real world had ever been, Takako chose that exact moment to walk into the common room.

"Tell me what?" Before anyone could say anything, the woman's eyes were drawn from her team to the television. Jo watched as a sort of quiet horror overtook Takako's face. It was only seconds later that Jo witnessed a person shatter.

4. STAND DOWN, SOLDIER

"TAKAKO, WAIT!"

JO wasn't sure exactly what she would say if the woman chose to listen to her plea and stop, but she still kept her pace behind her. In fact, the entire group from the common room had followed Takako into the hall the moment she'd turned on her heel.

In the end, Wayne had been the one to tell Takako what they knew about the destruction currently ravaging her home country. And, while Jo had anticipated a more emotional response, the way Takako had nearly sprinted in the direction of the briefing room hadn't exactly been unexpected.

Jo had done the same thing once, when she'd first woken in the Society. When she'd been desperate for escape and would have given anything to return home. Takako's desperation to affirm her perceived reality stemmed from a different source, but Jo recognized it all the same.

"There's nothing you can do, Takako," Eslar called uselessly from the back of the group. Takako seemed oblivious to the comment, possibly ignoring it. But if the expression on her face was anything to go by, she was lost in her own head. Even with a persistent pace, Jo felt like she was left frantically trying to keep up.

Luckily, Wayne seemed to have a longer stride than hers, quickly pulling himself around the group and in front of Takako. About a foot away from the front of the closed briefing room door, Wayne planted a hand into the hard line of Takako's shoulder, forcing her to come to a sudden stop.

"What are you going to do?" he demanded, pushing hard enough that the woman had to take a step back for balance. Wayne looked almost unnaturally serious. "What *can* you do? Shoot the mountain?"

"Get out of my way," Takako bit back, slapping Wayne's hand away and attempting to walk around him. Wayne easily blocked her path.

"You're being a dumbass," Wayne huffed, standing his ground.

It seemed weird to hear Wayne curse, opting for something biting and incredibly modern instead of his usual colloquialisms. It made the tension thicker somehow, and as the two faced off, the rest of the group gathered behind them, waiting to see who would end the stalemate first.

For a moment, it looked like Wayne would win, but something in their silent exchange must have chipped away at his resolve. Jo couldn't see Takako's face from where she stood, but she could see Wayne's, and as if a telepathic conversation had taken place, she watched the man's expression fall and a sigh escape the downturned line of his lips.

Then, to everyone's surprise, Wayne stepped aside, allowing Takako to wrench open the door and hurry into the briefing room. It was a move brought to an almost instantaneous halt, however, Takako's form pausing barely a foot inside as Jo and the three men filed in around her.

Seated at the head of the table, as if he'd been waiting for them to arrive, was Snow.

Jo was momentarily stunned, reminded instantly of how long it had been since she'd seen him: at the end of their last wish a few weeks ago. But her last real interaction was when he had taken her through the Door, a night she might never forget. Both compounded together pulled forward lingering questions, and now certainly wasn't the time to ask. Why had he shown her his magic? And what had he meant when he'd said "the truth about hers"?

He looked as ethereal as always, silver hair falling like moonlight over one of his eyes as he stared Takako down. It was neither the time nor place to be admiring Snow's beauty, but Jo felt suddenly awkward in his presence. It was like being back in high school around Yuusuke for the first time—before they'd established themselves as purely just friends—but so much worse.

Another string of wordless dialogue later, Takako tensed without warning, startling Jo out of the distraction that always seemed to overcome her around Snow. When she redirected her full attention to the situation at hand, it was to find Takako glaring at Snow, poised and strung tight as if in anticipation of an attack.

"Let me out, Snow," she said suddenly, voice low and harsh, practically a growl. Snow seemed unfazed.

"No," he replied simply, getting to his feet with a casual air that didn't fit with the strained and restless atmosphere at all. "There is nothing that can be done now and none of you should risk being tempted to spend your extra time unnecessarily."

"I have to help them," Takako grit out, hands tightening into fists at her side. Jo felt the pain in the woman's voice tug on her own heart. "I have to save them. That's what we do, isn't it? Save people?"

"Sometimes," Snow admitted, and Jo could practically taste the bitterness on the back of her tongue from everything left unsaid. Sure, *sometimes* they saved people, but sometimes they didn't. It depended on the wish. And even though Takako must have known that, Jo also had little doubt that, for Takako, making any desperate attempt to help her kin was the only conceivable action.

"Then let me go to them," Takako tried again, not pleading, not demanding, but hopelessly lost somewhere between.

"No," Snow repeated, holding his ground with an intimidating authority. If Jo didn't know any better, she'd say the temperature in the room had dropped, a crackling energy shifting between the two like a magical standoff. Then, Snow added, "It will be torture for you to see them and be unable to help."

"I won't ask you again, Snow," Takako said, tone hard. "Let me out."

Snow stayed silent, but his answer was clear. He would not move.

Unfortunately, Takako's response was clear as well. Suddenly, almost too quickly for Jo to see the transition, Takako was pulling a gun from the holster at her hip and pointing it in Snow's direction.

Jo was too stunned to do much more than gasp, but at least one or two of the men behind her shouted Takako's name, demanded she lower her weapon, even moved to act. To which Snow merely held up a hand in their direction, keeping them from interfering.

To his credit, Snow seemed completely calm in the face of Takako's assault, eerily so. In fact, he looked as though he were about to have a normal conversation with the Japanese woman, as if she wasn't currently pointing a gun right between his eyes.

"Get out of my way," Takako demanded, thumb reaching over to unclick the safety. In the near-oppressive silence of the briefing room, with nothing but their breaths playing shaky accompaniment, that single click was deafening. "You know I won't miss."

Jo wasn't even sure if Snow could be killed by a bullet; she didn't know if he could be killed at all, if any of them could be anymore. What did immortal spirits have to fear from death? But in that moment, all that mattered was that Takako believed in her threat and, as she took aim, it was obvious she intended to test that theory.

Before she could pull the trigger, however, Snow took a step away from the table, gathered his height, and stared down the nozzle of the gun. He took another step forward and Takako's steady hold on the gun began to waver. Snow reached out, grabbing the muzzle in a display of both confidence and fearlessness.

"Stand down, soldier," he said, almost gently. "This is a battle with no winner."

For a second, Takako didn't respond, gun still poised to fire. Jo held her breath, the whole room seemingly waiting at the edge of a proverbial cliff, wondering if they were going to fall off completely or simply stumble away from the ledge.

Then, as if a switch had flipped, Jo watched the tightness of Takako's back loosen, the straight line of her arms sag a bit at the elbows. Without a word, she re-engaged the safety on her gun, pulled it from Snow's grasp, and returned it to its holster.

"My apologies," she said, bending forward into a deep and rigid-looking bow. When she raised herself back up and turned towards the group, it was without an ounce of expression on her face.

They didn't even need to be asked; Eslar and Wayne stepped to one side and Jo and Nico to the other, letting Takako pass. She did so without a word, movements borderline mechanical.

It wasn't until Takako had disappeared from sight that Jo felt she could breathe again, and even when she did, her inhale was shaky, scraping at the back of her throat and burning deep into her chest. Takako's words still rang in her ears.

That's what we do, isn't it? Save people?

How were they supposed to do that when their hands were shackled by wishes that weren't even their own?

5. MUGICHA

SNOW ROUNDED THE table and started for the door, pausing briefly to utter a command directly to Eslar: "Look after her."

Jo kept her eyes pinned to the Door on the opposite side of the room. The steel was as cold and inflexible as Snow's words; neither had any heart. She clenched her fists, feeling like she was made of fire in a room that was now colder than ice.

"Understood," Jo heard Eslar say, though it sounded like he was now on some distant planet far, far away from where she stood.

She listened to Snow's footsteps as they left: boots clicking on the obsidian floor of the briefing room, muffled weight on the carpet of the hall, and eventually, nothing at all. Even if she could understand him, even if she *wanted* to understand him, she couldn't. What Snow had done had been in Takako's best interest, hadn't it?

Yet if that were true, why did it feel so heartless?

Jo still couldn't erase the anger she felt at the nearly militaristic way it had all been handled. People were dying—no, more than that; Takako hadn't joined the Society that long ago, which meant her *family* was likely dying. If there was any time for compassion in their operation, it was now. Yet all their leader seemed to give them was the bitter reminder that they were nothing more than slaves to the circumstances of their existence. Would it have really done so much damage to let her go through the Door?

A hand fell on Jo's shoulder, jolting her back from her thoughts.

"Coming?" She could tell Wayne was repeating himself, though how many times he'd addressed her was a total mystery.

"Where?"

"We're going back to watch the news," Nico said softly.

"No." Jo swallowed back the bile that rose up in her throat at the mere idea of sitting there again and watching the carnage. Turning her eyes away wasn't going to help, but neither was watching it. She was useless to everyone if she let her sanity crack now.

Out of the millions who needed it, there was only one person Jo could help right now. It was almost nothing, in the grand scope. But at least helping *someone* was *something*.

"You guys go on ahead," she encouraged.

"I don't want to leave you alone." Wayne, well meaning and thick-headed as always.

"I'm not going to be alone," Jo corrected him.

"Then who—"

"We'll leave you to it," Eslar interrupted Wayne. "Thank you for looking after her."

Someone has to, Jo thought bitterly. It seemed no one else was clamoring to rise to the task. "No problem."

Jo followed the three men back through the hall and to the Four-Way.

"Let me know if you need anything." Nico pulled her in for a tight hug, one Jo was eager to return. He was calm, calm enough to remind Jo that this was far from the first massive tragedy he'd ever witnessed. She wondered if she could be like him someday, taking turmoil in her stride, smiling all the same. It seemed an impossibly hard thing to do. The only thing that could be harder was the idea of doing it again, and again, and again.

Jo pulled away and assessed the man with the sunshine smile. He'd been born during the Renaissance, was old enough to have seen dozens of wars, immeasurable horrors, and he could still smile as genuinely as he did. She didn't know if it was admirable or terrifying. In what way did a heart have to contort to be able to do that?

"Will do." Jo dismissed him and her thoughts before they could linger in a place that was far too negative. This team was all she had; she couldn't allow suspicions to form surrounding someone's goodness. It was just the shock and hurt talking, she knew.

She turned right, heading up the stairs toward the recreation rooms. There was no sign of Snow in the hallway, even if she squinted all the way to the very end. Jo wasn't sure if his absence was relieving or disappointing. It was likely for the best, either way. She was emotionally off-balance, somewhat upset with the man's actions (even if she didn't really have any right to be), and not in the best headspace to exchange words.

Much to her surprise, and despite Takako's much earlier comments about what she did when she needed to "clear her head," both recreation rooms were void of watches—no sign of Takako at either.

That left one other option.

Jo headed in the opposite direction, back toward the Four-Way, up the other set of stairs, and toward her own room. However, instead of turning left at the end of the hall, she turned right and was faced with the nameplate that greeted her every morning: *Takako*. Taking a deep breath, Jo gave a gentle knock on the door.

Several seconds passed and wore at her resolve. There was no word, no response. She should leave the woman be.

But something wouldn't let her.

"Takako," Jo said softly, knocking again. "I know you're in there." She didn't, actually. But she couldn't imagine where else her friend would be. They didn't have *that* many options for privacy in the Society. "Please, open the door?"

Just as Jo had committed herself to sitting on the floor and waiting in the hall until Takako was ready to let someone in, the door finally cracked open. Takako stood rigid, half her body still hidden on the other side.

"Yes?"

"May I come in?" Jo asked, wishing it sounded stronger. She wasn't going to take no for an answer, yet wanted to let it be Takako's choice.

"Why?" The woman questioning her was nothing like the Takako Jo knew. She'd burrowed deep into this shell of curt responses. Not that Jo could blame her.

"Because I don't think you should be alone." Being honest came easier than she expected it to, and it seemed to startle the woman. Seeing her hesitation, Jo doubled down. "We don't have to talk. I can just, be there. . ."

As if merely being there could ever be enough, she mentally chided herself. But to her surprise, Takako stepped back and allowed the door to swing open wide enough for Jo to enter. She stepped in quickly.

She'd seen rooms like this in pamphlets for Japanese resorts, nice hotels, even in one of her former employer's homes. It was an open space, with ten woven grass mats making up the floor. Wooden beams supported cream-colored, sand-paper-textured walls on three sides. The fourth side had *shoji*—wood and paper—screens pulled open to a wooden platform that overlooked a small garden space. A pastel sunset glowed behind purple mountains.

It was the epitome of Japanese architecture. Yuusuke would've been proud of Jo for just how much of her Japanese she could recall without the use of magic: a *horigotatsu* in the center of the room, a *tokonoma* with a scroll displaying calligraphy, an oversized closet where Jo fully expected to find *futon* tucked away. Yet, as picture-perfect as it all was, it still felt lived in. There were little accents here and there displayed above the rest, placing personalization before the picturesque, and making it feel like a home.

Takako busied herself at an electric kettle. Her movements were measured and precise as she filled up two small cups and put them on a tray with Japanese rice crackers between them. Jo left her to it, stepping onto the wooden platform just beyond the *shoji* and taking a seat.

There was a crash and an expletive from behind her that had Jo turning.

"Are you—"

"I'm fine," Takako snapped. "I just. . . I'm fine." she said much softer, in that same barely-controlled way as she cleaned up the mess of tea that had just spilled across her small counter. Jo knew it was much the opposite, but said nothing as Takako lifted the tray, setting it between them. "The tea isn't much."

"*Mugicha* makes me think of home."

"Of home?" Takako said, startled. "I would've never imagined we would share a similarity on this."

"Why not?" Jo couldn't help but laugh at her ever-mechanical nature.

"Because you're from America."

"Lone Star Republic, technically," Jo gently corrected. She didn't have enough nationalistic pride to take offense. Especially since Takako had never actually lived in a time where the LSR existed.

"Right. . ." Takako shifted her cup from hand to hand. "Still can't imagine there's a big drive for *mugicha* in Texas."

"Well, yeah, fair. . . but plenty of people emigrate from East Japan." Jo looked down at the tray, selecting the cup closest to her. She wished she hadn't brought up the discussion of home, but it was far better for her to distract Takako with her own home than let the Japanese woman think of hers. So, Jo rambled away. "My friend, Yuusuke. You remember him I'm sure with the whole first wish debacle?" Jo cringed slightly. "His father immigrated to the Lone Star Republic for work from the California prefecture. That's how we met in high school."

"East Japan. . . " Takako said slowly, as if hearing it for the first time.

"Well, yeah. . ." Jo thought back, she didn't have to go very far. World War III hadn't ended all that long ago. And it wasn't like the details were very important. "I mean, technically, I think it's all 'Japan,' but everyone calls the annexation of what was California, Washington, Oregon, and Nevada 'East Japan.'" Jo took a long sip of tea. It was nostalgia in a cup. She and Yuusuke had let go of it long ago in favor of things with enough caffeine to kill a small animal. But it was the same rich, earthy taste she remembered from when they'd first become friends.

Despite herself, she wondered how he was doing now, *what* he was doing now. She shouldn't still care, but she hoped he was safe. And perhaps it was that hope against hope that had Jo sitting where she was now, understanding all too well what Takako was feeling—worry for people she should've let go long ago.

Takako was silent, a frown passing over her face.

Jo shifted to face the woman. "I'm sorry, I shouldn't have brought up Japan." How stupid could she really be?

"It's not that." Takako shook her head.

"Then. . ." Jo let the word trail off into an open-ended question. She wasn't sure if it was safe to ask anything. There were memories they all had of their past lives that were better left forgotten.

The other woman took a deep, slow breath—in through the nose and out through the mouth, as if bracing. "My wish."

"Your wish? What does your wish have to do with anything?" Jo brought up a hand to her mouth, having startled herself. Here she was, having just scolded herself for prodding Takako, and now she'd asked the one probing question the Society considered taboo. "Sorry, I shouldn't have—"

"It's fine." Takako shook her head. "I've been meaning to tell you, to seek your forgiveness."

"Forgiveness for what?" Jo had come to console *her*, and now Takako was trying to turn the tide. But Jo wasn't going to allow it. Or at least, she thought she wasn't, but her mind went a bit blank the moment Takako opened her mouth again.

"I destroyed your country."

6. TAKAKO'S WISH

"YOU... WHAT?"

FOR a long moment, Takako didn't elaborate. She simply reached for her own cup of tea and stared deep into the depths of it, face lined with too many conflicted emotions for Jo to count. Then, as if finally finding her resolve, she set it back down with a heavy *thud*.

"I admit, when you joined the Society and I realized you were American—or, from what had been America at least, I felt... a bit guilty," Takako explained, not that it made her previous confession any less nonsensical. "I guess you could say I took your country away from you. I destroyed what could have been, so to speak."

"What are you talking about?" Jo tried to smile, but it felt a bit disjointed, her confusion overwhelming her features. Took away her country? How? She'd lived in it for nineteen years.

Whether in attempts to explain, or simply to get the words out, Takako ignored her question for a moment, shaking her head. "I must have seemed standoffish at first, and for that I apologize, but I simply didn't know what to say, not knowing what I know. But I still wanted you to feel welcome. And, I suppose, I wanted to make it up to you somehow. Everyone else was so much better at it than I. . . But I guess they've had more practice."

The gifts, the kindness. That had been Takako's attempt at assuaging guilt?

Jo frowned, looking from Takako's face to her own cup. Despite the comfortably warm feel of the ceramic beneath her fingers, the tea still steamed, as if the cup should be much hotter to her touch. Jo wondered if it should be burning her, if it actually was, and the day had merely numbed all senses.

"I don't. . ." Jo shook her head, confused. She wanted to understand what Takako was saying, but she didn't know how to ask for clarification. She didn't doubt the genuineness of Takako's kindness, regardless of the underlying intention, but her reasoning still felt beyond Jo's reach. Her country had been just fine, hadn't it? The Lone Star Republic continued on throught Jo's short lifetime as it had always done. Not that she paid much attention to politics beyond her connections with the nation's dark underbelly. What wish could Takako possibly have made?

Jo's frustration must have become obvious, because eventually, Takako sighed, raking her hands through her hair and tugging on it.

"In 2010, our countries were at war," she began, and when Jo met her gaze, there was a despondency there that she was unfamiliar with when it came to the kind, but stoic, woman.

Jo remembered reading about World War III. History wasn't exactly her favorite subject, but the war had only ended in 2015, just forty-two years before Jo joined the Society (a narrow enough piece of time that the veterans never let anyone forget), so it was hard *not* to know about the war. A rising tide of nationalism had pulled the former United States in on itself, retreating from its allies and making stronger enemies of old nemeses that ultimately formed the "Commonwealth Powers."

"The war started in 2007, right?" Jo asked, more for her own confirmation, whilst trying to remember exactly when Takako said she'd been born.

Takako nodded. "It did. Japan was emboldened when the U.S. lent its support toward militarization—the de facto 'Warden of the East.' It was a potent blend with the determined drive forward on building the nation as a military power."

"And then there was the China-Japan war."

"In which, the use of Japanese force had the U.S.A. positioning itself against my country, and Japan siding with Russia." The way she spoke was clinical, void of emotion or any real investment. Takako spoke like she was the one reading a textbook, espousing facts and nothing more. Until her voice began to waver. "I. . . I was a soldier, and I was afraid." Her hand balled into a fist; Takako hung her head.

Suddenly, the woman's skill with a gun made a lot more sense. Jo reached out, taking her hand, and startling Takako into meeting her gaze. "That's okay. I can't imagine how terrifying it was. . ." She had never seen war. When Jo had grown up, the world was at peace. Well, minus the odd squabbles in North America's Midwest, where no one could seem to decide what was a territory of what, who ruled themselves, and which regions were allied.

"You don't understand. I thought—that is to say, there were rumors. . . That the U.S. would unleash biological warfare."

Jo didn't remember reading anything about that, one way or another. So she kept her mouth shut and just listened.

"That was when I made my wish."

In the silence that followed the barely-there confession, Jo found herself mulling over Takako's words. It had been long enough since Jo'd taken her last sip that her tea should have gotten cold. Instead, it was still the perfect temperature. She gave thanks to the small comforts magic could give.

"Japan was losing—or you thought Japan would lose—in your timeline, so you wished for Japan to win the war. And that's the world I was born into," Jo clarified, thinking of the odd events leading up to the Commonwealth Powers' victory: a series of tactical errors, miscommunications and weather phenomena that resulted in the USA's western fleet being condensed and subsequently decimated. That was followed almost immediately by a decisive and unforeseen strike on the eastern seaboard, which resulted in enemy boots on the ground.

It was too many unfortunate events to happen merely by chance. Takako nodded, as if reading her mind.

"I don't quite remember what I said to Snow anymore." Takako paused before Snow's name, grinding it out. "My memory of making the wish is hazy, like trying to remember a dream, but I do know that I'd been thinking about my family. My mother and father, my sister. I wanted them to be safe. At the time, winning the war seemed like the only way to ensure that, and I was willing to do anything if it meant securing their safety. My family—" Takako paused, taking a deep breath she let out on another rough sigh. "My family is everything I have, even if they no longer remember who I am." She buried her head in her hands. "It's not fair, none of it."

Instantly, with those words, Jo was brought back to the present.

She had never related more fiercely to another's sentiment. Her mother's blood still flowed through Jo's veins, even if memories of Jo no longer flowed through her head. As one-sided as those memories were now, Jo would treasure them for a literal eternity. Even Lydia, a sibling Jo never had the opportunity to know and born in a timeline where she'd never lived, now held a small place in her heart—a sense of gratitude that her mother was not spending her life without the companionship of a daughter.

Takako held a similar, undying love for her family. And right now, though Jo did not know for sure, she would bet that they were currently in the path of Mt. Fuji's fury. And Snow refused to let Takako even attempt to save them.

Another flash of anger sparked in Jo's chest at the thought, but she smothered it, forcing herself to stay calm, focusing on Takako and the turmoil she could now see swirling behind her eyes. She couldn't save Takako's family for her. If Jo was honest with herself, Takako's family likely couldn't be saved at all—everything in the world was at the whim of wishers. But at this moment, for what it was worth, she could at least offer her an end to her guilt.

"Look, Takako," she started, taking what she hoped looked like a casual sip of her tea. "I appreciate you telling me, your trust. But I honestly don't care one way or another what America could've looked like versus what it did when I lived there. If it was one single nation, or split up as it is. . . None of it matters."

As expected, Takako looked startled by the admission, and Jo couldn't bite back the smirk that tugged at her own lips in response.

"If America had won, I'd be working for the mafia, probably some descendants of Wayne's old friends. Take a moment and imagine how *that* would've been." Even Takako smiled slightly at the remark. "Regardless, my life wouldn't exactly have been different in a sovereign nation. I mean, maybe I worked with the Yakuza a bit more in the timeline you created? But hell, with the internet, I might have worked for them anyway."

"You don't know that. You might have been happier."

Jo just shrugged. It was almost a little odd to feel *nothing* for her homeland, as if it had never really been her home to begin with. "No, I don't *know* anything. But I highly doubt my family would have been well off either way, and I definitely would have been doing the exact same thing no matter what reality I'd grown up in. I know no different, and who my boss is never really mattered as long as the pay was right. Home, what's really important about it, isn't land or walls but the people who occupy them—it's the people who matter, and I would've had those same people in any reality. So you'll find no hard feelings about your wish here."

Takako didn't seem to know how to take that, so Jo added, "But if what you're looking for is forgiveness, it's yours." Jo squeezed the woman's hand lightly. "I don't blame you, Takako. But I forgive you for whatever you think you need forgiveness for."

For a long, drawn-out moment, Takako looked at their hands, not quite holding, but resting comfortably against each other. Then, Takako stretched her hand out beneath the touch and linked her fingers with Jo's, gripping tightly for a moment before simply settling into the hold. It felt like a thank you, so Jo took it as one, rubbing her thumb gently over Takako's.

Another, more comfortable length of silence passed before Takako spoke again.

"Megumi, my sister," she whispered. "I've been watching her grow, following her life as best I can from here. She's almost forty now. My niece and nephew just turned twelve last month. Twins, actually."

As much as it pained her, Jo could tell where she was going with this, could hear the way each word had been wrought in barbed wire and caught all the way up Takako's throat. She didn't want to be right, but Jo knew the universe was not that kind.

"Two years ago, the family moved from our sleepy mountain town to Shizuoka for work." When Jo looked up from their intertwined fingers to Takako's eyes, she was unsurprised but heartbroken to find them shiny with unshed tears.

"There's no way they'll be able to evacuate in time, especially not now, and that's if they're not—"

This part, Takako couldn't finish, but Jo didn't need her to—didn't *want* her to. Neither of them had seen the news since this morning. For all either of them knew, Takako's family was already dead.

There was nothing Jo could say, she realized. Nothing of value she could offer as comfort or solace or distraction. All she had was her presence, the promise of her nearness, to combat the crushing weight of suffocating solitude. For a moment, Jo allowed herself to think of what it would feel like if her own family was in the path of the volcano's wrath. What would she be feeling? Would she want to be alone?

The answer to the first question was too much to consider.

The answer to the second was no.

"Can I stay with you for a little while longer?" Jo asked, keeping her voice soft, letting every ounce of her own sorrow shine through. Takako didn't hesitate, nodding her head and closing her eyes tight when the motion caused her tears to fall at last. As Takako gripped her hand, Jo witnessed the second of two seemingly immovable mountains tumble.

"Please."

7. RESTRICTIONS

TAKAKO WAS FINALLY still.

Jo wouldn't have called the sleep restful; perhaps it wasn't even sleep at all, more like a forced stasis. Every now and again Takako's brow furrowed and she twisted, no doubt haunted by any number of ghosts, before settling again. But it was a reprieve, at least.

Takako hadn't entirely bought into the idea of closing her eyes at first, calling it a "pointless waste of time." But Jo's argument that sometimes wasting time was the best thing to do won out, and the Japanese woman had laid down her head and let her consciousness escape her.

It was the only escape they really had.

Takako had separated her two futon and given Jo the better of the two blankets, even though Jo would've lied out on bare tatami to make Takako more comfortable. With one hand, she still clutched at Jo's fingers. Throughout drinking their remaining tea in relative silence, and then talking about some stupid computer babble that Jo had practically invented for the sake of distracting her friend, the other woman had held onto Jo. Even as they'd fallen asleep, Takako held onto her between the futon as though she were a teddy bear—her comfort.

Jo closed her eyes, and when she opened them, she saw a different person altogether.

Yuusuke lay across from her, a memory painting over Jo's vision fresh and clear. It was one of their first jobs, holed up in some shitty motel room, the only thing two high school students just striking out could afford. He'd been paranoid, afraid of failure, nervous of the career paths they'd chosen for themselves. She'd reassured him then, stayed with him in his bed until he finally slept. Not quite a lover, but certainly more than a friend. Something that was a bit better than both.

Who had Yuusuke leaned on in her revised world? Who did he go to? Did he share that hotel room with someone else or no one at all?

Jo closed her eyes again, but this time a different sight greeted her. It was a flash—a blink then gone. But Jo could've sworn she'd seen a woman, screeching as Jo was taken away from her. Jo fluttered her eyelashes several times, but couldn't conjure back the sight, couldn't even conjure a memory of it. It was as if it had never happened at all.

Sufficiently too unnerved to rest as well, Jo carefully unraveled her fingers from Takako's, watching for any signs of disturbance. There were none. She remembered the embarrassment Yuusuke had endured the morning after he'd shown "such weakness" (his words) and, just in case, she'd save Takako some face without her asking.

Somehow, despite the invisible weights that had been chained to her shoulders, Jo managed to stand. Takako was undisturbed. Jo continued to watch for any signs otherwise, but her friend remained motionless up to the moment Jo closed the door behind her.

Jo pressed her forehead against the wood, taking a deep and shuddering breath. Eventually, it would stop hurting; it had to. Technically, she knew no one in the volcano's path of destruction. Technically, she knew no one in the world as it was. But there was something visceral about the pain. Something that, surely, every human felt at seeing another in such unavoidable agony. And it was a feeling only magnified by Takako's turmoil.

"How is she?" Like a godsend, Nico's voice pulled her from the well of suffering she'd been dipping into.

"How do you think?" Jo snapped despite herself, instantly regretting the tone. "I'm sorry, I'm just spent. I didn't mean that."

"No, no, it was a foolish question." Nico continued smiling on, even if it was a bit pitying, an underlying sadness beneath the soft expression. Nothing could discourage that man's smile, it seemed. He was the only ray of joy in the universe at the moment when the whole world needed him, and only seven others knew of his existence. "Why don't you come and sit with me for a bit? Take a break from all this. I just made some coffee."

"I can't possibly take your coffee." Her hands and feet didn't have ears to hear what her mouth was saying, as they were already crossing over to take the cup Nico had in his hands.

"Think nothing of it." Nico opened the door to his room, and Jo entered without further resistance. It offered the same atmosphere that was part home, part nostalgia for a world, time, and lifestyle she'd never known.

"Thank you." Jo murmured. Her eyes suddenly fell on his easel. "I have an idea."

"What's that?"

"You should paint Takako something."

"Jo—"

She bristled at the tone of his voice, not wanting to hear his objection. She didn't care if his muse didn't feel up to the task. Takako needed it desperately. "Something simple, just like you did for me. Something to remind her of home and family. . . Or, better yet, give her hope."

"I can't do that."

"What? Why?" Jo turned so quickly that she almost spilled her coffee. "Is this some rule passed down by Snow? Because if so, I swear that he's gone too far and you need to ignore him."

"I can't, Jo," Nico repeated.

It was like the glass of the framed photo she'd worked so hard to mentally create, the one that encompassed the happy smiling picture of Nico, of their whole team, fractured in that moment. "Why is no one else looking out for each other? How are you all okay to just stand by and be divided? And by what? Obligation? How do you never *question*—"

"Jo." Nico placed his hands on her shoulders. Even though Jo felt like her bones continued to vibrate under his palms, her mind was settled for the briefest of moments, long enough to actually hear what he'd been trying to say. "Even if I wanted to—*which I do*—I can't."

"But. . . *Why?*"

He led her over to one of his chairs, squeezing in next to her. It was a little smaller than a loveseat and the fit was tight. But instead of uncomfortable, it felt warm and safe. Jo pulled her feet up onto the cushion as he spoke, cradling her mug.

It was then she noticed that the mug was indeed *hers*. The one she always used. The one Takako had gotten Samson to make for her.

Nico had planned this.

Jerk.

"Has no one told you of restrictions, yet?"

"Restrictions?" Jo repeated. "No. Oh, let me guess, this is another bit of magic nonsense that doesn't actually make any sense but we have to abide by because. . . reasons?"

Nico actually laughed and the sound of genuine amusement was a balm even better than coffee—and that said something, because very few things were ever better than coffee. "Something like that, yes."

"Great."

He nudged her with his shoulder and Jo sighed softly, letting out her sarcasm before asking, "So, go on then. What are 'restrictions'?"

"Every magic has some sort of limitation on it. It varies from person to person, but everyone in the Society has something that restricts when and how they can use their magic."

Jo thought of Snow as Nico spoke. Could a power that great be restricted by anyone or anything? But she stayed silent on the matter. Snow had never outright said not to, but Jo couldn't imagine speaking to anyone else of the special place he'd taken her to on the other side of the Door. What he'd shown her felt innately private. She wouldn't violate that confidence, no matter how many other stupid rules he imposed on them.

Nico continued, "For example, Wayne's is obvious. The bet must be about money. A relatively generous restriction compared to mine."

"What's yours?"

"My power only works on a person once. To look at one of my paintings a second time would do nothing."

"*What?*"

He chuckled at her shocked reaction. "The person must be lost in the canvas. They can't over-analyze, or the magic won't take its hold. So, once a person knows how my magic works, even subconsciously, it can no longer be effective on them."

"How is that remotely fair?"

"Magic isn't fair." Truer words hadn't been spoken that day.

"So, what's mine?" Jo couldn't help but wonder

when she'd stop learning things about her new life. It'd been almost six months, after all.

"I don't know. You have to discover that on your own." Nico patted her knee and stood.

"Wonderful." Jo bitterly turned her attention to the wide window, signaling that she was done with the conversation. Perhaps, on a normal day, she'd have more patience for it. But today, there just wasn't anything left in the tank to deal with the nuances of magic.

Nico crossed over to his easel and the canvas that waited for him. Nothing more than a mass of color was stroked upon the negative space—an image of chaos that could only be called to order by the artist.

"What're you painting?" Jo asked. Her voice softened instantly with a change of topic.

"Julia."

As soon as he said the name, Jo saw it: the silhouette of a person yet taking form. She saw the early highlights of a brow and nose. She saw the mass of brown that would ultimately become hair. If Nico hadn't just told her that he couldn't use his magic on her again, she would've assumed it to be something fantastical to suddenly see the structure of the piece.

"Tell me about her?" Jo put her coffee mug on the floor and spread out on the sofa, though the stretch of cushions suddenly felt too big for one. She rested her head on the tall armrest, watching him as he set to work.

"My Julia?"

"Yes."

"She was my muse. The stars were born of her tears

and the sun of her smiles. She was everything good in my world and far more than I ever deserved. We lived in Florence. . ."

As Nico spoke, his words tickled something in the back of Jo's mind—something she'd read in the recreation room months ago about a Julia around Nico's time, the mistress of some pope. But the paragon of goodness and purity Nico was describing surely couldn't be the same woman. There had to have been dozens of Julias in Florence back then. . .

Nico continued to speak, and the words, alight with the flame of love kept alive after all this time, was a beacon that lured her mind toward an oasis of calm in the storm that bellowed just outside of the Society's existence.

8. WAITING GAME

J O WATCHED NICO paint until her eyes were bloodshot and he was rubbing stiffness from his fingers.

She'd stolen a heavy blanket from his bed somewhere around the time the conversation was dying, and had bundled herself up in it. It wasn't that the room was cold, but that she *felt* cold. Jo felt as if she'd been pitched out to the vacuum of space. The only tether she had to the world was the sound of Nico's voice and, when that gave out, his brush.

At about the four-hour mark, Jo wished she could sleep. But it refused to come to her. No matter how much her mind begged for the relief, her body refused. So she settled for unfocusing her eyes and pushing her mind into a void until Nico stepped away from the easel, stretching, indicating that he was finished (for now).

"I should pick up a hobby." It was the first time

either of them had broken the silence in—Jo tapped her watch—three hours.

"A hobby? Seems like a good idea. What would you do?" He swirled his brush in a jar of mud-colored water.

"I don't know, maybe you could teach me how to paint? It seems cathartic." Jo stood, folded up Nico's quilt, and walked over to set it on his bed. Not for the first time, Jo couldn't help but admire the man's room; the homey messiness and the warm colors mirrored the half-finished canvases splattered in paint and ink.

"I'm afraid we wouldn't have enough time for that." He placed the first brush in a different jar, and started the process on the second.

"Don't we have eternity?"

"I'm afraid," he said again slowly, "we wouldn't have enough time for that."

"Oh, *ha ha*, very funny." Jo rolled her eyes, walking over to the canvas.

It was further along now, the streaks of color more obviously swirling into the silhouette of a woman. A beautiful woman, young and smiling and caught in laughter. It was breathtaking, even without Nico's magic Jo's eyes were drawn to it and only it.

In many ways, the Society was a shame. Niccolo de'Este would never receive the acclaim he so rightly warranted. His pieces would never win awards or hang in museums; he would never be compared to Pollock or Van Gogh or Murakami. Instead, he would only ever be appreciated by a sparse group of seven—most of whom had questionable taste. It was far, far less than someone of his talent deserved.

Jo could already feel the tell-tale ache in her heart growing thicker, lecherous—the same ache that seemed to thrive on realizations directly linked to her new reality. No matter how accepting she was of it, there was no helping the occasional feelings of loss that cropped up even still. For all intents and purposes, Nico was only nineteen. He should be studying art on a full ride at some university somewhere (or whatever the Renaissance equivalent was). He should be selling pieces by the dozens at local art shows. He should be living, just like *she* should be living. But their lives had been taken, all in exchange for the realities of people who would never know of their involvement, their existence.

Just like magic itself, it wasn't fair. Jo sucked in a breath and thought with vehement sorrow that, even if they had all agreed to join the Society in their own ways for their own reasons, the prices they paid didn't seem to balance out.

"I tease," Nico said, oblivious to the torrent of thoughts that consumed her steps over to him and the easel. "Of course I would love to teach you to paint."

His voice was light, the banter easy, serving as a reminder that there was nothing she could do. She wasn't going to waste her time wallowing in righteous self-pity. "Fair" was hardly a driving factor in the whirring cogs and gears of the universe's clock, wasn't it? The members of the Society no more deserved their fates than the citizens of Japan deserved theirs, but that didn't make any of it any less real.

"Well, you may be right, a different hobby might suit me better."

"Then we shall find it together." Nico gave his hands one more wipe on his apron, though the motion was hopeless. The garment had just as much pigment on it as had soaked into his skin. His expression shifted, and there was only a second before he spoke, but a second was long enough for Jo to fill with dread at what she knew he'd say next. "For now, however, I think we should return to the rest of them."

A flash of panic ran down Jo's spine at the thought, the sudden realization brought her back to the reality that existed beyond the reprieve that had been Nico's room with a fierce and sobering shock. They'd been sitting for nearly six hours. Had the majority of the carnage already settled? Did the volcano, god forbid, erupt again while they'd selfishly escaped their unwritten duty of bearing witness to the world's horrors?

Surely someone was still in the common area watching the news. The onset of the desire to know exactly what had transpired over the last couple of hours was swift and almost visceral, as if she was now personally connected to the damage and lives lost. Whether it was Takako's legitimate association, or her own vicarious attachment, she felt instantly guilty for not keeping up to date.

"You're right. I want to see what's happened."

With that, Jo and Nico wordlessly made their way down the hall. Not unexpectedly, there wasn't just one person sitting on the couch in front of the television, but three.

Eslar leaned forward, elbows on his knees and chin resting on his laced fingers. He seemed to be almost unnaturally engrossed in the news (how he had the stamina completely eluded her), analyzing what appeared to be new footage with a frown. Jo wondered if he'd even left the couch once. Samson sat to his side, occasionally whispering things in one of the elf's long ears. Wayne was an island at the far end of the couch, his grim expression warding off company. No one seemed to notice Jo and Nico's arrival, and as she shifted her gaze from the men to the television, it wasn't hard to understand why.

Most of the broadcast seemed to circulate between reporters' comments about the carnage—of which there was a near indescribable amount—and actual footage of it. Mt. Fuji seemed to have finally settled. According to the scientists (for whatever their assessments were still worth) there were no further eruptions expected in the foreseeable future. That didn't stop the continual oozing of lava and thick blanket of ash that now seemed to cover the globe. It was hard to believe, even harder to hope, that Mt. Fuji would stay dormant for long, not when its eruption had been so unexpected and violent.

Even if Mt. Fuji never erupted again, the catastrophe had already left its permanent mark, not just on Japan, but on the entire world.

"Look what the cat dragged in." Wayne noticed their presence, his dry remark cutting Jo from the constricting tethers of grief that had already begun to form between her and the television. "We'd wondered where you two had gone."

"*He'd* wondered," Samson corrected bravely, but still very quietly and without raising his head.

"You could've come and got us," Jo said defensively.

"A reprieve is sometimes necessary," said the elf, who had barely moved from the television and still did not tear his eyes from it. "And there is not much to be done, for now."

Samson caught her eye, but seemingly wasn't able to speak until he'd ducked his chin again. "I made some breakfast for everyone."

Slowly, Jo walked the rest of the way to the couch, leaning heavily against it. "Thanks, Sam. That's very thoughtful of you," she murmured, distracted by the images flickering across the TV screen.

They were showing footage of the Hakone region now, still smoldering in some places, burning in others, but mostly just completely destroyed. With a sickening lurch, Jo found herself subconsciously comparing the sight to old photos she remembered learning about in her high school's ancient history class—the entirety of Pompeii sitting in ruins, whole families frozen forever in their last moments of life, completely unaware of it being taken from them. The images of the long-ago Roman city came alive vividly in her mind, like she'd seen it before. Jo attributed it to the footage she'd all but seen on loop now overlaying with her past school lesson.

She wasn't sure what was worse, seeing something like this coming, or being blindsided. For example, Shizuoka had watched their neighboring region fall to the might of a natural disaster, knowing all the while they were next. Multiple clips of a tsunami, triggered by the quake, only added to the still spreading damage.

It was truly becoming too much to bear, a relentless assault of one thing after another after another.

She didn't know how the men continued to do it, stare at the news with their somber tones, as if seeing something she couldn't. So, Jo didn't bear it. She turned away and stepped toward the kitchen, where Samson had laid out mismatched plates and platters filled with breakfast foods, willfully oblivious to the horror-movie cinematics only a few yards away.

Apparently, she wasn't alone in needing to step away, because Jo nearly jumped out of her skin at the sudden appearance of the orange-haired man at her side.

"Thank you for making breakfast," Jo said, mostly just to break the silence. Samson nodded, keeping his eyes set firmly on moving the platters so that they were in a perfect line. Jo grabbed some scrambled eggs, a few slices of bacon—careful not to disrupt Samson's adjustments—and then paused. This close, even Samson looked more uncomfortable than usual, his brows furrowed and face bordering on stricken. "Hey, Sam?" Jo whispered, taking in a breath when he glanced at her with noticeably wet eyes. "Are you all right?"

For a couple of seconds, Samson didn't respond, just looked at her with that same worried expression. It was a dumb question and she knew that; none of them were really "all right." Then he sighed, an exhale that Jo felt leave her own lungs in response.

"Yes," Samson mumbled, scrubbing harder at the

soapy pan. "I just don't like the waiting."

Jo wanted to ask him what he meant, but there was something about the sentence that felt final, a heavy silence following in its wake. She wasn't sure how she knew, but she was certain Samson was done talking. So, with one last murmur of thanks, Jo took her plate out of the kitchen, down the hall, and as far away from the television as she could get.

Takako was expectedly awake when Jo let herself quietly into her room. She was now in a seated position, but otherwise didn't seem to have moved much from her futon. So Jo placed the plate of food in front of her and took back her own spot on the adjacent futon as well.

"I don't know if you're hungry, but Samson made it." Jo offered, trying once again to simply fill the silence with anything but worry and tension. "At the very least, it'll feel good to fill your stomach with something hot."

Takako nodded at her, mumbling what sounded like a soft thank you, but she made no move to eat. Jo could sympathize; her own stomach tied in sickening knots. She didn't have the heart to mention the fairly recent development of a tsunami; Takako would find out soon enough.

As Takako stared off into the distance, Jo started to see traces of a similar expression on her face, the same concern that had been mirrored on the faces of the rest of her team. A concern Jo was slowly starting to realize ran deeper than just for the lives lost in Japan. Everyone was on edge, waiting for something, as if they expected the catastrophic after effects of Fuji to somehow reach them as well.

Eventually, Jo couldn't take the silence anymore, pulling her knees up to her chest and hugging them close. "Takako?" she asked, wincing when it seemed to startle the woman out of her thoughts. Takako hummed in acknowledgement, but seemed no less distracted. "Samson said he hated the waiting. What did he mean?"

Somewhere in her, Jo had known. Even as she asked the question, she knew what the answer would be. She just hadn't wanted to hear it. Or maybe her mind just rejected thinking it, as if that could make it any more or less real.

When Takako frowned in response, it was with no little amount of fresh pain in her eyes. She looked reluctant to answer even, raising one hand to her mouth as the other tapped a soft rhythm against the tatami. It took longer than Jo expected for her to string together a response, but when she finally dropped her hand, it was with a stoic and schooled expression. Even if the turmoil in her eyes hadn't entirely faded.

"He means waiting for Snow to call us to the briefing room," Takako said, a fraction of that carefully crafted expression crumbling. Jo didn't need to ask for clarification, but she gave it to her anyway. "With a disaster this big, there's no way someone won't make a wish."

"Of course someone will make a wish." That much was obvious. Hundreds of thousands of people were dead or gravely injured. "But what are we supposed to do? Stop a volcano? Even Snow knows we can't prevent a natural disaster."

Takako finally looked up. Jo had spent so long trying to get close to the woman, but now that she finally was, all she wanted was to be blind to the truth in her eyes. Especially as she said, with a blunt and grave certainty, "That doesn't mean we won't be asked to try."

9. LATE NIGHT VISITOR

EVENTUALLY, TAKAKO HAD requested to have some time alone, a request that Jo couldn't deny. Everyone had their own manner of processing and she wasn't about to dictate Takako's.

Jo didn't go very far. She didn't feel like wandering the mansion, didn't have the energy to do anything in a recreation room (despite all earlier notions of picking up a hobby), and couldn't continually impose on Nico. So when Takako gently kicked her out, Jo drifted across the hall to her own bedroom.

She laid on her bed, stretched out amid the plushness, occasionally watching the nighttime of Paris. When the sun rose, so did Jo, for no other reason than habit. She left her bed and with it what felt like all notion of ever being able to sleep again.

The next night, Wayne kept her company—

65

companionship only; it was impossible to feel any sort of *urges* under the present circumstances. Wayne was on the same page, it seemed, when he produced a bottle of whiskey from his room and they drank till dawn, thinking of new (terrible) "crew names" for the Society. The two winners were "The Timekeepers of Infinity" for most palatable, and "Witnesses of Truth" for most cringe worthy. At least it gave them a laugh, something Jo realized she hadn't done for days.

Another day passed. Another day of drifting from place to place, doing nothing of worth, contributing nothing to no one. Another day of waiting as she witnessed the rise and fall of the world from her new vantage of eternity.

It was then, on the third day, that sleep miraculously came to her. She wasn't sure if it was sheer will and determination, boredom, or the fact that even if her body didn't need sleep, her mind eventually demanded a reprieve. In fact, were it not for the heavy knock on the door waking her, she wouldn't have been certain she'd slept at all.

"This better be good," she mumbled into the pillow. She'd just been on the cusp of a dream—she'd swear it. It may well be a decade before she'd find herself able to actually shut her mind completely off once more.

Jo flipped her wrist, looking at the time that illuminated the strip of fabric. It was some time after three in the morning and two hours after everyone had broken off from the common room and gone to bed.

Jo pulled herself from the bed and shook the drowsiness from her mind. Who could possibly be knocking—

Her hand froze, hovering above the doorknob. If magic was a current of electricity, the metal of the knob was conducting it between her and the man on the other side. She could *feel* him there, and for the briefest of moments, an alarm bell rang faintly in the back of her mind. Something about this was ill-advised, the alarm warned. Perhaps, it was because there was something akin to her now dream-like memory of meeting Pan, an ominous threshold from which there was no going back from.

But Jo willfully ignored it all and opened the door.

Snow, even untouched by the Paris skyline that illuminated her bedroom windows, still radiated moonlight. His silver hair swept over an eye, but seemed looser and rougher at the edges. His eyes were sunken, hollow.

This wasn't their fearless and stoic leader. This was the man in agony she'd seen through the Door months ago—the man she'd forced herself to all but forget. There was clearly no path forward to discovering anything more about him.

No path, until he presented one to her.

"I don't know why I'm here." His voice belonged to someone who'd spent hours screaming at the shadows in the corners.

"Come in." She moved on instinct—on an invisible tide that ebbed and flowed between them. If he was the moon, then she was the sea, pulled along by the mysterious aura that he wore like couture.

"I shouldn't."

"Why?" It wasn't a particularly good argument, so his lack of fight when he did surrender was all the more glaring. While she was used to his feet seemingly never touching the ground, the wounded, once-majestic creature now walked with the heaviness of a body robbed of all ethereal grace.

Snow closed the door behind him, leaning against it as if to draw space between them. There wasn't much, and it pulled her a half-step closer in. . . what? Fascination? Concern? Sympathy? He was all of it wrapped in the most beautiful enigma she'd ever seen.

"I shouldn't be here," he repeated.

"Well, you are, so that's that," Jo said as gently as she could through her exasperation. "Snow. . . What happened?"

"Warning you is pointless." He pressed his eyes closed and hung his head. "It will do no good. You can't stop it, none of us can."

"Stop what?"

"And now, now we must do this." He shook his head again and the long bangs all but concealed his face. "Why did I come? Telling you will do no—"

Jo summoned magic she didn't realize she possessed and silenced him with a touch.

It was the most delicate, timid touch she'd ever given. Lighter than a butterfly landing, her fingertips on his cheek. Right first, then left.

He was warm. Warmer than she thought he would be for a man who looked so much like his namesake. Had he been this warm when he'd taken her hand at the Ranger compound all those months ago? Had he been this warm when she'd helped him most of the way back to his room after he'd allowed her to witness his magic?

When he didn't flinch or pull away, the pads of her fingers made shallow indents in his skin as she pulled his attention forward. *Look at me*, she wanted to say, *let me see you*. Her lips were still, voice silent, but everything about her was alive. His presence had done for her what sleep could not; it rejuvenated her.

Perhaps it was some residual magic that lingered between them from his pulling her into the Society, but this man made her feel something indescribable. Something she'd never felt across universes or realities. In a fake world outside of time, this was real.

It was something she'd been missing all along. Something she longed for. Something that was almost like. . . a reunion.

"There's been a wish, hasn't there?" she whispered.

He nodded and pressed his eyes shut again, as if in pain.

"Tell me." He'd have to sooner or later and if he did it now, he'd have practice keeping his composure for the rest of the group.

As if reading her mind, Snow took a shuddering breath. Then another, slightly more stable one. And then, he found length in his spine and strength in his shoulders. He rose to his full height and looked down at her. His carriage wasn't overbearing, nor was it the aloof comportment she'd seen him muster so many times before.

He looked like a stumbled Atlas, finding the will to

stand and carry the world on his shoulders once more.

"We are to prevent all loss of life."

"Wh-what?" Appreciation for him telling her in advance hit Jo like a Mac truck. She would've never been able to keep herself together in the briefing room when he broke the news. She could already feel it ripping at the seams of her facial composure. Scenes of wide-spread carnage from the news they'd been watching for nearly a month all flashed before Jo's eyes in a visceral assault. "It's too much this time. It'll be impossible."

"We'll think of something." He glanced away.

"No, we won't." Jo grabbed his hands, taking a full step closer to him. Their hips were almost touching now. "Snow, this isn't hacking into a mainframe or getting revenge on a mob boss. This is a volcano. It's already happened, we can't just get a do-over."

"We can." He tilted his head to her, eyes locking.

"What. . ." Jo's voice had fallen to a whisper.

"I've done all I can."

She searched his face, her fingertips still mapping the curves of his cheeks and the line of his jaw. "Are you all right?" Jo wanted to groan at herself for the question. He gave her that cryptic response and all she could ask was if he was all right?

"I did. . . all I could, Jo." He rephrased his statement, weaker, almost trembling in breath between the words.

"What did you do?"

"You have no idea what you're asking." Snow's mouth pressed into a hard line, but didn't move away. If anything, he felt closer. He leaned forward. She was sure now: he was closer than he'd ever been.

"Then tell me." Jo pulled him but there was no more space to give; their legs were touching, chests brushing. "Tell me something real. Tell me what *this* is."

His eyes widened and Jo felt hers mirror them. Was she even asking about the wish or his ever-elusive magic anymore? Or was she seeking validation for the pull between them?

"Jo. . ." All words failed him just as they were eluding her.

Grammar and structure melted away as his silver eyes bore into hers. Jo swallowed hard. There was one thing left in her mind, a singular request that would not let her breathe again until it escaped.

"Stay with me tonight?"

"What? Why would you ask that?" The rasp of his voice was thickening to a velvety chocolate paste.

"Don't let me be alone, not knowing this," she begged softly. "It's been torture waiting, and now I have to wait with knowledge I can do nothing with. Stay with me, at least until the others are stirring."

"I can't do that." Even as he spoke, their separate personal space was condensing into a singularity that would suck them both in. "You know I can't."

"I don't know anything. You won't tell me *anything*. . . The one thing that I do know is that I want you here."

"And I—"

When he cut himself off, swallowing down whatever he'd almost confessed, Jo found herself hanging on those two words to the point that a groan of frustration rose in her throat. Eventually, true to all prior form, Snow ended things with the tact of a four-year-old.

"I need to go." For a man who could usually put the grace of a ballerina to shame, he'd suddenly turned into a boar. Snow half-pushed, half-steered her to the side.

"Why? Tell me one thing, Snow, please!" Jo demanded, voice raised, even as he opened the door. "Don't shut me out again!"

He shot her a near-painful look, equal parts glare and nervousness, before his composure returned and he leaned forward. Her treacherous heart beat faster almost instantly.

"This wasn't the way it was supposed to be." Something was at the point of breaking, and it wasn't just the way his last couple of words cracked and shattered. "Staying distant, because of your magic—right now, this is all I can do."

He was pleading with her to understand but giving her just enough to have only the vaguest idea that felt more like a shapeless blob than a tangible thing labeled "understanding". Still, one thought came forward. A singular memory.

"You'd said something about my magic before, after the first wish." Jo stepped closer, trying to pin him in place. "What did you mean then?"

"I can't tell you."

"Why?" Jo wanted to punch him and kiss him all at the same time.

"This is the only way we can protect you. Somewhere, you know that's true."

It was like being transported back in time. Had he

not said something similar to her long ago? If he had, her mind couldn't locate the memory; everything had gone soft. "What? Why would I need to be protected? And from what?" she asked no one, because the man who held all the answers had run from her once again.

10. SEVEN-HUNDRED AND THIRTY

I T WASN'T EXACTLY a surprise to anyone (least of all Jo, given the prior night's encounter) that they were ushered into the briefing room the next morning. That didn't mean Jo wasn't instantly filled with dread over the fact. Breakfast was bypassed, the television blank and silent, and like a funeral march, everyone filed in to take their seats.

Snow's words had circulated in her brain clean through to the morning and played underneath his appearance in the common room, announcing their presences were required in the briefing room.

Though when Jo looked around the table at the rest of the group, she would have sworn by the atmosphere that everyone else already knew. Everyone seemed to share the same exhaustion, the same forlorn expression. Everyone except Pan, that is; she just looked mildly amused.

Jo frowned at the now hazy memory of their last encounter that was stinging at the edges of her mind. Pan's eyes landed on hers and Jo promptly looked away. Nico had been right, Pan was likely just making trouble for trouble's sake. Well, Jo wouldn't give her the upper hand. She forcefully shifted her attention back to the matter at hand.

We are to prevent the loss of all life.

How were they supposed to deal with such an impossible wish?

To prevent something on such a drastic scale, especially when so much damage had already been done. . . there was no way. But Snow had acted as though they had no choice but to try. Despite herself, Jo couldn't help the nervous intrigue worming its way into her stomach. Did he truly have the kind of power that could prevent a volcano from erupting? Could they even hope to close the Severity of Exchange on something like that? How exactly would they handle the fact that the life had, already, been lost?

As if on cue, Snow weaved his way in one fluid and authoritative motion from the doorway to the head of the table. It had already been quiet in the briefing room before, but with Snow's arrival, the quiet seemed to shift into an almost tangible thing, heavy and expectant. Like some grotesque, pregnant monster ready to pop.

"You all know why you're here," Snow started, looking to each of them in turn. When his eyes locked briefly with Jo's, she swore she felt her heart stutter. Now was *not* the time to recall the deeply vulnerable man who had come to her the night before. If she reached for anything of that memory, she'd reach for her frustration at his vagueness first. After a second to steel himself, that same detached expression settled like a second skin over his features. Snow lifted a hand. "Let us begin."

Much like every wish since Jo's arrival at the Society, she watched with undeniable fascination as the table came to life, changing and sifting through forms and images until settling on one everyone recognized instantly. They'd been watching the same pictures flash across various news broadcasts for days. Except, where Jo had begun to expect destruction and heartache, all she saw was life, normality, and a country untouched by catastrophe.

"What is this?" she heard herself say, though she didn't recall giving her lips the express command to move. Her body continued on its own accord, and Jo felt herself inch forward in her seat, as if getting a closer look at the images might help her understand them better. "A recording? Or—"

"As of roughly nine hours ago, our current timestamp has been updated," Snow offered, as if that explained anything at all. It was a simple statement with an impossible implication that her mind rebelled against. Surely Snow didn't mean—

"Snow." Eslar's voice was low, almost scolding, despite its usual tenor. "What does this mean for the Severity of Exchange?"

Before Snow could answer, as though Eslar's interjection had awoken them from a stupor, everyone at the table seemed to come back to life. Jo blinked blearily, trying to join the rest of them.

"How far back did we go then?" Wayne asked at about the same time Nico said, "What were the protocols of the wish?"

The questions seemed almost frantic. The only people not chiming in were the usually silent Samson and a rather shaken-looking Takako.

All at once, it came rushing back.

Prevent all loss of life.

Without realizing it, Jo had gotten to her feet, the movement bringing the sudden buzz of the room back into a tense hush. She understood in one sudden moment of clarity what he had meant when he had said he'd "done all he could."

"You rewound time," Jo demanded, looking past the footage of a destruction-free Japan to stare down their powerful leader. "You reset to before the disaster."

"I did." There was no hesitation in his voice, but that didn't mean it wasn't without its unspoken consequences. Snow gave a wave of his hand and the image of a young boy appeared on the table. As was the case with their wishers, there was some basic information laid out (it always reminded Jo of a character bio from one of Yuusuke's video games). "Our wisher is Shiro Yamada from the Hakone region. His circle was made of many once-living things, ashes—" Snow didn't clarify further. He didn't have to. "Thus, the scale of his wish is. . . quite large. His wish is for us to ensure survival of any and all Japanese citizens in Mt. Fuji's path."

"So we're not meant to stop the volcano," Jo

elaborated for him, mostly just to get the words out into the open, prove to herself and everyone else that the pieces had fallen into place: a jigsaw puzzle glued to the board. "We just need to save the people?"

"An evacuation? That could work, perhaps. . ." Nico frowned, looking from the table to Snow and back. "But what's the current timestamp?"

"A month before the eruption."

"A month. We have a month to get hundreds of thousands of people out of the line of fire." Jo balked, running a shaking hand through her hair. With a desperate flick of her wrist, she wrestled her watch free of her hoodie's sleeve. There, in soft, illuminating proof, was the number **766:00**. Seven-hundred and thirty hours added to the time she'd collected from their past few wishes. One month's worth of hours. He wasn't joking about any of it.

"I've used nearly all of my magic usually reserved for the final wish-granting on this reset," Snow went on, seemingly unaware of the panic slowly filtering into the room. "Which puts the Severity of Exchange at a much higher percentage than normal. It will require far more field work than our usual wish—"

"No shit," Wayne all but spat, leaning heavily back into his seat.

"—but should not be impossible," Snow finished as if he hadn't even heard Wayne speak. Jo felt practically sick with the onslaught of fresh nerves, too many questions piling on top of each other. What would happen if they failed? How were they supposed to evacuate such a large area so quickly? What were they even going to *do?*

"It's not enough time to move *everyone* and prevent the loss of *all* life," Takako whispered, more to herself than to anyone. It was almost a shock to hear her voice after so long, even more so to see the look of frustration marring her usually stoic face. "What happens if. . . We won't have enough—"

A soft twinkle of laughter cut Takako off instantly; all eyes turned to Pan with a start. She was leaning back in her chair like she hadn't a care in the world, even going so far as to raise her bare feet to the table, crossed at the ankles. When she wiggled her toes to get comfortable, her nail polish seemed to change color.

At the look of amusement on her face, Jo felt a stab of shock and annoyance deep into the center of her chest. An annoyance that morphed quickly into a defensive anger as the girl clicked her tongue and spoke.

"This is absolutely priceless." She giggled, stretching lithely before working her fingers through the fine strands of blue hair curling in long waves around her head. Just yesterday it had been short and spiked, layered in tones of purple, hadn't it? When Pan looked at her, Jo felt herself bristle. "What's got everyone so worked up? I mean, it's not like anyone is dead." Then, gaze still locked lazily on Jo, she winked one cat-like eye. "Yet."

If Jo thought the previous silence had been suffocating, this one was borderline lethal. The weight of her own surprise nearly consumed her. She might as well have choked on the bitter taste of her instant fury.

Everyone seemed to suffer a similar loss beneath the blatant display of indifference. Everyone except Jo.

She swallowed back that fury and let it burn all the way down like a $2 gas station energy drink.

"Excuse me?" The words were more felt than heard, a seething hiss of a whisper past clenched teeth. Pan just continued to watch her, the obvious tilt of a smirk pulling at the corner of her lips.

"If everyone is so afraid of the consequences, then simply make sure to lessen the Severity of Exchange. You don't want to put so much strain on poor little Snow. He's already done so much for you and used up all his normal magic allocated for a wish. No help there to save you all." Pan shrugged, twirling a curl around her finger over and over again. Jo didn't know if the woman-child was actually oblivious or simply apathetic, but either way, she seemed to easily ignore the waves of Snow's anger that roared overtop them all. *Why did he stay silent?* "I'm sure it's hardly so difficult as you seem to be making it. Just get it done and make sure it's *perfect*."

For a long moment, Jo didn't quite know what to say to that. Was she joking? Even if she was, did she not realize that humor was *definitely* uncalled for in this situation? Either way, Jo felt a pang of pure hatred rush down her spine. If not just for herself, or for the team, then for Takako.

"Just get it done?" Jo repeated, pushing away from her seat completely and walking along the curved length of the table in Pan's direction. She thought she might have felt Wayne reach out to hold her back, but her focus was zeroed in on her target, her retort already spilling past her lips. "Who the hell do you think you are, acting like this is so *simple*? We got to witness *exactly* what would happen if we fail. We got to watch the death toll rise and the carnage spread, and you don't get why we're afraid? You don't understand why we might be a little less than nonchalant about all this?"

Jo found herself suddenly standing right in front of Pan's chair, leaning into the woman-child's personal space in a way that should have been disturbing if not, at the very least, intimidating. Jo felt something visceral and sinister spike deep within her, fueling her outrage. Looking at Pan was like looking in a mirror but only seeing the worst reflected back. "No. You wouldn't understand, would you? Because you spend all of your time in your room taking month-long naps you don't need, and god knows what else, instead of actually doing your damn job like the rest of us."

Pan looked completely nonplussed. "Then don't fail," she said, grinning with an ease that made Jo want to slap her across the face. "I'm sure, of all of you, Takako understands that best. Don't you, pet?"

Jo hadn't wanted to say anything, hadn't wanted to bring too much painful attention to Takako's family, to the raised stakes, to everything she had to lose if they failed. But hearing Pan comment so frivolously set Jo's blood to outright boiling.

"How dare you!" she yelled, slamming a fist down on the table between them before pointing squarely into Pan's chest. "She's suffered more the last couple of days than any of us. And you just expect her to write that off, pretend she hasn't had to grieve and move on enough to deal with all of this? What right do you have to be so. . . so *patronizing*, you fuc—"

Suddenly, Jo felt her center of gravity being forced backwards, an arm flailing out to grasp at the hand currently gripping tight at her shoulder. "Jo, enough." Eslar's voice was in her ear, not quite scolding, but not soothing either. She hadn't even realized she'd been nearly nose to nose with Pan until Eslar was practically dragging her back to her seat.

The look of smug amusement on Pan's face, the embarrassed resignation on Takako's, and the mix of disappointment and caution on Eslar's, all fought for Jo's first reaction. Not that any of those could possibly be right. Surely Jo wasn't in the *wrong* here. . . was she?

"You're just going to let her talk to us this way? Like the lives of these people don't matter?" Jo shook her head, finally pulling away from Eslar's grip. "Whose side are you on?" And then, as a more important question tickled the back of her mind, Jo became all too aware of the gazes currently pointed everywhere but at her or Pan. Jo tightened her hands into fists at her side, looking not at Eslar or Pan or at anyone else. No, with these words, she pointed her accusing stare right at Snow.

"What is wrong with you people?" *Why are you all so afraid of her? Why are you letting her treat you this way?* Jo wanted to say, pointing over her shoulder accusingly, ready to demand answers if not from Snow than from Pan herself. But Snow just shook his head and Jo felt herself pause.

Maybe it was the brief flash of something in his eyes, something a bit broken and definitely pleading that she could have simply imagined, or maybe she had just grown tired of fighting a clearly losing battle. Either way, Jo found herself rolling her eyes and plopping down with a huff into her seat. Snow nodded, taking the opportunity to jump back into the logistics of the wish, the time limit, and the necessity of their involvement.

But Jo was only half listening, instead looking almost continuously over at Pan.

This wasn't over, not by a long shot, but by the stretch of Pan's grin, it was obvious the woman was already stewing in her own victory. Jo would dig answers out of the very walls of the Society if she had to; somehow, she would figure out what made this woman so special, so frightening.

Pan was a puzzle that simply couldn't go on unsolved.

11. IF LOOKS COULD KILL

"ARE THERE ANY other questions?" Snow asked the room.

Everyone shook their heads, Jo included.

"I propose we remain here and begin to work out a plan of attack." Eslar took the initiative when the rest of the group remained silent. "There is no time like the present."

"There is precious little time, period," Wayne added, and Jo found herself silently agreeing.

"Then I suggest you all get to it." Pan got to her feet with a languid stretch and a very bored-looking yawn. "I trust you all will not disappoint." And with that, she turned to leave, no more helpful than she'd been during any other wish before.

Jo couldn't hold back the rush of aggravation burning through her stomach. Whatever mysterious hold Pan had over everyone else, she was not about to have over Jo as well. Thankfully, it would seem she'd blissfully missed the meeting where they'd all sat down and agreed to fear the woman. "Classic Pan," she scoffed. "Bowing out of all the heavy lifting as usual." Jo half raised her voice. "Good thing none of us want you here anyway."

With a slow and inhuman fluidity, Pan turned back towards the group. A smile curled from ear to ear, spreading like sizzling butter across her face. It reminded Jo of the Cheshire Cat from the long ago stories of *Alice in Wonderland*. "Well, it looks like someone in this group has a bit of fight left in them. Aren't you a gem who makes her mother proud?" Jo stood to meet her, awaiting her approach, another confrontation, but Pan didn't make any motion toward her. Instead, she continued toward the doors. "I'll leave you to it, Miss Savior, since you seem so ready for a challenge. Maybe, if you do a good job, I'll even let you challenge *me* someday." Pan threw her head back and laughed, as if the idea was pure humor and little else.

Jo watched Pan's every move as she sauntered out of the room. She couldn't think of a comeback fast enough and the woman was gone in a blink. Jo curled her hands into fists.

"Sit down, doll, or you're going to scare us all into submission." Wayne's voice startled Jo back to reality.

"If looks could kill," Nico mumbled to himself.

"What, are we just supposed to sit here and take that?" Jo thrust her hand in the direction of the doors leading back to the innards of the mansion. "I don't get it. I don't get how you can let her act like thousands of lost lives are nothing." Her question from before had gotten no answer, so maybe if she stated them as fact, demanded and begged even, she'd finally get one. And oh how she needed one.

"They're not lost yet," Eslar reminded her firmly, ignoring all remarks about Pan.

Jo snorted at the elf. "*Yet?* Like it's possible for us to actually do this?"

"That is a matter I think we should all remain here to discuss." Eslar, too, could rephrase his earlier statements. He had not moved from his chair, but Jo suddenly felt like the willowy man was towering over her. She wasn't ready to back down yet. She was still seeing red.

Her eyes swung from Eslar to Snow. She didn't know why she was bothering with the subordinate when the ruler was among them. "You are our leader. Stand up for us! Stand up for Takako. Do *something*."

"I can stand up for myself."

Jo froze, Takako's tone sending ice up her spine; it almost pained her to move her neck and look at the woman. When she did, it was to find cold, dark eyes staring her down with an expression caught somewhere between insult and disappointment. "I do not need you or anyone else to do it for me."

"Takako, I—" Jo began to plead softly. Her temper had walked her foot right into her mouth.

"What I want is for you to let go of this misplaced righteousness and do as Eslar says. That way, we can figure out a way to prevent the loss of all life—my family included. If you are truly my friend and ally, you will work toward this as well."

Jo sank into her chair and wished the cushion would swallow her whole. Pan had been the asshole, so why did Jo suddenly feel so terrible?

She hated this, all of it. She didn't want to let her anger at Pan go, nor her curiosity at why the woman had such a hold on all of the team.

"You're right," Jo mumbled, trying to swallow her pride and find a normal voice once more. "I'm sorry, I— Fighting amongst ourselves over some insensitive comments won't help anyone. Let's just. . . focus on the wish." She'd never managed to figure out the whole "being the bigger person" thing that was meant to come with adulthood.

"Now that's settled," Snow spoke deliberately, as if trying to radiate his displeasure. Jo folded her arms over her chest; she wasn't going to let him have the satisfaction. "I shall leave you all to it."

The room was silent once more for the morning's second departure. The clicking of the doors closed left just the usual six of them.

"Oh no, please. Let us handle it. Thank you for the help, Snow. We greatly appreciate it," Wayne remarked snidely from Jo's side. It seemed she wasn't the only one rankled.

"Snow has done enough for us." Eslar, ever the peacekeeper.

"Oh? Like getting us into this mess?"

"It's not as if he chose this for us." Eslar fired the

statement with such certainty that Jo sat a bit straighter.

Snow didn't choose the wishes? Was that true?

"I wouldn't be so sure," Wayne continued, oblivious. "I wouldn't put it past him."

Or Pan, Jo added mentally. Between Snow and the candy-haired creature, Jo would put her money on Pan being the one who'd pick a wish like this.

"Isn't picking the wish good, though?" Nico said softly.

"What?" Wayne balked.

"We can save a lot of people. We can do real good. Isn't that what we wanted?"

"Not if we don't stop arguing like children." Somehow an irritated edge had come to sharpen the typically direct timbre of Takako's voice.

"Takako's right." Jo rested her elbows on the table, leaning forward. As much as she wanted to know more about Pan, and Snow, and everything else, there was nothing to be gained yet on those fronts and far more to be lost by infighting. "So, what are we going to do?"

"We just have to move a few hundred thousand people." Wayne leaned back in his chair. It was his turn to sulk now, it seemed. Jo and he were similar in so many ways, they could create a dangerous feedback loop of frustration if they weren't careful. "Could just ask them all one by one, we have a lot of time." Wayne looked at his watch and then put on an all too sweet tone to say, "Excuse me sir, madam, you're about to die in hellfire. If you could just—"

"Enough, Wayne," Eslar snapped, rubbing his temples.

Jo put her forehead down on the table and let the rest of the team squabble around her. The moment she closed her eyes, the newsreels she'd watched for a week played before her like an ominous premonition. How could they get all those people to move? What methods had she seen utilized in state- or country-wide evacuations? Hadn't she assisted in one before, for a past boss or a cover-up? Surely there was something she could do, something she was overlooking. . .

She shot upward and, judging from the surprised looks the movement inspired, she'd had her head down for longer than expected.

"Great of you to join the class, dollface."

"It's simple," Jo said quickly, ignoring Wayne. She had more important things to discuss now.

"What is?" Eslar asked. But when Jo spoke, it was directly at Takako. "All we need to do is hack into the evacuation system. Create a few falsified statements, issue a large-scale evac. It should just be a push of a button or two and then every man, woman, and child will get alerts on their bio bands." Jo held out her wrist.

"You can contact every person just like that?" Nico seemed somewhat surprised.

"Warning systems were commonplace back in the early 2000s," Takako mumbled, chewing on the thought. "They've only gotten more sophisticated over time. . ."

"It could work," Jo urged. "We do it quickly, and then there's plenty of time for everyone to move. By the time they realize the evac wasn't government approved, everyone will already be out of the blast zone. And even if people try to go back, news of the actual disaster will start spreading. Everyone stays put and everyone stays safe."

"You're sure you can do this?" Eslar folded his hands and rested his mouth against them, his bony knuckles resting just below his nose. "We don't have a lot of time on the calendar."

"Leave it to me." Jo flexed her arm like she was about to flex her skills with a computer. "I can do it all from the recreation room, even. It'll be easy peasy."

Eslar turned to Takako. "What do you think?"

Jo looked back to her friend and ally, realizing that for this mission, Takako had become their de facto leader. Snow would always have control over them, but this was personal for the woman, and that seemed to go above everything else. Takako locked eyes with Jo, who swallowed hard, giving a nod as if to say, *I can do this. Let me.*

"I give you my trust." Takako nodded as well.

Pride swelled through Jo's chest and then went right to her head, the pressure of anxiety hardening it into a dizzying weight right between her temples. Jo had pulled off far more complex jobs, certainly. But she wasn't sure if she'd ever had a job with stakes quite this high.

12. EASY PEASY

I CAN DO this, Jo repeated like a mantra as she left the briefing room. *I can do this. Easy peasy.*

"Hold up!" Wayne's voice called after her. Jo paused just inside the hallway leading toward the rec rooms.

"Yes?" Jo glanced down the path he'd stopped her from going down, trying to not let the mental pathways being forged in her mind get off-course.

"Do you. . ." He shoved his hands in his pockets, mulling over his next words in a display of a surprising amount of tact for the man. "Do you need help with anything?"

"I'll be fine." Jo gave a small smirk. "Not sure how much your nickel would be able to help anyway."

He didn't back down so easily. "It's a lot of pressure, and a big task. You made it sound simple but—"

"That's because it *is* simple." Jo wasn't about to

let him introduce doubt to her mind. There wasn't any room for it. "All I have to do is access multiple databases that service the government in storing private bio-band information. Bypass security protocols. Plant and activate evac warnings at the highest possible threat level. And make it all look legit enough that no one questions."

"Doesn't sound simple to me, doll."

"Turning on a computer doesn't sound simple to you," she countered.

"You have me." Modesty? She didn't usually expect that from the man. "Maybe not my help, but someone else's? We could be boots on the ground for you."

"I have this," she insisted. No doubt, no fear. She could do what needed to be done, it'd be easy. "In fact, I don't want everyone else risking shifting things unexpectedly and making it harder for me. Just take a breather."

"Odd hearing you worried about the ripple effects of the Severity of Exchange."

Jo shared a brief laugh with him. "Well, we all have to grow up sometime, right?"

"So I'm told. Still waiting for it to happen." The conversation stalled, no more momentum to carry it forward, but Wayne persisted anyway. "You sure?"

"I got this."

"Because we're a team and—"

"Wayne, I got this." Jo sighed softly. "If Takako can believe in me, can't you?"

"Okay." He shrugged. "If you need anything Missus Lone Wolf, you know where to find us."

"I won't hesitate."

He could've at least made it look like he believed her. Made it look like he had faith she could pull it off. But Wayne didn't give her the courtesy, and departed with a small pat on her shoulder.

"It'll be easy peasy!" she called, but he was already too far to hear. "Yeah. . . Easy peasy," Jo insisted once more to herself. She knew what she had to do; she'd even explained all the steps for Wayne. But even with the steps laid out before her in perfect, simple-to-follow pathways, Jo still couldn't help but repeat them over and over, drilling them into her own head. She spared no effort in attempting to convince herself that this was just another day at the office. Just a few things to hack into, a few scripts to run, nothing major.

Jo's hands were slick with sweat when she fumbled with her watch. It forced her to take a breath, and still her slightly trembling fingers to get it off. She was not unfamiliar with failure, but never before had she been so afraid of it.

She wouldn't fail. She wouldn't let herself even consider it. Lives were at stake, and Takako's faith in her acted as both a balm and a boost of adrenaline. She wouldn't let her down—wouldn't let any of them down.

With renewed determination (and a roller-coastering confidence that she did her best to keep in check), Jo finally removed her watch and placed it on the recreation room's side shelf.

The same impressive set-up of tech greeted her the moment she opened the door. In fact, it seemed even more elaborate this time—the desktop from her last visit updated with yet another monitor. There were also wall-mounted televisions giving a constant playback of Japan's current news broadcasts (now serving as a reminder for rewound time). A cooler in the corner filled with RAGE ENERGY begged to be drunk. Even a comfy-looking futon was on one side, offering the promise of a brief reprieve should one be needed—and Jo was already bracing herself for that particular inevitability.

These rec rooms really knew how to provide.

With an almost running start, Jo threw herself into a rolling chair, wheels nearly skidding as she slid to a halt in front of her updated setup. As usual, her favorite programs were already up and running on a few screens; the others downloaded with software written in Japanese, though she had to blink a couple times to read it.

Over the last couple of months, her ability to understand both written and spoken languages outside her native tongue had become almost second-nature. Even though Jo had studied Japanese in school, she wasn't always the best student (especially in any classes that didn't deal with programming). It was almost as if she had to flip the switch from her mind trying to actively translate it, to allowing her passive magical ability to take over.

It looked like everything she needed to get started was right within her reach, just waiting for her to dive in. Which was why she couldn't quite figure out the reason her hands continued to hover, trembling just slightly, over the keyboard.

She didn't have time to doubt her abilities, or to feel overwhelmed and intimidated by the task at hand. She needed to have this hack pulled off yesterday, and instead, all she could do was stare at the news broadcasts hung on the wall above her head. Everything looked so normal, so peaceful in comparison to the footage they'd been forced to swallow for the last few days.

Somewhere in Shizuoka was Takako's sister, her niece and nephew, all alive and well and completely oblivious to the oncoming disaster. A disaster that they had no way of stopping. But they *did* have a plan, and Jo *did* have a chance to save their lives—to save thousands upon thousands of lives. So, despite the way her hands still quivered, despite the way her heart had taken up what felt like permanent residence in her throat, despite Wayne's words stubbornly lodging in her mind, Jo got to work.

Within moments, she could feel it. It wasn't just the sensation of her magic bubbling back to life, helping her see alleyways in the dark web or data-routes that seemed otherwise invisible, but her own confidence spiking.

This was her thing. It was the one thing that she could hang her hat on, be confident in, and no one else could take from her. It was the value she brought to the Society. She could tear down walls and shred any defense that kept her from her goal. Nothing could be put before her that she couldn't break.

If anyone knew how to get these evac warnings put in place, it was her and no one else.

The rush of magic-fueled adrenaline was

intoxicating, thrumming beneath her skin like the buzz of an electric current. Her eyes bounced from screen to screen, fingers setting up a constant staccato rhythm against the keys. Second by minute by hour, she experienced her plan unfolding.

It started with a quick hack deep into the Japanese government's residential databases and ended with complete control of all citizens' bio bands—which Jo was very careful not to alter in any unnecessary ways. From there, it was simply a matter of uploading the evac codes into their wireless drives and waiting for the warning to go into effect. All dominoes lined up and waiting to be knocked over.

This time, as Jo took a breath and hovered a finger over the 'Enter' button, her hand trembled not with nerves, but with eager anticipation. She could do this; it would all work out. She'd covered all her bases, made sure every detail was accounted for. Now all she had to do was find a computer on the other side of the Door (with a USB port), activate the evac warning, and wait.

Wayne was sitting on a couch just beyond the Four-Way, heading toward the common room, when she crossed back toward her room, as if he'd been waiting for her. His eyes drifted up from the tablet he'd been thumbing and caught hers for a long moment. Jo gave a quick nod before he could say anything, and continued on.

She didn't need help; she needed the USB from her room and the trust of her teammates. There wasn't anyone else who could do this. It all fell to her and she wouldn't fail them.

The USB stick was right where she'd left it after their last wish. Wayne was right where he was before—both times when she crossed back to the recreation room and then back toward the briefing room. Both times, he'd said nothing and made no motion to stop her.

As she left the mansion and stepped onto Japanese soil, Jo thought of Takako and her family, of Mt. Fuji and the decimation of the surrounding regions. She thought of every line of code, every hack, every digital footprint she'd put in place to lead the citizens of Japan out and away from future tragedy.

Tokyo buzzed on as normal, giant billboards of brightly colored *anime* and video game characters taking up entire skyscrapers. She'd chosen Akihabara as her point of entry—the "electric city." Yuusuke never stopped ranting about the gamers that could be found in arcades and computer cafes there and, sure enough, here was the place where she found some hole-in-the-wall computer café with towers that still sported USB ports.

The attendant looked at her, albeit somewhat suspiciously given her mastery of Japanese, but made no motion to bar her from renting out a space. Her corner procured, no prying eyes on her, Jo plugged in and began running her scripts. Her heart beat on overtime as she navigated the real-world channels, and it wasn't until the last dredges of her magic fizzled that Jo felt she could even take a breath.

Returning to the Society felt almost like a dream, her body dragging and her mind clouded from overexertion.

Jo couldn't bring herself to head to the common room yet. Blissfully, Wayne was no longer waiting for her, and she could sneak back to the recreation room unimpeded. Even though she'd taken her watch to head back to the real world, the room was just as she'd left it—monitors broadcasting the news included.

Taking up a seat on the futon, Jo watched, waiting for her actions to take root. It took a little longer than she'd expected (or intended), but eventually alerts began popping up on every channel. Jo lifted the remote, clicking to another news station.

"Come on. . ." she whispered—begged to the newscaster. "Tell everyone that—"

"This just in—" a title graphic swooped across the screen, interrupting the woman for a moment "—we are receiving reports of wide-scale evacuations across the Kanto region of Japan. Preliminary protocols are advised to be followed…"

Jo leaned back against the futon with a pleasant sigh. It was working. Things would escalate, dominos would continue to fall, more evacuation zones would be alerted and rising danger warnings would prompt people to move.

Perhaps it was the relief of success, or simply the release of the constant state of mental and magical concentration, but Jo felt instantly heavy, wracked by a wave of exhaustion. A dizzy haze settled over her as she glanced wearily at the bottom of one of the screens.

Her plan had taken nearly thirteen hours to execute, including the one and half she spent back in the real world.

Jo stood, rubbing her shoulders with as much pressure as she could muster (which still wasn't enough) and took in her workspace. At least half a dozen cans of RAGE were sprawled around the keyboard, and when she finally pulled her attention to the music still blaring from her headphones, it was already a quarter of the way through a repeat of her favorite playlist.

She returned the headphones back to their hook, her fingers protesting the mere idea of even grabbing something. Her knuckles brushed the monitor she'd been working so furiously on in the process, and it flickered off. Jo paused, staring at it. She tapped the screen once, twice... three times, before it finally flickered back to life.

"You gave all you had, too, huh?" Jo gave a small laugh. "Fine, have a rest." She clicked off the single monitor and started for the door. As was usually the case after a long session, she couldn't even stomach the sight of a keyboard. She wanted to be anywhere other than that tech-filled dark room.

So Jo headed for the only place she could conceive to be the exact opposite—the open and bright common area.

The door to the recreation room closed before she ever noticed that the monitor had sparked to life only briefly, before fizzling out entirely.

13. HOTSHOT

THE MANSION WAS quiet and the world outside its windows was dark—leading Jo to believe that it was, indeed, nighttime. Her watch corroborated the fact, reading just after midnight. But Jo still felt like she had to sneak through the halls.

Jo departed from the recreation room and scooped her watch off the shelf, fastening it back over her wrist. The expanse of hall leading to the Four-Way was void of windows. It wasn't until she was walking down the stairs and heading toward the common area that she even got a sense of time. Of course, she could've checked her watch, but that was just so *logical* and her brain was far too sluggish for such taxing solutions to life's simple problems.

Dawn was just cracking over the mountains in the distance, rays of sunlight arcing over their peaks and shining brightly—blindingly—over the pool. It filtered in as vibrant streaks through the columns on the opposite wall of the entry to the common area. For once, the room was silent.

"Well, I guess I'll have to make my own coffee," she lamented dramatically to no one in particular. At least, she intended it to be no one in particular.

"I could summon Nico for you." Eslar's voice rose up from the couch, only to be followed by the man himself.

"Sorry, didn't see you there." The apology was half-hearted. She'd definitely prefer Nico's brewing skills to her own. If Eslar insisted, she certainly wasn't about to stop him.

"How did it go?" Eslar got right to business, forgetting mention of Nico entirely—much to Jo's disappointment. "Wayne reported he saw you leaving a while ago."

"Not *that* long ago." Jo shrugged as she slowly fussed about the kitchen.

"You did not answer my question."

"Yes sir, sorry sir." Eslar didn't seem to appreciate her joking, so Jo returned her voice to a less militaristic tone. "All seems to be well."

"It must be, if you're here." He shifted back onto the seat of the couch, the back of his head to her, tilted down.

The television was off, which meant something else was occupying his attention. Jo strolled over, confirming her suspicions. "Hey—sorry, didn't meant to startle you."

"What else do you require, Josephina?"

"Josephina? What are you? My mother?" Jo leaned on the back of the couch. "Do you have one of those you'd recommend me? Preferably one not in. . ."

"Elvish?" he finished for her, confirming her supicions.

"Yeah."

"You want to read?"

"You don't have to sound so surprised." She walked back to the kitchen, hoping to hide the small amount of offense she took at the shock in his eyes.

"I do have one I'd recommend. I actually think you'd enjoy it. It's one of Samson's favorites, actually. . . But it is in Elvish."

Jo poured herself a cup of coffee. "Bummer." Well, there went the idea of cutting herself off from tech for a few blissful hours.

"Why does that bother you?" An offended tone took up residence in his words.

"I can't read—*oh*." Jo brought up her palm, smothering her face for a second with a groan. The elf had the audacity to give a low chuckle. "I'm exhausted okay! I forgot I had translation magic." She leaned against the counter, cradling her mug, and clarified, "It'll work on languages that. . ."

"No longer exist?" The words were steely, almost practiced, almost in a manner she'd expect to hear from Snow. "Yes."

"Then pass over the words."

Eslar stood, departing the room for several minutes (long enough for Jo to finish her cup and wash it) before returning with a tome in hand. There were a few runes stitched into the leather of the front. Jo blinked at it several times: nothing. Just when she was beginning to get paranoid that her mind was too taxed to mentally translate anything, they shifted.

"*The Bow of the Goddess*?"

"An old folk tale about a man who was gifted a weapon by the Goddess of the Hunt, making him her chosen champion in her war against the Goddess Oblivion."

"Sounds like fun." Jo shrugged.

"Does it?" He seemed skeptical.

"I want something that I've never seen before to cleanse my mental palate. And I'm fairly certain I've never seen anything like this before."

"The likelihood is slim," Eslar agreed before strolling over to the couch. Jo started for one of the chairs by the pool that she and Nico usually sat out on, awash in the morning's sun. She thought the conversation over, but then Eslar added, softly, as if debating if he wanted to say anything at all, "Keep it as long as you need. Let me know what you think when you're finished."

"Yeah, sure," Jo mumbled, staring at the elf. It felt almost like… friendship? Closer than she'd felt with the man since their first wish.

Jo took up her seat, and a few hours passed in blissful silence. Her mind soaked up the words. All too soon, she no longer even saw the script-like runic language, and instead, became absorbed in the story that hailed from a time when magic was real and gods seemed just a little more possible.

What was shaping up to be a surprisingly peaceful morning was, unsurprisingly, ruined by Wayne. Jo didn't even hear him come in, but he must've made a direct line for where she sat. "Wow, doll, you look like hell."

Jo startled, nearly dropping the book. Her eyes drifted up to where he stood at the edge of her lounge chair. "Good morning to you, too?"

"I take it you were successful?"

"Right to business I see." Jo closed her book and set it aside. "I'm trying to hold you in suspense, is it working?" Really, what Jo wanted to say was "turn on the damn TV."

"Should I get Takako first?" Wayne posed the question loudly enough to be fielding Eslar's opinion as well.

Jo stood, making a show of stretching, hoping she didn't have to be the first one to speak. She didn't know what the right answer was here. But something possessed Eslar to look her way. *Why did this come down to her?* She swallowed hard. "She'll find out one way or another. I think she should be here. It could be a relief to wake up and see everyone evacuating."

"I'll get her then." Wayne scurried off.

As he did, Jo made her way over to the couches, sitting diagonally across from Eslar in what had become her usual spot. She focused on situating herself on the cushions, looking at the elf from the corners of her eyes. Eslar must have come from a time with no notion of awkward looks, because he ignored her deftly. Or maybe he just didn't care.

Jo opened her mouth to speak, just as he did the same.

"How are you liking the book?"

"Oh, fine. . . I'm kind of a slow reader, so I'm only at the part where the God of Fortune is meeting with the Goddess of the Hunt to discuss crafting a weapon."

Eslar hummed, nodding, flipping the page of his own manuscript.

The book wasn't what she wanted to talk about, and he must know it. Jo swallowed, glancing toward the door. They were alone, but for how long? She had to chance it. Things were going well between her and one of the oldest members of the Society; this was as good an opportunity as any. "Should we get Pan as well?"

To his credit, Eslar was unrattled. "Do you really want to subject Takako to that again?"

"As she said, she can stand up for herself."

"Can you trust yourself around her?" Eslar raised his narrowed his eyes, no doubt referring to the temper Pan brought out in Jo.

"Trust myself not to do what? Is there something I should be worried about?" The memory of the woman-child with a blood-red sky behind her flashed unbidden before Jo's eyes.

"She brings out something in you."

"And why do you think that is?" Jo knew why: it was because Pan was a barely tolerable twat, nothing more or less.

"Perhaps it's because Pan is the oldest among us, and

the closest to Snow," Eslar said, almost nonchalantly. But the casual words were obviously loaded.

Before Jo could probe further on *exactly* what he meant, especially about the Snow bit, Wayne returned with not just Takako in tow.

"Good morning, Jo." Nico gave her a cheerful smile, quickly crossing over. "How is it that you don't have a cup in hand?"

"Because I've already had two cups."

"Then I take it you don't need a third?" he asked, heading into the kitchen.

"Blasphamy good sir!" Jo said dramatically. Nico chuckled, and gave a nod, already making espresso. It was the only spot of levity she could find before her eyes fell on Takako, who sat heavily next to her.

"How did it go?"

Jo opened her mouth to answer but Eslar responded by (finally) turning on the TV instead.

Everyone stopped all movement the moment a newscaster appeared.

It took a moment for Jo to properly hear the broadcast. She wanted to chalk it up to having focused for so long on translating Elvish. But that wasn't the case.

It was her mind reeling as the words she'd expected to hear and the ones currently being spoken clashed in severe counterpoint with each other. She even found herself reading the notices at the bottom of the screen over and over again, as if maybe she'd discover that her magical, internal translator was somehow out of whack.

But no matter how hard she tried, the words

continued on unchanged. *The world went on unchanged.* And that was entirely the problem.

". . . Japanese Government has issued a statement explaining that there is no scientific evidence to support such claims and all scientific agencies responsible for monitoring potential natural disasters did not issue the warning either. Therefore, Prime Minister Nakamura has deemed the evacuation call a cyber-attack, and requested that all citizens ignore the recent evacuation requests as they look into the organization responsible for these hacks."

Jo was on her feet. Her heart raced. Her hands balled into fists. Her face flushed not with anger but sheer horror.

"Currently, they are not linked to any terrorist group and appear to be a rogue attack set to strike fear into the populous and cause chaos. While the motivations are still currently unknown, the Prime Minister has sworn to uncover the truth, vowing to allocate emergency funds to the PSIA to ensure the safety of the citizenry. In light of the news of his swift and decisive action, Nakamura's approval ratings have risen nearly 33 percent, a steep rise just before the elections. . ."

The newscaster's voice faded to a static buzz. As if all language magic had worn off beneath sheer, appalled disbelief, Jo could barely understand the words at all anymore. Only one statement cut through the humming between her ears.

"Nice try, hotshot."

She spun on her heel, staring down Wayne. "I did everything perfectly!"

"Clearly not." Eslar looked up at her, as if challenging her to try to intimidate him. As if accusing her for spending so much time lounging when there was work to be done. *Not that she'd known.*

"The last time I looked in the recreation room not more than three hours ago, things seemed to be going smoothly. People were beginning to move. I-I set up the evacuation notices, I planted information in scientific databases—"

"Come on, doll. You didn't think those scientists would try to validate where that information was coming from?"

"Do not take that tone with me." Jo scowled, her attention returning to Wayne. "Do not speak down to me." She felt her blood boiling. "Where were you and your flipping coin while I worked all night?"

"You told me you didn't need—how did you put it? Me and my nickel?" he fired back with rapier-speed and accuracy. It was that thing between them again, a natural escalation that kept them feeding easily off of one another. Unfortunately, this time it wasn't directed at a common enemy, but each other. "You chose the job and took it on for the team. Don't pawn off responsibility."

He had a point. *The bastard had a point.* Jo ran a hand through her hair, snagging on tangles. "I'll fix it. I'll fix it," she muttered.

"How?" Wayne asked. "You have more answers in that magic hacker bag of tricks?"

Her brain was on overdrive. It was running through everything she'd done the night prior, looking for a way to improve, looking for a fix. Simultaneously, Jo was looking forward. Even with the post-hack-a-thon exhaustion making her brain fuzzy, she desperately sifted through direction, information, viable courses of action.

And she was coming up empty.

Minus her little hiccup at the beginning (and, even then, everything had worked out just fine in the end), every other wish she'd touched had been a series of successes. Now, she was failing at the moment it mattered most. Jo dropped her hands to her sides and sighed. Her pride had gotten her in this mess. She'd been a fool for thinking she could do it all on her own. So she couldn't assume more pride would get her out.

"I don't know. . ." Jo confessed to them all. "I *thought* I did everything right. I was so sure I could do it." Her eyes fell on Takako. Shame and guilt filled her stomach, pushing two words up past her throat and out of her mouth. "I'm sorry."

She looked back to the TV. Jo heard it for the first time again, but the words remained washed out. They were all repeats from before.

"I don't think this is a total failure," Takako said, finally.

"How?" Eslar stole everyone's question from their halfway open mouths.

"They say scientists are looking for any foundation to the emergency being called." Takako's words were careful, clearly trying to draw the line between optimism and pragmatism. "We just have to make sure that they're given a reason to find what they're looking

CIRCLE OF ASHES ✍️

for. We need to prove to them that the emergency needs to be taken seriously."

A ray of hope sparked in Jo's chest. Perhaps there was a way yet to salvage the situation. On reflex, her mind immediately went to how she could hack and code her way to a solution.

But she pushed it aside.

"Let's get everyone together in the briefing room." She couldn't do this alone. None of them could. Wayne had been right; she just had to learn it the hard way. "We need a new plan, team."

14. THE CRAFTSMAN'S PLAN

"**A**LL RIGHT." JO started the moment everyone had situated themselves in their usual seats in the briefing room. It probably looked a little presumptuous for her to be standing at the head of the table, but Snow was (as usual) nowhere to be found, and she simply couldn't help herself. She needed to prove not only that she could offer the necessary support for this wish, but that she recognized the benefits of the other members of the team in accomplishing it. Her failure had settled thick and heavy in the pit of her stomach, and she wanted to do everything she could to remedy the weight.

"Some of you, most of you, know. . . But the attempt at forcing an evacuation using the bio bands was a failure," Jo spoke directly to Samson as he was the only one missing from the common room earlier.

Samson nodded, sinking slightly into his chair under her stare. Jo quickly averted her eyes, as not to put so much unintentional pressure on the shy man.

"The government has labeled it a terror attack and the evacuation has ended before it could even really begin. So, we need to re-evaluate our next steps. . ." She let her voice trail off, hoping that someone would offer the solution she didn't have.

For a second, the Society simply looked among themselves before settling as a unit back on her. It was Nico, in his usual kind tone, who finally spoke up, "Well, we still need to get people to evacuate."

"Exactly," Jo said, pacing a bit like a teacher trying to get her students to come to their own solutions on a project. Really, she was just hoping she'd find her own exceptional solution somewhere in the three feet of space she was traversing. "And how do we do that now that the evacuation has been discredited?"

"If we knew that, doll, we would have figured out a plan of action already," Wayne interjected. "Or perhaps you would've done it." Despite the way it made Jo bristle, she ignored the smart remark. If he was trying to be playful, he was grossly misreading the room. Instead of letting herself be egged on, however, Jo merely threw him a distinctly unimpressed look before waiting for someone else to offer a more helpful opinion.

Thankfully, Takako seemed to have no problem offering support. "We need to show them proof of why evacuation is still the right course of action. There's attention being paid to it now, so it may not take much to validate the concerns you planted. We merely need to give it credit that can't be ignored."

Before Jo could pick up on that, Wayne leaned heavily back into his chair with a bitter sounding laugh. "Oh damn. I forgot to record all the terrible broadcasts coming up so we can just play them on repeat for those who don't have the luxury of time travel."

"Wayne," Eslar scolded this time, earning if not a chastised look from the man, then at least a moment of silence. A silence which Jo wasted no time filling.

"Scientists are already looking for proof of the unidentified claims, the news said as much. Even if they don't know how the records that triggered the evacuation notices got there, it's been enough to peak their interest," she continued, leaning against the table and doing her best interpretation of Snow, trying to look each person in the eyes, one at a time. "So why haven't they offered up any of their findings?"

For a long moment, everyone seemed to consider the options, but eventually, Takako uttered a soft murmur of recognition. "They don't *have* any findings yet, right? Or they would present them."

"That's what I'm thinking." Jo wasn't sure if they had zero findings or just inconsequential ones, but she nodded anyway; it fit everything that had been said so far, and was the best direction forward. "If the scientists had something, there's no way they'd let the government call off the evacuation knowing the danger Fuji poses."

"Then what are we going to have to do to make sure they arrive at findings worth sharing and evacuating over?" Eslar asked, more to himself than the group, one dark green thumbnail caught between his teeth as his eyes narrowed in concentration. "And make sure they reach these conclusions with enough time for all the people that need to move to do so?"

Things looked about as hopeless as ever, but Jo couldn't help but feel a small swell of pride as everyone began floating ideas across the table. Perhaps her contribution hadn't been a total failure after all.

No, it'd been an epic mistake. Jo couldn't let herself lose sight of that, or the monster of pride would crawl onto her back and whisper in her ear again. Getting everyone back on track was, at best, repentance.

"Oh!" Nico sat up, not quite slamming but definitely placing his palms heavily on the table. His gaze instantly sought out Jo's, an enthusiasm there that was both endearing and motivating. "What if they have no findings because they don't have anything strong enough to perceive them?"

Jo mulled that over. "You mean, they don't have the technology?" It seemed outlandish that, out of all of the technological advancements her time period had under its belt, *this* would be the one thing that had fallen through the cracks. They had androids petitioning to live normal lives, indistinguishable from humans, but not better earthquake detecting materials?

"Let's say they don't have proper measurement tools for correct prediction information. We'd need a stronger seismograph—something that can measure deep-layer tectonic shifts and then predict future movement based on these micro-movements." Eslar continued, frowning as well in deep, disgruntled thought.

Jo actually took a small step away from the table, taken aback with surprise. The elf was from a time period that was so long ago, and so far from her own, that it was utterly inconceivable to Jo to even imagine. Yet, he could navigate technology better than most from Jo's own times. As annoying as he could be in his occasional role of "team mom," Eslar was truly something else.

"I can do that."

All eyes turned to Samson, his brow furrowed and eyes distant, as if he hadn't even realized he'd spoken. Jo could see one hand tapping an unnatural rhythm against the table as his other fiddled with a cube shaped object held a few inches away from his lips. His fingers shifted with practiced ease, a soft magical aura emanating from him that Jo could feel all the way from the other end of the table.

The silence following his statement stretched long enough that Eslar had to cut back in, clearing his throat to get the craftsman's attention. Samson jumped slightly, though his hands continued to fiddle; the cube seemed to mold beneath his fingers like a sentient clay, becoming something Jo could not yet envision. "Samson?"

"I can make what you need," he clarified, eyes downcast, though not in a way that emanated any sort of self-consciousness. Instead, they seemed to shift about the open space in front of him as if already trying to work out a spatial understanding of his newest project.

"It- It will be simple," he went on. "Enough to convince anyone—scientist, government, prime minister. It should cover all of our bases, dig deep enough into the necessary seismic data that the evacuations will be irrefutable. Just tapping into the AI supercomputers for high-level calculations. . . Modifications, really. Nothing new. Just improving what's there for them. I can do that. Yes, I can, no problem."

For a long moment, Jo didn't know what to say; it was the most she'd ever heard come out of Samson's mouth at one time. But she wasn't about to waste it. With a quick clearing of her throat, she nodded and tacked on the best look of motivated authority she could manage.

"You heard the man. He's got the proof machine on lock." She must really be getting used to the world of magic if she'd take that simple explanation from a thousand-year-old man as proof he could create such a thing. "So, now how do we get that machine into the hands of a scientist who can use it?"

From there, all discussion focused on hashing out logistics. If there was anything Jo had learned throughout her time as the Shewolf, it was the benefit of laying all the "best cards" out on the table, working out a foolproof methodology, and playing it like a poker game she had no intention of losing. They had aces up their sleeves—magic—and with it, there was no way they *could* lose.

This was merely about getting somebody to look at their hand and recognize the win.

Wayne and Takako took it upon themselves to

masquerade as researchers looking to sell the updated seismograph machine to the head seismic facility, capitalizing on the recent interest in such a device. With Wayne's magical abilities, conning their way into the office of the right people would be "a piece of cake"—or a piece of something from the 1920s that Jo promptly forgot (Tomato Pie, perhaps?). Then, it would simply be a matter of falsifying documents on Jo's end just to tidy things up if anyone looked for evidence that Wayne and Takako were indeed part of a legitimate company. Another night of hacking the appropriate registries, creating documentation for the machine's functionality, and their validity.

And, if she was thorough and careful, another night of opportunity for Jo to redeem herself.

15. KEN AND GOOFO

The door to the rec room opened with an icy breath. Jo instantly pulling her sleeves down over her hands.

Inside, the same set-up greeted her as last time: monitors, futon, and a freshly stocked mini-fridge of RAGE Energy. She blinked, allowing her eyes to adjust to the dim lighting. It all looked pristine once more, as if waiting for her to make a mess all over again.

There was, however, one new addition. Draped over the back of the chair at the computer desk was a brand-new hoodie. It wasn't her usual all black fare, but a deep navy ensemble with a slightly off-blue pattern over it that reminded her of abstract snowflakes.

Jo ran her fingers over the fabric, trying to place the material. It was softer than wool, higher quality than a cotton. . . cashmere? Not quite. It was different than anything she'd ever touched before and yet so similar to something she could've sworn she'd felt—likely a designer dress at a department store, the sort of thing she could look at and dream of but never afford.

"Really?" she asked no one but the seemingly sentient walls, trying to talk away the odd feelings it evoked in her. "You can give me a new hoodie, but you can't make a room that's less icy and can still have all my tech?" Jo slung her arms into the sleeves, waiting for a reply. There was none. Then again, she was a bit glad of the fact. She may be settled into her magical existence, but she had a feeling a talking mansion would take it a step too far. "Either way, thanks, I guess."

Jo plopped herself into the chair. She didn't run into the room this time or slide up to the keyboard with momentum. No, Jo leaned back, stretched out her legs, sank into the (surprisingly soft) hoodie the room had given her, and stared at nothing for several long breaths.

As if somehow knowing that she had yet to start in on her task, there was a knock on the door. Jo turned and what felt like a now distant memory came back to her—*was the last person to knock on the door Pan?*

She swallowed, making sure her voice was even and strong. "Come in."

Part of her hoped that it was Pan; Jo wouldn't mind a few minutes alone with that girl-creature to give her some uninterrupted pieces of her mind. But while that may be something Jo would *like*, it was also perhaps not the best idea given that the mere thought of the supernova-haired woman still set Jo's blood running hot. So, ultimately, she was glad it was just Wayne. As quickly as they could rise each other to anger, it also seemed they could put each other at ease.

"Hey, doll." Wayne swept over her with his gaze. There was something uncanny about that look. Even though Jo knew her hair was a mess, there were likely bags under her eyes, she was in a sweatshirt about four sizes too big, and Wayne had noted earlier that she "looked like hell," he could still look at her as though she was the most magnificent creature he'd ever beheld.

"I really should figure out a pet name for you." Jo gave him her own up-and-down. His sleeves were rolled, collar slightly unbuttoned. But his vest and pants were tailored to perfection, a sort of casual prestige that only men like Wayne could muster, even if it lacked a little of its usual magic. "You call me doll, so, how about. . ." She tapped her lips with a hum. "Ken?"

"Ken?" Wayne seemed startled.

"Yeah, you call me doll, like a Barbie Doll. Ken was her boyfriend."

"Boyfriend?" He arched his eyebrows.

Jo laughed at the idea, so loudly that she could hear her voice echoing in the hall. "No, Wayne, just *no*. Not like that. We covered all that, remember? I was just thinking of a male version for 'doll'."

Wayne slid his hands in his pockets, an endearing smile on his lips. "I rather like my name. I don't think I want to take another man's, even if it means a term of endearment from you."

"Not Ken, then?"

"No." He shook his head. "How about goofo?"

"Goo-what-now?" Just when she thought he

couldn't get any weirder.

"Goofo," Wayne repeated, as though it would somehow make it more obvious. "Zelda Fitzgerald called Scott that, real romantic-like."

She could only laugh.

"So goofo is a no?"

"Obviously." Jo grinned at him. "Don't really want anything 'romantic-like.'"

"You're the one who went there with boyfriend talk."

Jo gave him a half-hearted roll of her eyes. "I guess we'll have to keep looking."

"I guess so."

There was a brief moment where they just smiled at each other. Shoulders relaxed, as if forgetting the tension of the wish that loomed over them every waking moment now. "Thanks," Jo mumbled. "I needed that."

"Needed what?" He seemed genuinely confused, though a smile still tugged lazily at his lips, betraying him; he might have had a better idea than he let on.

Jo shook her head, dislodging the thoughts. She couldn't let herself get comfortable and forget what was on the line. Comfort would make her relax, and relaxing led to sloppiness. The weight of the stress on her shoulders was necessary right now. "Nothing. Anyway. . . What can I help you with? I doubt you came here to talk about goofo."

"I didn't." He took a step in, finally, just enough to allow the door to mostly close behind him. "I wanted to apologize."

"Apologize?"

"I was a bit of an ass."

Jo could draw things out further, make him really say what he'd done wrong. Prove his remorse. But she knew sincerity when she heard it. So she just waved a hand through the air, as if clearing any negative thoughts or feelings from the space between them. "It happens. Don't worry about it. We're all under a lot of stress."

"Speaking of. . ." Jo knew where Wayne was going just by his tone. He didn't have to say anything further, but he did anyway. "When you're done in here, I thought perhaps you may need to blow off some of a little steam."

"And you're offering your services?" The corner of her mouth pulled into a smirk despite herself. They hadn't actually done anything since Paris (if you ignored heavy flirting now and then), and while the itch hadn't turned into a full-blown ache for touch, Jo supposed she wouldn't mind some physical companionship for an evening.

So, why wasn't the idea more appealing?

"Only if you'd like to make use of those services, of course." Wayne gave an almost lecherous wink.

"I'll think about it, *Ken*." She dragged out the pseudo pet name, knowing just what it'd do.

He gasped and stepped away, hand pressed to his chest in only semi-faux insult. Jo laughed at his offended stare, her mission accomplished. "Well, now you've ruined the mood," Wayne huffed.

"I couldn't resist."

"I hope you're satisfied."

She was, but spared him and didn't rub it in.

He left, the air between them settled and friendly once more. That said. . . their flirting was fun, but it felt a hollow, like an echo of what could've been there but wasn't quite. Stress, Jo decided. The stress wasn't making her want anything. Certainly, that was it.

Jo placed her hands on the keyboard and set to clearing that stress right from the root. The monitors flared to life. Well, all but one. Jo stared at it dumbly. It was the same one as before. She reached up and tapped the power button.

Nothing.

Jo tapped it again. Then gave a few raps on the side of the screen. It turned on with a suddenness that nearly blinded her. Squinting, Jo quickly adjusted the brightness, and set about her work. The mansion made everything realistic, down to the occasional technology glitch, it seemed.

The banter had, somehow, re-sorted the random tangents that cluttered her mind. Things were running smoothly again. Her magic felt like a marathon, rather than sprints. Jo drew on it at a consistent pace in the background of her mind, greasing the wheels but not using it for momentum. Her own talent was enough for that.

Overall, she moved more slowly, but with unwavering purpose. It wasn't fueled with arrogance and fear like the frazzled machete-like approach she'd taken last time. No, Jo was beginning to wield her magic like a scalpel, striking only where she needed with absolute precision. Like this, absolutely nothing could stand in her way. It was as if just touching something caused it to unravel.

There were only two cans of RAGE ENERGY left in the fridge when Jo departed the recreation room for the third time in three days. Her more measured, direct approach yielded results. Isn't that what Yuusuke had tried to tell her years ago? Approach it like playing the long-con, not the quick attack?

At least, she thought he'd said that. Trying to recall moments from her past life, her "real" life, was starting to become more and more difficult.

It was like trying to pick apart a hyper-vivid dream from a similar memory. Whenever her mind drifted to specifics, they seemed to waver and shift like two cells layered on top of each other. Was it Yuusuke's advice she was following, or someone else whose name and face she'd already forgotten? When images of a long beard, a crowned head, and ornate clothing flashed across her mind's eye, was that a memory, or a phantom image from a distant but lingering dream?

Jo rubbed her eyes. Being part of a society outside of time probably just had some unfortunate side effects, that's all. And surely the supremely hazy memories of her best friend, the man she'd given up her existence for, were purely a result of exhaustion and not an actual loss of clarity.

Even if she worked fewer hours this time, the session was no less intensive than the last. Her mind felt like pulp, one even Eslar's bedtime story may not be able to save.

Jo looked down the empty hall. There were no

sounds echoing, no footsteps nearing, and the door to the other recreation room was void of a watch. It compelled her to check her own—just past three a.m., for whatever time was worth. Basically nothing, other than the arbitrary habits they still observed.

Which meant everyone was likely holed up in their own rooms, passing the time doing whatever they did. She knew where to find Wayne just like she knew he'd not mind her barging in on his space. Jo leaned against the door with a sigh. The thought was no more appealing than it was last time. Their conversation earlier had, indeed, sparked something in her. She wanted touch, but not Wayne's.

Jo pressed her palm to her forehead with a sigh. What *did* she want then? Or rather, *who*?

When her hand pulled away, Jo looked left, not right, toward a white door at the opposite end of the hall. She was too old to be playing games like this. She knew what she wanted and she was in control of her emotions—most of the time.

But this? This was some odd magnetic vortex that drew her forward with an inexplicable force. Jo found herself toe-to-toe with Snow's door, facing off like it was some wild beast. She remembered the last time she'd stood before his door, the cryptic answers that followed all the questions still swirling in her mind like unspoken taboos. Then there was the time he'd come to her in the night, making things all the more confusing.

Jo's hand hovered. But when it fell, her knuckles didn't meet the wood of the door. Jo's fingers splayed out over the grain. She tipped her head forward, only realizing how warm she'd grown once her forehead met the cool, unblemished surface.

She was better than this. She wasn't some lovesick teenager with raging hormones, debating how to get laid. Hell, she had a hot 1920s heartthrob waiting in a bed for her.

"I don't know why I'm here," Jo whispered.

Her eyes opened with purpose. No, she knew *exactly* why she was there. She knew what she wanted. She didn't want cheap sex or empty intimacy. She wanted more than an itch scratched. She wanted to explore a connection with someone who had somehow managed to pull her in with nothing but a look. Snow and she weren't anything, yet infinite possibilities stretched between them like a vast ocean.

Jo had a staring contest with the door as if it held all the secrets of the man within. But even if it did, it wasn't betraying them to her. She started down the hall in the opposite direction, hands balled into fists.

Fine, she wanted Snow. She wanted to chart that sea of "maybes" and "what ifs" between them, even if it ultimately led nowhere. She was big enough to admit it to herself. Now, it was just a matter of figuring out how and when she was going to admit it to him.

16. USEFUL SKILL

J O DIDN'T GO back to her room that night.
It wasn't that she didn't *like* her room. It was lovely, like a picture. But it was also a picture that reminded her of the one night she'd spent with Wayne. Furthermore, like a picture, it was something that had little use. There was a bed (for all the sleeping she couldn't do), a desk area (pointless, given everywhere else in the mansion), the wall where she'd hung her painting from Nico (nice, but she didn't spend hours staring at it), and a small computer (that she'd long since deemed insufficient compared to the recreation room).

So, instead, Jo returned to the seat by the pool she had begun to frequent. Eslar's book from earlier was still there, waiting for her right where she'd left it. Small orbs strung along the entrance into the living and kitchen areas lit the patio with just enough light to read by. While her mind felt too mushy to really grasp any of the words that her eyes fell over, it was repetitive, mindless, and blissfully passed the time.

Right around dawn, shifting from the kitchen behind her alerted Jo to the presence of someone else. She shifted in her chair, poking her nose around the side to see what other ghost was lurking about in what had become an unofficial "quiet time" for the members of the Society.

Samson didn't seem to notice her at all, which gave Jo an opportunity to observe him. His motions had a fluidity that reminded Jo strangely of Eslar. It was a sort of grace Jo could only dream of mustering, and beyond the most virtuoso ballerina she'd ever seen. There was something that looked *magic* in the way he simply existed that no one else could seem to command.

He appeared to be busying himself with a few ingredients from the fridge, and unlike his usual demeanor, he was doing so with an easy confidence, his back and shoulders free from tension. His brown hands moved with delicate precision, and Jo was instantly reminded of the fact that she'd never actually seen the craftsman's magic at work. She could only assume it was an impressive sight to behold, given how nearly everything else about him was.

She realized then, watching him go about fixing himself an early morning snack, that out of everyone on the team, she knew the least about Samson. Beyond his position as the crafter and his five-star cooking, Jo hadn't interacted with him much, and her questions surrounding him and his origins were plenty. Rivaled only by her questions surrounding Pan, perhaps.

Before she could announce her presence to the easily startled enigma, Samson turned (as if sensing being watched) and looked directly at her. As expected, he seemed momentarily stunned, maybe even frightened, and nearly dropped his plate. Jo was quick to scramble from her chair, rushing to his aid. Samson barely caught one end of the dish, holding it shakily. Out of breath from the quick sprint, Jo held the other side firmly for a moment.

"Sorry about that, I didn't mean to scare you." At this proximity, she could see the flecks of gold in his wide-set eyes. Guilty for startling him and then encroaching on his space, she let go of the plate. As if by magic, his hold was now far sturdier.

"It's all right," he replied, though not without slouching a bit and looking quickly away from her face. "I usually don't find others here at this hour. Well, maybe Eslar, but not today it seems."

"Yeah, we all kind of hide away at night, don't we?" Jo chuckled, though it was mostly humorless, dying off quickly and replacing itself with an awkward though not uncomfortable silence. Samson seemed no more interested in striking up conversation, so eventually Jo cleared her throat and tried again by using the plate as her inspiration. "Making some breakfast?"

For a beat, Samson seemed almost confused by the question, but then he glanced from her face to his plate and recognition filled his eyes. "Oh, no. This is for later. Maybe I will want to snack then, maybe not. Making food, eating food, just. . . food helps me think, and I intend to spend the entirety of today, if not longer, working on the machine."

An idea struck Jo at the words, and while part of her thought it might be overstepping, especially with Samson's obvious preference for solitude, she rolled with it. Finding excuses to spend time with Samson outside of the kitchen had been near impossible so far, and he certainly didn't offer any opportunities of his own volition. Jo wouldn't let the present chance to learn more about her teammate and friend pass her up, especially now that her part of the wish was once again complete. The idea of simply sitting around twiddling her thumbs or re-reading the passages of Eslar's book while she waited had the potential to drive her mad.

"Would you like some help?" Samson merely blinked, so she added, "With the seismograph, I mean. I can hand you tools or something. I don't actually know how your crafting magic works, but if you need a second set of hands. . ." Her voice trailed off at his expression. Samson continued to stare at her for a long moment, face open and surprised. In fact, he stared long enough that Jo began to feel a little self-conscious about her offer. "You don't have to say yes if you would rather work alone, I just figured I'd—"

"Yes!" Samson cut her off, the word escaping him a lot louder than Jo was used to hearing from the soft-spoken man. When he realized his outburst, he slouched into himself again, a rosy blush spreading across his face. "Yes, please. I would appreciate the help."

Which was how, for the first time, Jo found herself in Samson's room.

Like most other rooms in the mansion, it was a mash-up of different aesthetics that Jo would usually presume to conflict, yet somehow, went together. Wide, rustic-looking beams that reminded her of an old-timey cabin stretched across the roof. Their dark stain was offset by the plastered and whitewashed ceiling and walls. Over the cement floor, various pelts had been thrown, and atop them long steel worktables stretched the length of the rectangular room. The whole left side seemed practically littered with tinkering tools on open counter space; the phrase "organized chaos" came to mind.

Despite the slight messiness and industrial notes clashing with natural, however, the whole room felt incredibly warm and welcoming, cozy in a way that only a properly lived in and well-loved place could be. Even the view beyond the paned window over the counters on the left was soothing. The glass was slightly frosted at the corners and looked out over high snow drifts.

Curiously, there was a secondary door on the right wall; Jo's room only boasted one entry and exit.

"What's in there? Storage?" she couldn't stop herself from asking.

"Oh, that. . ." He trailed off as he wandered toward the door. For a brief moment, Jo worried she was asking about something personal. She was grateful just to be in his space at all; she shouldn't pry. But her concerns proved unfounded as he stopped, suddenly turning, head bowed and picking at his nails. "It's my room."

Duh. There was no bed, no personal items in the

workshop.

"Would you like to see it?"

"What?" The question came out purely in surprise, but Samson's shoulders seemed to droop further. "No, I mean, yes." Jo took a breath and gave him a big smile as his head rose timidly. "I don't want to invade your space, but I'd love to see it if you want to show me."

Relief overtook him, and Samson quickly opened the door, ushering her over to look inside.

Jo hovered in the doorframe. The truth was, there wasn't much room for her to go any further. Her original suspicion of a storage closet wasn't far off. A narrow bed took up the entire wall to the right, the door opening against it if pushed too wide. To the left was a hearth, crackling and warming more furs and blankets piled over a small but comfortable-looking chair.

A shelf was directly at her left, piled with books and other trinkets—some she recognized from Samson's fidgeting. Across from that was a narrow work table, the chair before the hearth seeming to serve a dual purpose depending on where its owner wanted to sit more. There, an array of feathers and shafts of wood were piled; a quiver hung on the wall above.

"Arrows?" Jo asked, daring to taking a step in as Samson moved aside.

"Yes." He focused entirely on the quiver as well, speaking more to it than her. "I was a fletcher, in the Age of Magic."

"A fletcher? Someone who makes arrows?"

"And bows." Samson nodded, walking over hastily. "I would do quivers too. Sometimes even leathers or chainmail. I had a small smithy where I could make the heads too. Look." He pulled open a drawer, pulling out a small point of lead and twirling it between two fingers. "This one was my favorite."

"It's very lovely." She made a show of inspecting the arrowhead. Jo didn't know the first thing about archery, but she did know when someone was proud of their work and she didn't want to discourage him by not showing enough excitement. "And deadly-looking," she added, not knowing which was a better compliment for such a thing.

A dusting of rose covered his cheeks and Samson quickly looked down, stashing it back into the drawer. "Then there's—"

"What's this?" She hadn't intended to interrupt him, it just sort of happened. Jo lifted a finger, pointing at a single arrow in the quiver. Slightly taller than the rest, the feathers on its end seemed to shimmer with their own light; every time she shifted her eyes, they seemed to take on new colors in stark contrast to the pale, almost golden wood used on the shaft. "Did you make this—"

"Don't touch it!" He grabbed her wrist and Jo felt the bones crunch. She tried not to wince, but may have failed, given how quickly Samson pulled away. He clearly didn't know how much strength was in his hands. "Th-That was a gift. . . I think. . ." Samson had a staring contest with the arrow for a long moment as if waiting for it to confirm his suspicions, before turning and starting for the door. "We should get to work."

"Yeah. . ." Jo mumbled, rubbing her wrist. She took

one glance back at the quiver and its mysterious contents but quickly tried to put it from her mind. Judging from the way Samson acted, it must have something to do with the wish he'd made. Hadn't Takako said that her wish now seemed hazy, too? With how long Samson had been in the Society, it would be no wonder that his recollection of the circumstances that had brought him there were faded.

Jo closed the door to his room behind her, determined to put it all far from her mind. She considered leaving briefly. But a stool had been pulled out next to where Samson was already beginning to lay out supplies. Jo accepted the unspoken invitation and settled herself down among the bits, baubles, and tools that lined the back wall. The plate of food he'd made was at her elbow (he must have set it down during her initial inspection of the place), still untouched.

Samson grabbed a work apron from a hook on the wall and gathered up tools and mismatched electronics, piling them at the center of the table. There was an air of preparation to what he was doing. His extreme focus pushed away the last of the awkwardness from the incident in his room and Jo let it fade as well. If he wasn't letting it bother him, then she wouldn't let it bother her. After several long minutes, Jo, intrigued, couldn't help but get back to her feet and walk over for a closer look at what he was doing.

The man said nothing. Frankly, Jo would've put her money on him completely forgetting that she was even there. Samson looked over the accumulated items in front of him, hands flat on the table before him and eyes bouncing from item to item with an electric focus. When Jo got close to him, she felt it instantly—magic rolling off of him in waves. Then, with a quick breath, Samson got to work.

If she'd thought his motions had been precise in the kitchen, they were even more so now. He lifted scraps of metal, plastics, and silicones, turning them into amalgamations greater than the sum of their parts. The way he handled what had now been transformed into bits of electronics and rudimentary machinery seemed almost inhuman, robotic.

Jo couldn't really comprehend what he was doing, tools and hands and magic working together to combine and transmute the items into something new, but she couldn't tear her eyes away either. Magic was invisible. There was no glow, or spark, or thread tying it all together. Yet there was also a force that could *almost* be seen in the way it all moved and shifted.

She had never seen Samson so in his element before. He looked in control, confident—emanating a breathtaking sense of purpose and passion. Watching Samson create something from pieces of nothing until familiar shapes began to form was like watching an artist paint or a musician play. Slowly, Jo could see a framework being laid out. Surprisingly, the way she saw it was not with her own sensibilities of tech, but an intuition that came with the unique magic she'd been gifted with.

"Wait."

His hands froze at her word and Jo swallowed the instant guilt that swelled at disturbing him.

"There's. . ." She struggled to describe what she saw. It was an understanding in a language that only she could comprehend. Trying to fabricate it into common words that would be useful to him was a struggle. Luckily, Samson was no stranger to struggling for words, and he was a more-than-patient listener. "This here. If this connection gets wobbled too violently it could break."

"But there wouldn't be excess movement unless—" It dawned on him the same moment Jo thought to explain it herself.

"Unless someone tried to sabotage the experiment. Or a violent earthquake hit. Or Wayne was his usual clumsy self."

He looked down, assessing what Jo had assumed to be the possible roadmap he'd been following. "Well, then, if I connect this like that. . ."

"No, it's still weak here." She leaned over him to point.

"Here, then."

Jo's magic fizzled between her ears. Her eyes scanned the board he was working on over and over again, until. . . "Yes, that's secure."

Samson leaned back with a smile of triumph. Then, in a flurry of sudden movement, he grabbed her hands. Jo leaned away, not because the contact was unwelcome, but because she'd never been touched by him so intently before. "Your magic is useful to me!"

Jo couldn't stop the burst of laughter in both amusement at his statement and in relief that she truly hadn't put him off by inquiring about his room. "I'm glad," she said earnestly. Perhaps he'd just invited her for the company, but Jo was pleased that her ability to break things could also be of use to their crafter in reverse-engineering for failure.

"I have so many things I want to show you. . ." His eyes scanned the room.

"Let's focus on this for now." There wasn't time to be distracted. "Then, later, I can take a look at whatever you want."

Samson gave a nod and set back to work.

Jo continued to hover over his shoulder, pointing out potential errors the second her magic picked them up. It was like a duet perfectly balanced between someone born to build and another born to destroy. Without having ever realizing it before, they were a near-ideal counterbalance to each other.

Their magics playing off each other gave her an easy sort of air with Samson that Jo had never quite felt before and that bred confidence. Except. . . that wasn't right, was it? Something in the back of her mind told Jo that she *had* felt it before. She knew this feeling even better, truer—different, with someone else. . . But why?

"So how long have you been a part of the Society?" Jo asked by way of distraction. Unlike her other interjections regarding their (now shared) project, Samson's shoulders tensed this time, though his hands never stopped moving, fingers shifting elegantly over one of his tools. When he didn't respond for a while, Jo frowned. "You don't have to answer. I was just curious— you'd mentioned the Age of Magic before and I don't quite understand all the timelines, not really. . . Sorry,"

Jo mumbled, feeling guilty for prying yet again.

"I don't mind," Samson said, though his voice was tight and his eyes stayed pinned to his work. "It's simply a. . . difficult question."

Before Jo could tell him to ignore the question entirely, he went on.

"I was born in 1333, before the Age of Magic ended. As I said, I was a fletcher at the employ of a local duke. I made my wish when. . . well, I've been with the Society since the year 1354."

"That's. . . a long time," Jo whispered lamely, mind rebelling against the possibility. Samson just chuckled, his hands coming to a momentary stop. He kept his eyes on his project, but they looked far away, witnessing a distant memory, maybe.

"It has been," he said. "Though Eslar has been here for much longer."

A strange look came across Samson's face at the mention of the elf, a look that despite its openness, Jo couldn't seem to define. It sparked another thought that she wasn't sure she should voice, but once new information was within reach, Jo couldn't help herself.

"You must have spent a lot of time together. In the beginning."

At this, Samson couldn't help glancing in her direction, eyes wide with surprise. After a few moments, however, his face softened, the ghost of a smile pulling at his lips. He turned to face her more completely, leaning against the table and turning his back to the project. It was the first thing in hours capable of taking his attention away from the device. His eyes held a sadness in them that Jo couldn't fathom, and for the first time since meeting the awkward and kind man, she felt as though she could see just how old he truly was.

"Perhaps we would have, were it not for me. We were each other's only companions for many years—save Pan and Snow," he said eventually, crossing his arms over his chest, stopping the slight rattle that suddenly seemed to overtake his hands. "But time does not heal all wounds. Not even after hundreds of years. And I—my wish—did the unthinkable to him."

Jo wanted to ask what he meant, she couldn't imagine Samson hurting a fly, let alone someone like Eslar. But he'd already turned back to the table, the atmosphere in the room heavy with tension and the sudden, obvious desire for silence. *This* must have been why Wayne had cautioned her against asking about wishes all those months ago. Part of Jo wondered if she should leave, but she didn't move. Jo continued to study what she now knew was the second oldest member of the Society (ignoring Pan and Snow, as most seemed to do on such topics).

"Jo?" Samson said her name just as she'd pushed away from the table. He continued his task, but motioned with his chin toward the side counter of tools. "Will you pass me my pliers? I think they're somewhere by the screwdrivers. Then I'll need you to look at this again with that magic of yours. I think I finally have it sorted."

Jo blinked her own surprise, then found herself smiling. It felt like a peace offering, and even though she had more questions now than answers, she took it easily, handing him his pliers and settling back in to check his work.

17. ESP

J O REMAINED WITH Samson until his fingers were red and raw and her eyes were bleary.

Somewhere along the way, she'd lost all understanding of exactly how the pieces fit together. They were mapped in such a way that only Samson's mind (and magic) could comprehend. But Jo had absolute faith in the man and his command of his project. She focused on doing as he asked, looking at this or that, making sure there wasn't an obvious way she could see the machine and its various mechanisms short-circuit, break, or otherwise come apart—short of smashing it with a hammer, or exerting enough of her magic on it. The more she worked with Samson, the more confident Jo became that she could destroy anything she wanted if she merely exerted enough force of will.

Samson leaned away from the table, wiping his

brow. "I think that's it." He tilted his head this way and that.

"I got nothing else." Jo affirmed. She tilted her head to the side, looking at the machine. As much as she didn't want to come off as questioning Samson's work, she also had a curiosity that couldn't be satiated. "Shouldn't it have rolls of paper, and a needle?"

"Everything is internal here—digital. All the sensors are contained within so they have the least chance of being acted on by external forces. It was a modification I made early on, given your insights."

Jo gave an approving nod and slung an arm around his shoulders, giving them a friendly squeeze. "Well, I think you've done a great job."

Samson tensed initially, but relaxed before Jo could pull away. "Thanks," he mumbled. "And thank you for your help with this."

"Anytime you need me to figure out how to break your things, I'm here. I did promise help with some of your other tinkerings." *And I won't pry about your personal matters next time*, Jo promised mentally.

"I'll keep that in mind." Samson nodded. "For now, you should take a breather from this wish."

"What?" Jo stiffened. "Why?" She knew she'd messed up, but she'd been doing all she could to fix it. To be denied participation now—

"Because you have been working non-stop. Give your mind a rest."

"But—"

"I'll get this to Wayne and Takako. They can get it to the scientists." He lifted the contraption, starting for the door. Jo was close behind.

"Are you sure?" Jo asked, cautiously believing that this decision truly came from a place of concern over her mental wellbeing and not some sly tactic propelled out of frustration for her ineptitude at the onset of the wish.

"Working on a wish is exhausting. Let us share some of the load," he said over his shoulder.

"My mind is mush," she admitted. "But I feel too wound tight to even relax a little. I doubt taking a break from the wish would make it any better." If anything, it could honestly stress her out more.

"Perhaps you should try anyway?" It was odd to see Samson so pushy. Jo took it as a sign of true concern, and a marker for the fact that she should actually listen to him. He certainly would know what he was talking about.

"Well, I *had* been talking to Nico about picking up a new hobby," Jo said as the door closed behind them.

"Like what?"

"He asked the same thing, and like I told him. . . I have no idea." Jo grinned and, much to her pleasant surprise, Samson grinned back.

"If that's the case, then maybe I shall put forward my suggestion of continuing to work with me on my projects."

"I'd like that," she said quickly, as if he'd think about the words for too long and then take them back, realizing what he'd offered. "Whenever you need me, Samson. It's not like I don't have the time."

They both shared a laugh at that, Samson's

significantly quieter than hers.

"Until then, then." He gave a nod, taking a step backwards toward Wayne and Takako's rooms.

"Until then," Jo affirmed, turning on her heel and heading in the other direction.

Her head was in a haze and her body felt energized. Taking a bit of a break actually *sounded* good, but she desperately did not want to be excluded from any steps of the wish. Jo was a mess of contradictions and obsessing over redeeming herself wasn't helping anything. She needed a break, needed something else to look at for just a little while that would occupy more of her thoughts than Eslar's book.

She'd hoped to find Nico in the living room (he was always one for a pleasant distraction), but Eslar was the lone ghost haunting the space as usual. Jo's eyes scanned the empty room, coming back to the elf who now stared at her.

"How did it go?" Eslar asked.

"What, do you have ESP now?" Jo asked, walking over to the kitchen.

"If only."

She snorted at the elf's comment. It was the most casual levity she'd ever heard from him. Jo wandered into the kitchen, opening and closing cabinets. She wasn't actually hungry, so making something was merely another way to pass the time, another habit of humanity to indulge. What new habits of the immortal could she take up instead?

"Well?" Eslar followed up when the silence had dragged on.

"How did what go?"

"Your work with Samson," he clarified.

She paused, turning to face the elf on the couch. "Really, how did you know I was working with him?"

Eslar shrugged.

"Are you sure you don't have ESP?" she asked again.

"If only," he repeated in kind. Jo found it just as amusing as the first time and she shook her head. *"Well?"*

"It went all right." *She hoped.* "In case you somehow don't mysteriously know all the details, I was helping him test the machine—" It was far more technical than a standard seismograph and deserved a better name, Jo just wasn't up for thinking of one at the present moment. "And he seems confident it'll work."

"Good, we need it." Eslar turned back to the television.

Jo turned as well, leaning against the counter. The T.V. was loud enough to fill the room.

"The prime minister will be giving another press conference on the current steps being taken to prevent further acts of cyber terrorism and protect our nation's digital borders. . ."

"Cyber terrorism," she repeated. It was a distinction she'd never earned before, yet Jo couldn't find any pride for it.

"They seem to be clinging to that label in regards to your hacking."

"Don't remind me." Jo turned away from the broadcast, eventually deciding on coffee. Ten hours without coffee did not a happy Jo make. At the least, the grinding, brewing, and pouring would keep her distracted from the news for just a little while longer.

". . . scientific community agrees that there is no evidence to support the evacuation order. . ."

"Yet," Jo spoke over the newscaster.

"We hope," Eslar added.

Hope was an odd choice of words. It stuck out to Jo like an HTML tag that hadn't been enclosed properly. An anomaly that was intentional, functional, yet wrong. Hope wasn't going to complete their wish. And if they didn't complete it. . .

"Eslar," Jo poured herself a mug and crossed the room to the elf as she spoke. "We all *hope* it works. . . But what happens if it doesn't?"

He looked back to the television.

Jo placed her hands on the back of the couch, hovering over him. "Eslar. . ." she prodded, giving him space to interject. He said nothing. "You're the oldest among us." Jo chose the direct approach. "Surely you must know what—"

"We've never not completed a wish."

Jo straightened away in surprise. "Never? Out of all the wishes the Society has ever granted?"

"No."

"So what happens if we fail?" Jo asked, her voice falling into a weaker hush than what she would've liked. He said nothing, his face passive, his eyes avoiding her at all costs. "Eslar—"

"I do not know," he cut her off. His intensity only made Jo more suspicious.

"But—"

"I can only assume it wouldn't be good."

"Why?" Again, he was silent. That cool distance he always managed to keep finally set Jo's blood to boiling. She took a sip of the too-hot liquid in her cup. "Eslar, what do you know?"

"Nothing."

"Bullshit." The word flew from her mouth faster than Jo could catch it. But seeing it land in the shock on the elf's face, she didn't regret it. "You know—"

"I know nothing and I do not wish to be bothered any longer." He huffed and threw open the book in his lap, looking between it and the television with a determined ferocity.

Jo abandoned the elf and her mostly untouched coffee, storming out of the room in a huff. If he wouldn't tell her, she'd find someone who would. There were only two people who were older than Eslar: Pan and Snow. Jo would rather eat her hoodie than speak to Pan. Plus, she didn't want to bother with anyone or anything else when she could go straight to the source. She'd avoided him long enough; what better excuse than this?

At the Four-Way, she heard voices in the distance— coming from the briefing room. Jo's feet stilled and she squinted down the dim hallway. The door was ajar enough at the end that she could hear Samson's voice, but she couldn't make out his words.

That same frantic, nagging feeling wormed up her neck from earlier and Jo started up the side-stair with purpose.

Jo stood before Snow's door for the first time in

weeks. How long *had* it been exactly? The last time she was here was after her failed hack-a-thon. But she'd walked away that time like a coward, her tail between her legs. She couldn't even knock.

Not this time, Jo vowed to herself.

She wouldn't be denied and she wouldn't be turned away. She wanted—*needed*—answers, and it seemed there was only one man who could give them to her. Jo raised her knuckle and, in equal parts anger and curiosity, but mostly sheer force of will, rapped on the door a few times.

Just like the last time, it took Snow several agonizing moments to respond (long enough that Jo almost walked away). But when the door finally opened, Jo's mouth did with it. She was going to ask him everything she wanted and not tolerate any kind of subversion.

But her mind went blank the moment she saw him.

He wore a knee-length silken robe in white that seemed to accentuate his lithe figure, with tight-fitting trousers of some variety underneath. If it didn't somehow work so perfectly on him, Jo would've made a joke about looking like a second-rate rock star.

But it *did* work perfectly for him. He looked like a vampire with an ethereal edge. A sort of angel-meets-demon forbidden combo that Jo couldn't decide if she'd rather be smited or saved by. She'd honestly take a little of both, given the option.

Snow stared down at her. She could tell he was trying to withdraw, trying to keep his face passive, but he failed (miserably). Jo saw the confusion, inquiry, and. . . something more.

How long had it last been since they'd even just seen each other?

Too long, echoed through her chest before she could think of the actual answer.

Jo opened her mouth. She'd come here for a purpose. She'd come to pin him down and force him to tell her the truth about the Society. And yet, what slipped from her lips was a mirror to him that felt wholly necessary, like some subtle code they'd unintentionally created that meant nothing to anyone but them.

"I don't know why I'm here," she whispered. But what she really said was, *let me inside*.

Snow stared, blinking in momentary surprise. The haze lifted and his eyes flicked over to the door at Jo's left, his right. The black and ominous door that belonged to Pan.

Wordlessly, he wrapped a hand around her shoulder and half-tugged, half-ushered her into the great unknown of the Society that was Snow's personal space.

18. A STEP UP FROM PRINCE

S NOW'S ROOM WAS unlike anything she could have imagined, and yet, in an odd way, it suited him perfectly.

"What are you, some kind of prince?" Jo scoffed, pleased her snark had returned.

She wasted no time in walking the perimeter, admiring the lux decor. Because it really *did* look like something right out of her childhood fantasies of royalty. Even in the dim lighting, Jo could see the immense amount of detail that went into every aspect of the architecture and the effects it housed; The lavish, four-poster bed bore a thick, dark purple comforter embroidered in colors and patterns she couldn't quite place. The latticed windows overlooked an ornately landscaped lawn—complete with two fountains, winding paths begging to be walked, and neatly manicured shrubbery.

Inside, there was even a fireplace front and center. It was composed of stone pillars and carved designs; a happily crackling fire gave the room a flickering, orange glow. Yet, for as much light as it gave, there was very little heat to match. The room was comfortable, if not a little cool.

It felt like stepping right into the fancy bedchamber of a king's castle. Well, at least her nickname of "King Snow" didn't seem so far off.

"I used to be." Snow's voice pulled her out of her musing at once. She turned to face him, expecting him to have followed her farther inside, only to find him still standing by the door, hand on the doorknob as if debating whether or not to let her stay. Jo crossed her arms over her chest, the mere thought of him pushing her away again settling beneath her skin like the annoying buzz of a bad caffeine hangover.

"Used to be?" she asked, looking him up and down before raising an eyebrow at his tense posture. Snow's head was slightly bowed, brow furrowed in thought and silver hair falling like a veil over his eyes.

"You asked if I was a prince," he said eventually, straightening back up and finally taking his hand away from the door handle. Jo guessed she was worth keeping around for a little bit longer. *How nice of him.* "I used to be. Of a sort, at least. Well, it's what some called me."

There was something about the way the words fell from his lips that stilled her sass and made Jo's heart ache. Even as he stood before her, tall, collected, and distant, she could see something in his eyes that spoke of painful memories. If he hadn't done his damndest to keep her tiptoeing all this time just on the edge of curiosity and understanding, she probably would have hesitated in prying. But, much like that night in her bedroom, he seemed almost desperate for something— and Jo herself was desperate to know what that something was.

Jo let her arms uncross and her hands fall to her hips. With an overdramatic glance about the room, she asked, "Is this what your 'sort of' princely quarters looked like then?" Whether or not he could tell she was trying to lighten the mood, she didn't know. But when his lips cracked into the barest hint of a smile, she considered it a success either way.

"I have made some adjustments over the years, but. . . mostly, yes."

Jo could see him physically relaxing under the meaningless chatter, and while she hadn't forgotten her purpose for coming here, the sight set something warm to bloom at the center of her chest. She'd had a glimpse of the stress Snow had to endure months ago in the chamber where "he'd died," and she could only imagine what else he kept secret from the group. Like, for example, what happened when they failed at a wish? But knowing she had at least a miniscule ability to put him at ease blunted the urgency of the inquiry more than she'd want to admit, and kept her tongue on safer topics.

"So what were you like, then?" Jo walked up to him with a bit more of a saunter to her step then she'd intended. She licked her lips, ignoring the way her heart sped up as his eyes dipped down to watch. "As a prince?"

"Surely you did not come here to inquire about needlessly long lineages, debates over technicalities of what makes royalty, or to hear tales of what messes all of mortal-kind were making at the time that I was left to oversee it." At one point, he must have met her step for step, easing into her personal space without her noticing. They were only about a foot apart now, but Jo swore she could feel his presence like a physical press against her own body.

"Not exactly," Jo said, though it came out more as a whisper. Her gaze dragged up the firm plane of his chest, barely visible through the slit of his robe, to rest on his face. His steel gaze scanned her face from behind the fan of his hair.

"Then what *did* you come here for?" Snow asked, and if Jo didn't know better, she could have sworn there was something implied beneath the question, like a fisherman casting a line into the dark unknown of the sea—if she'd even dare let herself read into it that way. She had so many questions, had come here ready to demand answers, and in the end, all she could manage to do was take a deep, shaky breath.

Jo licked her lips again—why was her mouth so dry? "I'm not sure, I just don't know all that much about you, you know? Or the Society, or the wishes, really," Jo added hastily, not wanting to give up entirely on her original mission. She wasn't here for him. She definitely wasn't here for him. She couldn't let him, or her heart, get any misconceptions about that.

"*Hmm.*" Snow's hum wrapped around her like a fog,

making it hard for her to think, or see, for that matter. Slowly, he took another step forward, their toes almost touching. She could feel the warmth of his body like its own touch, could see every detail within the contours of his absurdly beautiful face. "You know more than you think."

"Tell me about it? About your kingdom and your, how did you put it, 'needlessly long lineages?'"

Something clouded and sad drifted through Snow's eyes at the question, though his smirk stayed firmly in place, keeping Jo from panicking. "I was not born, but created."

"What?" Jo whispered, oddly nervous.

"It was the Age of Gods, before the Age of Magic."

"I thought you said you were from the Age of Magic. Back in the Ranger Compound."

Snow thought a moment. "I believe I merely said magic was real at such a time."

"Way to be technical." Jo rolled her eyes. Age of Magic, that was the time when Eslar and Samson had made their wishes. What was the world like before then? "Was it common, in your time? To be made?"

"Not quite. They called me a demigod." His smirk had fallen into a small smile, still sad, but sweetened some with nostalgia.

"Demigod? Age of Gods? Sounds like a step up from prince, Mr. Modest," Jo teased, trying to laugh.

"I preferred to be their prince for just that reason. It seemed much. . . simpler." His eyes wandered to the window.

She suddenly wanted to change the topic to

something else, anything other than that time. It sparked a sort of yearning in her that Jo didn't want. "So how does a demigod like you end up in a place like this?"

Snow stared at her for several breaths, so long that Jo almost began to feel awkward. It was expectant, like he was waiting for something. But Jo didn't know what it was, and he just shook his head. "It all started with a dangerous magic, a split goddess, and the bravery of someone I loved."

All at once, Jo's original purpose flooded her senses, the opportunity for answers standing barely inches away.

Just one straight answer, Jo willed herself, though it hardly settled the frantic beat of her heart or the heat steadily pooling in her chest, her stomach, lower. *Just get him to give you one straight answer about something important.* The rest would come if she could get that out, surely. She could be satisfied for a while if she got something from him, anything.

"Snow," Jo began, more firmly. "What magic? *Whose?*"

She should have expected it, considering her track record with the infuriating man, but it still settled sour and unexpected in the pit of her stomach when Snow's expression went blank. He took a step back.

"That's enough storytelling for one day, I believe," Snow said, his voice cold. Jo couldn't help but bristle.

With a huff, she took a step forward, regaining the distance he'd put between them in a single step. "You can't keep doing this." She frowned, putting her hands on her hips and looking up at him with what she hoped was an intimidating glare. "You can't keep opening up just to push me away when I get too close. Or, I don't know, just take an interest in you like a normal friend, at the very least. This back-and-forth game of emotions—it's not fair to you, and it sure as hell isn't fair to me."

Though Jo saw his resolve crumbling just slightly at the corners, Snow refused to back down. "It would be best if you left."

"There!" Jo snapped, digging a finger into his chest. "Right there! If you don't want me around, then why let me in at all?"

All at once, the atmosphere in the room shifted, a heavy but not uncomfortable weight settling between them. Snow's expression hardened to the point that it cracked, then softened, and his eyes scanned her expression. Slowly, slow enough that Jo could have backed away if she wanted to, Snow raised a hand to her face.

The touch was light, barely there, but it set Jo's cheeks aflame, her heart nearly leaping into her throat. His thumb rubbed a single line against her cheekbone, the tips of his fingers resting against her neck. It reminded her vaguely of how he'd touched her in the Ranger compound. But this. . . *this* was different. There was a familiarity to it, a boldness, a (dare she think it) slightly sensual nature to such a light caress. Jo couldn't help but wonder what it would feel like when—if—he ever actually did touch her.

His words were barely more than a whisper. "It's been so long." It had been, since he'd last touched her.

"I wanted to have a solution for you this time, one that would work."

"This time?" Jo whispered back, leaning into his touch. "A solution for what?"

Somewhere deep in the back of her mind, she really wanted to know the answer. But all she could seem to focus on currently was the feel of his fingers, the warmth of his body. She could smell a hint of him in the air between them, crisp like rain or a fresh bar of soap, but as he leaned in closer, there was something like cloves resting subtly underneath. She could drown in his presence, she realized, and while the thought should have scared her, all it made her want to do was lean in the rest of the way, press her lips to his, and—

All at once, his presence was gone, and when she blinked away the haze of desire, it was to find him back by the now-open door. At first, he said nothing, simply stood there waiting for her to leave, and while she wanted to be angry, more than anything else she was just. . . hurt.

"Why did you stop?" she asked, because she couldn't help herself. "You want it, too. . . don't you?" She didn't know if she wanted to hear the answer to this, not when her heart already felt so dangerously invested, but once it was out in the open, there was nothing to be done. "You feel it. I know you do, you must."

At this, Snow frowned, his grip on the door handle visibly tightening. "Don't get involved with me. Not. . . Not now. It's too dangerous. I need more time. Especially at present."

The confusion and hurt from before began to morph

once again into anger. "What does that mean? What does any of the cryptic shit you say actually *mean*?"

"I'll do my best to explain things when I can. For now, trust me, the less you know, the better," he said softly, mostly to himself, as if he was the one who needed convincing. Snow blinked, a slow fall and rise of his eyelids, then straightened, as if catching himself in a spot he hadn't ever intended to be—all traces of his previously open demeanor completely gone. "The wish has yet to be completed. It would probably be best for you to use your time more wisely."

The sincerity in his first comment evaporated at once amid the heat of Jo's anger. "Yeah, all right." She sighed, stalking past him and back into the hall, though not without taking one last glimpse at his face. "I get it, King Snow—or is your proper title 'demigod' now? Either way, sorry to take up your precious time."

She wasn't sure, but for a split second, she could have sworn he looked upset to see her go.

19. NEEDS AND BRODIES

JO THREW HER watch on the shelf outside one of the recreation rooms and stormed in.

She expected to find her usual hacker set-up. But what Takako had said about the rooms (now seemingly forever ago) held true—the rooms gave what was needed at the time. Or, at least it seemed to be trying. Whatever magic the rooms used to pick up on specific needs, it was obviously trying to provide what it thought might help Jo take the edge off.

Unfortunately, Jo had never really been one for bondage.

So, after taking a moment to stare at the rather outlandish sex-dungeon inside, Jo walked back into the hallway and slowly closed the door. She might have needed to let off some steam, but maybe not *quite* in the way the room was offering. Still, she opted for giving it another chance, inching the door back open and peeking inside.

Jo choked on an inhale at the sight before her. This time, instead of a BDSM lair, it was an almost perfect replica of Snow's room. So eerily similar that Jo felt inclined to glance down the hall and prove to herself she hadn't blacked out and wandered back to Snow's door instead. She hadn't.

"No thank you," she insisted (though she didn't know if it was more to herself or the room), pulling the door shut and taking a deep breath. "I'll give you one more chance. Something simple, please." Jo opened the door. "Much better."

It was the same replica of her apartment bedroom she'd first woken up in when she came to the Society. There was the hamper of dirty clothes, the wallpaper of posters and out-of-date calendars. And—what she needed most—a familiar bed.

At once, Jo jumped onto the sheets and let out a mighty groan of frustration. She felt like a kid throwing a temper tantrum. Basically, that was what she was. But it was a cathartic outlet for her frustrations; better than letting them stew and risk taking them out on someone else in the Society.

Her initial agony unleashed, Jo gave a hefty sigh.

"Why?" she asked to the silence in the room. "Why am I like this?"

There was a fire in her stomach that shed light on a vacant ache between her thighs. Jo closed her eyes, letting a hand trail down her chest, absently rubbing against her stomach.

He'd been so close; the smell of cloves still lingered

on each soft inhale. Whether it actually clung to her clothes or was instead a psychosomatic memory, she didn't know. What she *did* know what that all he did was touch her, the lightest and simplest of gestures, and she'd nearly drowned. And she wanted to, she realized. She wanted to drown in him, wanted to feel the crash of his waves beneath her skin and further, deep, deep within.

She wanted him to fill her completely.

She wanted him to erode away the haze of confusion that surrounded them and finally relinquish the truth.

Without really giving it much thought, Jo slipped a hand beneath the waistband of her jeans. Her breath caught in her throat as her fingertips skimmed the line of her underwear, a teasing implication. The frustration from earlier was still palpable, her fingers coming away damp when she reached further between her thighs.

Part of her tried not to think about Snow, desperately reaching for any other fantasy, any other face that might get her to where she wanted to be. But another part of her knew it was pointless. When she finally gave in to the sensation she'd been longing for, relaxed into the rhythmic friction she'd been craving, it was with an unavoidable fantasy behind her eyes.

Snow's hands on her bare skin, his lips grazing her jaw, her collarbone, her chest. His body pressed against hers, as hot and needy as she was, grasping for the same release.

Snow's tongue instead of her fingers.

She wanted to breathe nothing but that damned scent of cloves.

It didn't take long before Jo was arching off the comforter, mouth slack with panting breaths and barely concealed moans. When she finally slumped, heart clamoring up into her throat and hammering away, it was with an even more frustrating thought: despite the urge that had hurried her hand, she still felt supremely unsatisfied. In fact, the aftermath mostly just left her feeling slightly hollow, her hands cold even as her face grew hot. She was either very sick, or she might be—

Jo groaned again, a sound which turned into a loud proclamation of, "No!"

She refused. Feelings of any sort beyond the carnal would only complicate everything. Especially feelings for the one member of the Society who had the emotional aptitude of a toddler. Then again, she wasn't really in a position to judge someone else on their ability to express emotions.

What she needed was to scratch this itch and be done with it—*that's all it was*, she insisted, *an itch*. Her head would clear and she'd be back to normal, of that Jo was certain. But Snow refused to help and her own attempts hadn't done the trick, so that left one last option. Pulling herself up, Jo yanked open the door, grabbed her watch, and went in search of a worthy distraction.

Hands in the pockets of her hoodie, Jo descended the stairs to the Four-Way. Her feet moved on instinct, pulling her toward the common area. She could hear the sound of Takako's voice echoing towards her and Jo's heart skipped a beat. As if by some act of kismet, she and Wayne were back. Her feet picked up speed, and Jo sprinted into the living room to find the Society—sans Pan and Snow—all gathered around the large island in the kitchen.

Takako and Wayne stood, while the other three men sat.

". . . they seemed receptive to the machine," Takako was reporting to Samson. "There was little issue once it was hooked up and they saw it working."

Jo's eyes switched from one member of her team to the next. Wayne stood, hands in his pockets, looking every inch the epitome of self-satisfied smugness. He was in more modern clothes than he usually wore, no doubt fresh off his mission to Japan. It was a simple black suit, clean-cut as usual, but with a 2057 flare— no pocket square, pencil-thin tie, his usually gaudy cufflinks replaced by simple silver ones that arced over the hem of the cuffs.

He looked. . . good. Really good. Good enough to satisfy the needs of any hot-blooded female.

She couldn't really say if what she was about to do was necessarily a positive decision, but it was certainly better than sulking.

Without a word, Jo crossed the room in wide steps.

". . . preliminary tests came back—oh, hello, Jo." Takako was the first to notice her.

Jo gave the woman a nod, hoping things didn't come off as too rude. She was on a mission, and didn't have time for anything else. This was the distraction from the wish (among other things) that she'd needed.

"Hey, dollface, wh—" Wayne was cut off with a soft *"oof"* as Jo grabbed him by the wrist, tugging him away from the room. "I guess the lady needs a word with me," he called over his shoulder.

Jo didn't even listen for any comment or reactions. She was too focused on the one thing that was certain to finally clear her head.

"Everything jazzy?" Wayne asked.

No, everything wasn't. Her stomach was in knots, her head hurt, her chest ached, and all she wanted was *relief.*

Jo opened the door to Wayne's room and pulled the man inside.

A penthouse suite greeted her, if the lavish furniture, expensive layout, and floor-to-ceiling panoramic view of New York City were any indication. A lush, tan carpet spread the length of the floor from wall to wall, disrupted only by the glass stairway that swirled up from its center to a second story. Leather couches in a deep maroon took up the corner with subtle but well-placed lamps on either side.

Jo didn't have much time to take in anything further. Because for all its luxury, the space felt lived in—comfortable, even. And comfortable was something Jo had every intention of making herself.

The door barely had a moment to shut before she had him pressed against it.

To Wayne's credit, he didn't startle. His hands fell on her waist, thumbs stroking up her stomach, fingertips already indenting her skin. His eyes searched her thoughtfully, the beginning of a crease forming at his brow and chasing away the drunkenness that had already begun to weigh on his eyelids.

"What is it, doll?" he asked, and Jo willed herself to focus on the part of his voice already dipping thick and low. The genuine concern lingering beneath, she ignored vehemently.

Instead, she pressed their hips together, relished the feel of the growing firmness in his pants, and took a deep breath.

He smelled so different.

Jo shook her head in a futile attempt to dislodge the scent of crispness and cloves from her nose. "Just shut up and kiss me."

But when Jo leaned in, eyes already fluttering closed, she wasn't met with hungry lips and panting breaths. Instead, she was brought up short by a hand pressed firm and unrelenting into the meat of her shoulder. Jo looked up at Wayne in confusion, startling at the seriousness that had now fully overtaken the man's expression.

"Wayne?"

For a long moment, Wayne only seemed to scan her face, looking for something that Jo couldn't even begin to place. His frown persisted, lips drawn in a hard line that was utterly uncomplimentary to his usually kind expressions. It drew on long enough that Jo began to feel self-conscious, pulling herself away from his now half-hearted embrace to hug her arms to her chest.

The motion seemed to snap Wayne out of whatever analysis he'd been conducting, an exasperated sigh falling from his lips.

"Look, doll," he said eventually, reaching out to pull one of her hands away from her chest and linking his fingers with hers. He gave them a squeeze, smiling in a way that somehow managed to be both fond and also pitying. It made Jo's heart warm even as her hackles rose. "I'd like to think we're both still on the same page here, but you might have the wrong idea."

Jo's chest squeezed painfully, suddenly not wanting to hear another word. This wasn't what she'd come here for, and he knew that. So then why wouldn't he just give her what she needed?

"We *are* on the same page," Jo said, and if the scoff at the end of her words sounded less than believable, Wayne didn't comment. He did, however, take a step back the moment she went in for another kiss. Even if he didn't let go of her hand, something in Jo still fractured a bit.

"We covered this before," Wayne explained, rubbing the inside of her wrist with his thumb. The motion soothed her, though only enough to hear him out instead of running away in embarrassment at the feeling of being so utterly rejected. "I'm here for you if you want to have fun. But this. . . *this* doesn't feel fun. There's more than that here. I don't know what's on your mind right now, doll, but I don't touch broads that can't even see me when they look at me."

"I can see you right now." *You enigmatic ass*, Jo wanted to add, but didn't for the sake of her cause.

"No, you're looking, doll. But you're seeing something else." He gave a small shake of his head. "I don't touch brodies like you with a ten-foot pole."

Jo's heart jumped into her throat, words spilling from her mouth like vomit as she scrambled into the defensive. "I don't know what you're— There's not— What did you just call me?"

At this, Wayne had the audacity to laugh, using his free hand to run fingers through her long, dark hair. When he rested his palm against her cheek, she couldn't help but lean into it, keeping her eyes locked with his in determination.

"A brodie is a mistake, doll face," he said, letting go of her hand only to wrap his arms around her waist and pull her in closer. "And whatever it is that's got you all caught up? If I had to put a name to it, I'd say it definitely screams 'brodie'."

The genuine look of sympathy finally had her breaking eye contact. Jo's breath caught, wavering slightly. Sure, she knew that a quick release, however satisfying, wasn't really what she was looking for, but she didn't know what else she could do.

Jo took a breath, feeling Wayne's body shift alongside hers. It felt intimate but casual, like a hug from a very close friend. She didn't know if it made her want to laugh and lean in or go back to the recreation room for another tantrum.

"I'm more than happy to help you," Wayne said suddenly, low and sincere. "But I don't think you want my help."

"Try me," Jo challenged reflexively, feeling her face heat when Wayne only smirked.

"My advice?" He was right, they weren't on the same page. Because the help she wanted did not come in the form of ominous advice. "You're chasing a fool's yearning. Doll, you and I? We're friends, thick as thieves, have been—on my side at least—from the moment you woke up. We work that way. And yes, we fell into bed once, still enjoy a good flirt. But all of that works because we know it's casual and not what defines us. It's auxiliary, in no way an expression of something deeper."

Jo couldn't stop a blurt of laughter at his directness. She heard his own satisfied, amused, huff before he continued.

"Eternity is way too long not to get any when it's wanted."

"You're telling me." She turned her head towards the skyline outside the flat's floor-to-ceiling windows, watching the faint oranges brighten into full-blown dawn.

"Which is why, if you want something casual, that itch scratched and nothing more, you can seek me out." He paused, and Jo could hear the echo of his earlier statements. This was not just scratching an itch, but trying to fill a square-shaped need with a round peg. It was forceful, brash, and likely not to work. He knew it. She knew it. But Jo still wished they could both just ignore it and try anyway. "But feelings? They complicate things. They make things messy. And you don't want a mess on your hands for eternity. Stay off that path before you get too far down and stick with casual, dollface."

Jo tensed. Careful not to dislodge his arms from around her waist, she turned to look at him, taking in the kind smile and knowing gaze. He meant well, she could tell that much. Hell, she couldn't even tell him he was wrong. Hadn't she been thinking the same thing about the complexity of feelings in the recreation room? And yet. . .

"You think it's a mistake?" she whispered, barely able to get the words out for fear of what they might mean.

"I do. And don't misunderstand," he added hastily. "This has nothing to do with wanting you all for myself or some other nonsense. I think we covered my feelings toward you rather completely." Her face must have conveyed her easy belief because he continued without pause. "I just don't think you want to get entangled with anyone here romantically, least of all our leader."

Jo ducked her head into his shoulder. So it was that obvious? She should've guessed. Even if it wasn't, Wayne would know. He knew better—and more intimately—than anyone else in the Society.

"I think I'll just. . . head out then, okay?" Jo mumbled, though she made sure to punctuate the words with a soft squeeze to his arms, making sure he knew she wasn't upset for being turned down. Wayne squeezed back, even going so far as to place a kiss on her cheek. Jo scoffed, making a show of wiping at her face. "Gross. Didn't you just say I shouldn't risk sappiness with people I was stuck with for eternity?"

He merely laughed, and Jo was thankful he spared her any further harsh, but valid, advice.

"Thanks again," Jo waved from the doorway, waiting just long enough to watch him bow, maybe a little ironically, before closing the door behind her.

She made it about halfway to her room before

slowing to a stop. The idea of being alone, of stewing in her own thoughts after such a blatant realization about her feelings, made an uncomfortable sensation prickle beneath her skin. Over the past few months, when she didn't want to be alone, she'd seek out Wayne, but this was the first time that she'd felt this odd pull in her chest after leaving him.

Hesitantly, Jo glanced down the hall, past Wayne and Samson's rooms, to the door marked with an intricate name plate and decorated with a beautifully painted bird.

Jo started for the door before she could convince herself not to, hoping everyone had dispersed from the common area; she didn't think she could bring herself to drag another man from the group. Nico's room was a place she already found herself associating with safety, warmth and calm and understanding. She could watch him paint or listen to him talk, or just sit next to him and read. She wouldn't feel guilty for going to him right now either, like she would with Takako. Out of them all, he seemed to have the clearest picture on matters of the heart.

Yet, just as she was about to knock, the man in question spun out the door, nearly bumping into her.

"Oh, I'm sorry, I didn't see you there! I didn't hit you, did I?"

"Just missed me." Jo shifted her weight from foot to foot, trying to catch her balance after the quick dodge. "It was my fault entirely, I was the one right outside your door."

"No harm, no foul." Nico smiled and stepped

away from the door and started down the hall toward the Four-Way. Jo hovered. She wasn't trying to be awkward, it just sort of happened when the one place she'd been heading was now walking away from her. But Nico's friend magic was the greatest of the group, for something compelled him to stop and look back at her, still hovering. There was a curious look about him that all too quickly turned kind and knowing. "Did you need something, Jo?"

"Oh. . ." Suddenly feeling very silly, Jo quickly shook her head. "No, I was just. . . I was. . ." *Literally not doing anything at all and running from my problems*, her mind finished.

"Well, then," he said as if she had actually spoken a complete sentence and not just garbled sounds. "If you're free, would you like to join me?"

"Where?"

"To my home."

20. JULIA

HOME? DID SHE hear him right?

"Well, this is home. I'm going to my old home, technically," he clarified as if reading her mind.

"Florence, you mean?"

Nico gave a nod in affirmation.

"Shouldn't we stay here for the wish?" Samson had told her to take a mental health break, but just how much of one was really needed? "What if someone needs us?"

"We won't be long and we won't be using any time on our watches. Additionally, I already cleared it with Eslar."

"Cleared it with Eslar," she repeated. "It's no wonder the elf has a big head, he practically runs the place."

"Careful, or with those ears he may hear you."

A laugh escaped her in the form of a snort. Nico's easy way wore her down quickly. Samson had said to take a break, but all she'd done was run from one place to the next, hopelessly working herself up further. Really, she hadn't taken that break yet, Jo decided.

"Well, if you're sure it won't be an issue."

"I'm sure." Nico waited for her to catch up before starting down the stairs.

"So, why Florence?"

"I must see my muse on occasion. Furthermore, it gives me the opportunity to stroll through some art supply stores, see what artists are using these days, give me some ideas."

"I thought you couldn't take things back from the real world?"

"You can't," he affirmed.

"Then. . ."

"The mansion is very good to me." The answer seemed mysterious, but Jo heard it for what it was: another "because magic" explanation. "I find often that after I go on these excursions, I'll have some new supplies in my room with which to work, or the recreation room will take on a new shape for my practice."

"Reality is what you make it," Jo paraphrased one of the first things Wayne had said to her upon entering the Society.

"Well said."

Jo pulled open the door to the briefing room, holding it for Nico. She hated being in there the instant her foot met the obsidian floor. The usually chilly air was now bitterly cold, as if the mansion itself was angry for the wishes being passed along to its occupants. While the idea of a semi-sentient mansion was somewhat off-putting, it was nice to think of someone standing up for them, even if that someone was a building.

Nico paused at the Door. Jo's eyes fell on his hand as it began punching in the coordinates. He was three numbers in when the fourth button stuck. The man paused, staring at it in confusion. He pressed it again, finally freeing it from its depressed state. The motion reminded Jo briefly of the flickering monitor, but the thought vanished from her mind the second the Door opened.

Italy.

It was a country of postcards made real. They stepped into a shadowed street made of stone. Condensed buildings stretched up in walls of plaster and warm-hued paints on either side of them. Doorways, square and arched, indented by wooden doors with heavy knockers stood just off the street. Metal pleated doors, most bearing some sort of graffiti, covered garages. Up ahead there was a sign with a big white P on a blue background; behind her a café was just beginning to open up, popping the umbrellas above the few outdoor tables in a fenced-off section.

"What do you think?" Nico asked, starting off in a direction only he knew.

"It's lovely." The way the buildings were built on top of each other, clearly constructed and renovated at very different times, had her thinking of Paris. Yet this was wholly different. "Quieter than I thought it would be and it seems. . . I don't know, real?"

"How so?"

Jo tried to think of the best way to rephrase her odd statement. "Like the people here aren't. . . I don't know, fake?"

"How would they be fake?"

"Not touristy, I mean." She finally landed on what it was. "This feels like a real street where real people live."

Nico laughed loudly. Yet the sweet sounds of his amusement did not resonate or echo. They existed only for her ears. "Of course it is. And, I will say that the people who live in touristy areas are also real."

"Obviously." Jo shook her head, laughing a bit at herself. "I don't know what I was saying."

"It's inviting?" he suggested.

"Inviting, that may be a good word for it. . ." Jo half-mused, half-agreed. He held up his right hand horizontal, so his fingers stretched parallel to the ground. Nico pointed at the base of the line between his middle and ring fingers. "If the Cathedral is here—" Jo had seen the famous Duomo of Florence from Nico's room back in the mansion. "The Ponte Vecchio is here." He moved his finger down and to the left. "It's a very famous bridge, I'm sure you know of it."

She gave a sort of non-committal hum and a nod. She hadn't heard of it, but didn't want to risk discouraging the man.

"Up here—" he moved up from the initial placement of his finger to the base of the line between his ring and pinky fingers "—is the Palazzo Medici."

"And that's where we are?"

A chuckle, though Jo didn't know why the question was funny. "No, this humble little street is not the palace of the Medici." He moved his finger to the right some—east, if the top of his hand was north, from the Palazzo. "We're right around here."

"I guess I see why it doesn't feel too touristy, then." Jo wasn't sure what else to say, though she didn't want to give the impression of not appreciating the quick geography overview. "But it's lovely here."

"This was to be my street."

Jo nearly stopped mid-step just as they had begun walking again. His street, his home. She tried to imagine Nico wandering the stone pathways of Florence in a very different time. Even though she knew next to nothing of the Italian Renaissance, she had an easy time conjuring up notions of Nico bustling from place to place, struggling with canvases nearly as big as he was.

"In fact, that building—" He stopped at a cross-section, pointing down an alley. "The blue one, was to be our home. In my time, it was owned by the Medici family and was to be my atelier. We would've been comfortable there. A better life than most of our status, certainly."

"We. . . You and Julia?" Jo clarified delicately. Even if she felt closer to the man now than ever, his past was still a topic Jo would tread on lightly.

"Just so." Nico nodded, a faraway look overtaking his eyes. "She was my muse, my inspiration. A woman whose outer beauty could only be matched by her inner."

Jo remembered the last time she'd been in Nico's room, the portrait he'd been composing so carefully. She had no doubt that it was still out on the easel where he worked, waiting for its artist to return. "Your muse. You said we were going to see your muse." She'd thought he'd meant the city. He must've, surely; there was no way Julia was still alive. Unless she had some modern-day descendant that Nico kept tabs on.

"Yes, in due time." He began walking again. "I have two other stops first."

"The art store, and—?"

"The Medici archives."

That sounded familiar to her, and not because he'd just spoken about a Medici palace. But Jo stilled her questions for a while. Nico was patient, and had already displayed a tolerance for them, but she didn't want to wear him out. Furthermore, there was something to be said for simply walking through a new place and letting her mind be distracted by all there was to take in. Even if the sounds were dulled and the smells were muted outside of time, there was still much to see.

"This is my favorite art shop in the city."

They ducked into a small doorway that led into a narrow hall before quickly unfolding into the densest collection of art supplies—*anything* supplies—that Jo had ever seen. Every square inch of space was taken up by boxes in storage, some with the fronts ripped off to display tubes of paint within. There were cases and cases of brushes in every shape and size. Most of them looked identical to her, but the way Nico inspected them informed her that they were far from it.

186

"How did you become an artist?" Jo asked, running her fingers over a series of markers precariously perched, zero fear of actually knocking any over.

Nico paused, thinking a moment. "How much do you know about artists in the fifteenth century?"

"Assume I know nothing." Jo grinned. "And even if I did, who's to say it would be the same between your time and mine, with all the wishes separating us?"

"Fair point." Nico chuckled, continuing along. "I find that modernity has idealized the notion of artist. In my time, we were seen as having little difference from any other craftsmen, like tailors or cobblers."

"But art requires so much talent."

Nico paused at this, bringing a knuckle to his chin. "Do you think so?"

"Of course," Jo insisted. "And you must, too, otherwise you wouldn't have laughed at the mere notion of my picking up painting."

He laughed and something about the sound reminded her of a sun shower—an impossible delight. "Much of art can be learned, despite what one may say in jest. It's a technique. Just like a musician learns their instrument, I learned the canvas."

Jo remained skeptical that it'd be so simple, but she kept the thoughts to herself, allowing him to continue.

"Apprentices would work under the master, whose name usually went on the majority—if not all—of the work. He'd also oversee commissions, and tend to the shop duties. I was one such apprentice, until my work caught the eye of one of the Medici daughters and I earned a patron outright."

"Apprentices working under a master, huh. . ." Jo looked at a wall of markers. She'd never imagined there could be so many colors. Her eyes were drawn to one on the upper right, a soft, gray-bluish white. On the colored cap were a number, letter, and the name of the color: SNOW.

Just like that, she was back to thinking of him, completely distracted from whatever else Nico was saying. Wayne's warnings rang loudly in her head. Everything with Snow seemed confusing at best, agonizing at worst. How bad could it get if she pursued something and was rejected? Unless she already had been rejected, and was willfully ignoring the fact?

"Not unlike us, *hmm*?"

"I'm sorry, what?" Jo blurted, startled. Nico was suddenly at her side.

"Apprentices working for a master."

"The Wish Granter's Apprentices. . . sounds like a movie or something."

"I suppose it does." He started for the door. "Speaking of masters, on to our second stop."

"Did you get what you needed?" Jo asked as they rounded the corner on the way out.

"I believe I did." Nico beamed. "Some positively stunning new colors are being produced. Now, there's something you may enjoy, the science of paint colors. . ."

The conversation on the way to the Medici archives remained light, and mostly focused on Nico and his extensive knowledge of art supplies. Jo wasn't usually one for museums, but she found the experience to be much more palatable when there was no ticketing process, security screening, waiting in line, pushing around people, or ropes to keep her from getting close to the art.

They strolled to the Da Vinci wing, out of time and completely unhindered. Nico spent several minutes studying the recently discovered sketch, critiquing it in more ways than she would've thought imaginable for what looked to Jo like a scribble on a piece of ancient notebook paper—a very very talented scribble, but scribble none the less.

Seemingly satisfied, Nico led their departure, heading away from the Duomo and further north. The longer they walked, the quieter Nico became, until he hardly said anything at all. Usually, Jo would assume it was a result of him talking almost all day, mostly at her. But this felt different. There was a solemn weight to his silence, like someone in a deep meditation. Jo's lips remained still as well, not wanting to jar his thoughts.

They stopped before a small iron gate wedged into a tall wall, barely wide enough for a person to slip through. It wasn't locked, but it looked as though it hadn't been opened in some time. Through the bars, Jo saw the wall of a church—characterized by stained-glass windows lining the stone.

But the stone she focused on was on the ground.

Nico plucked his watch from his pocket, holding it out and clicking a nob.

"I thought you said we weren't using time."

"Just a minute. . . only for the gate." He ushered her through, closed the gate. But surprisingly, did not click out of time. Jo followed close behind him, curious.

The courtyard felt like it was another world altogether. Jo had walked through realities, but this was a different sort of magic. This was a power she couldn't comprehend or wield, even if she tried.

Vines clung to the side of the church, markings on the stone indicating where someone had attempted to cut back the foliage. Awnings and rooftops cast the ground in near-perpetual shadow, the grasses under their feet struggling to grow. Stones seemed to be in no particular order. The newest looked as if it had seen a thousand rainstorms since it was placed.

There were no footprints save Nico's. There were no epitaphs on the tombstones or mementos left. Just little weather-worn nubs insisting on remembrance to an earth that threatened to claim them once and for all.

In the shadow of the church, in the back corner, Nico made his way to a gravestone that had been sheltered enough from the elements, preserving some of its engravings. The name written confirmed Jo's suspicions, but even if the letters had been expunged by time, the carving of a woman's face would've been recognizable to Jo anywhere.

"Julia," she whispered.

"My muse." Nico knelt down before the grave. He ran his finger through the dirt and quickly scribbled a star on the corner of the tombstone. Then, and only then, did he return to his watch, clocking out of time. "My compass star, always guiding me home, ever lighting my life."

"She was truly stunning."

"My wish was to save her, you know."

Jo didn't know. She had made the broad-stroke assumption that his wish related to Julia based on the way he spoke of his lost love and a few other comments Jo had interpreted. Still, the details were obscure.

"Save her how?"

"I was not the only one to notice the ethereal nature of my Julia." Nico ran a hand over the top of the tombstone, as if caressing it. "There were others, of course. But she only had eyes for me, and I for her. At least, until someone too powerful turned his gaze to her."

"Who?" Jo's voice had dropped to a whisper. Her research came back to her—the mention of a mistress.

"Pope Alexander VI."

"A pope?" Jo hadn't wanted to be correct in her assumptions of possible connections. "I read. . . I mean, weren't they all pious and whatnot?" She didn't actually know; the Catholic Church had been absorbed by the state of Italy during World War III in a play for its global reach and resources. While it still technically remained its own entity, it had long since fallen from public consciousness in the countries of North America as anything more than a puppet of a foreign power.

"Supposedly—ideally. But ideals are like the subjects of paintings. Lovely to look at, but categorically untouchable." Nico trailed off and sighed. "The Vatican had commissioned me for a Madonna. Foolishly, I used Julia for reference."

He hung his head. Such a sad weight settled onto the shoulders of the man that Jo nearly tried to hoist him back upward. But she found herself pinned in place by the gravity of Nico's sacrifice.

"The pope was known for his mistresses, you see. It was one of the worst-kept secrets in Italy. I should've known." He turned to her, eyes shining with grief even after all the years that had passed.

"It wasn't your fault," Jo whispered in response to that probing stare.

Nico huffed softly, shook his head, and looked back down at his empty hands. "They sent for her, so that she could impart further 'inspiration.' They took her from me, making it as if we had never promised ourselves to each other. My Julia, my light, was to be extinguished as nothing more than a new toy for that wretched man."

"So you made a wish."

Nico nodded gravely. "I had heard about it, whispers here and there. But I finally located a woman who could grant me the details I sought, someone who designed herself as a high sorcerer. After that. . . it was simply a matter of casting the circle."

Jo wondered what he used to cast, but he didn't say and she didn't ask. She could guess well enough, given the severity of his wish.

"And Snow saw your magical lineage, so you ended up as a member of the Society." She couldn't help but wonder if he'd been presented with the same impossible choice Snow had given her.

How did Nico choose? Life in a world with his Julia, but she would live in unimaginable pain. Or life in a world where his beloved would never think of him again, but thrive?

"I did. But the pope was assassinated and my Julia walked free before any harm was done to her. She lived a good life here in our Florence, eventually marrying another and having a whole brood of children." Nico smiled, but Jo wondered how much sorrow he'd felt over the years—watching his love, his betrothed, marry another with no recollection of his existence.

"And you still love her, after all that," Jo whispered mostly to herself, so she was startled when she got a response.

"Immensely. There is no time or world where I love her less."

"I wonder. . . what that feels like."

"Have you never been in love?"

Now, there was a question. Jo had certainly gotten around, experimented, had her fun, but love? Actual heart-pumping, world-shaking love? She thought she felt that for Yuusuke once, but the feeling wasn't returned and it fizzled way too easily back into friendship to have been much of anything more.

"Not really," she finally admitted, to herself as much as him. It seemed almost. . . sacreligious to attempt to lie, even to herself, in a place like this. Before a love like the one Nico still carried. "Not a love like yours at least. . . I don't think I'd know it even if I saw it."

"Why is that?"

"My parents divorced when I was a kid." Jo shrugged, turning her eyes skyward, blinking. Instead of seeing clouds, she saw spats between her mother and father, the precursors to the day he walked out.

"I'm sorry to hear that," Nico said, offering the usual platitude. "But that hardly means you don't know, or can't know, love."

Jo chuckled and shook her head. "No role models at home to equate to true love, really. . . And it's not like there's much room for it in the mob. Love just means people who can be hurt to get to you. It's safer to act alone."

"I don't think so."

"You haven't seen what they'll do to people who fall out of line." Jo met his eyes, mostly as a challenge—one Nico did not attempt to meet.

"I may not know what they'd do," he conceded one battle, and continued another. "But I do know that love is its own form of protection—to have another that will look out for you, no matter what. To have an unquestioning shelter to retreat to when the world becomes too much to bear."

It was Jo's turn to be quiet. She couldn't argue with a man who had given his life for the woman he loved. Hadn't she done the same for Yuusuke? Perhaps even if their love hadn't been romantic, it was genuine.

"I still wouldn't know," she mumbled in direct contradiction to everything in her mind.

"Lying does not become you, Josephina." Nico called her out with a gentle smile. Jo returned it weakly. He was the only man who could have her smiling while backing her into a proverbial corner at the same time. "And I mean that in all areas."

The smile fell from her lips. "Huh?"

"I think you know exactly what love is." He finally

began walking back toward the gate, the transition in conversation begging a physical transition back to what their lives now were. "And I think you're looking to find it."

"I don't know—" A look from Nico had Jo changing gears mid-sentence. "I can't."

"Why not? The foundation is clearly there, waiting to be built upon."

"We are talking about the same Snow, aren't we?" The idea of there being the opportunity for something genuine between them seemed so outrageous that she had no choice but to clarify. The contrast between Nico's counsel and Wayne's was so disparate, Jo felt something like a short circuit sparking in her brain.

"Who else?"

"Snow is. . . he's. . ."

"If you doubt yourself when it comes to seeing the ways of love, fine. But you have made it clear you don't doubt me. I know what a love that transcends time looks like."

"Getting a little heavy, aren't we? It's not like he and I have even broached the subject of a date, even." Jo laughed, feeling nervous energy creep up from somewhere deep within. She wanted to change the topic, desperately. And yet. . . didn't. She had originally sought out Nico for clarity and all she felt was more of a mess.

"Have faith in yourself, Jo," Nico encouraged. "You know what to do."

"Wayne thinks it's a bad idea. Too risky," Jo mumbled.

"I have no doubt. There's no denying it is risky, and Wayne treasures this team—we all do." Nico took her hand and looked her right in the eye. The other hand was held out, waiting, as the Door appeared over the gate, but Jo kept her attention solely on his face. "Trust me Jo: some people are well worth the risk of putting yourself out there and being hurt."

As he turned to input the code on the door, Jo took one more look at the cemetery. There were no flowers on the graves here. No mementos from loved ones. No mourners weeping. It was clearly a place that had been mostly forgotten by a world that had long since moved on from it.

But one man remembered. One man, outside of time, cared enough to show Jo that there was one force greater than circles, or wishes, or magic. It was the only force that could triumph over them all, lasting when all else was dust and stars on stones. Love.

She could never again question if such a thing would be worth it.

21. MAN MADE RECKLESS

WHEN THEY RETURNED to the mansion, Jo went promptly to the common room to find someone who could give her an update on the status of the wish. The length of time she'd been out of commission—occupied with her own issues—now bordered on selfish. But she and Nico found the main areas of the mansion quiet.

"Everyone must be busy," Nico observed, already heading over to the kitchen.

Jo had a mug in hand before he'd even procured the beans. "I hope everything is going well." She looked around the empty room once more. "Do you think we were gone too long?"

"We were hardly gone a few hours. All will be well," Nico assured her with far more confidence than Jo could muster.

That nagging fear of being useless still sat in the

back of her mind. If there was one thing she refused to be in this new life of hers, it was useless. The moment she became useless was the moment her sacrifice meant nothing, and all her magic potential to help the world would be wasted.

"I think I'll stay here," she said, as Nico moved to depart. "Just in case anyone needs me."

"Relax where you're most comfortable. We'll find you as needed," Nico assured her.

"I'm comfortable here. My usual chair is open and there's this book Eslar lent me that I should really finish." Jo paused and forced a smile. "Knowing him, if I don't finish it and give him a proper report, I'll get a talking to."

Nico laughed. "Then I shall leave you to it."

She watched him walk away. There was a downward slope to his shoulders that usually wasn't there. Was he going to work on the painting of Julia? Jo swallowed the lump that had been lodged in her throat since the church.

After an hour of not really reading (all that clung to her mind was something about a forest clearing and a carving), Jo could take it no longer and wandered back to the Four-Way, walking to the top of each stair and peering down the empty hallways before heading back toward the now-occupied briefing room.

Eslar startled at her entrance, his eyes wrenching away from the Door as if he'd been staring at it for some time. Jo cradled her mostly-empty coffee mug between her hands and leaned in the doorframe, aware of Eslar's eyes on her as she did so.

"Everything all right?" she asked when it became apparent that he was not going to be the one to break the silence. For a long moment, Eslar merely stared at her; if Jo didn't know better, she'd have said she was being analyzed. But eventually, he took a breath, letting it out on a sigh and looking away.

"I should ask you the same." He looked back to the Door. "You wandered off."

"Nico said he had your permission." Not wanting to throw Nico under the bus, Jo added quickly, "But maybe I should've asked, too."

"You don't need my permission, so long as you're not affecting the Severity of Exchange."

Damn straight I don't, Jo wanted to say. Instead she passed her mug from hand to hand and pretended to take a sip. He didn't seem irked, so Jo let the matter lie. "I take it we weren't the only ones who left?"

"Wayne has returned to Japan to follow up on a few things," he said, standing.

"How's it all going?"

"Let's find out," Eslar said, simply, walking towards the double doors back to the mansion and motioning for her to follow. Jo took the last swig of her coffee and did as told, hurrying silently behind Eslar (every one of his long strides was two of hers) until the two of them were standing in front of the common room's large TV. Eslar grabbed the remote and turned it on, the news station from the last couple of weeks still broadcasting the already-familiar anti-terrorism footage.

Except now, new content flashed intermittently.

"It would seem as though things are going smoothly."

"Yeah," Jo replied, though mostly out of reflex; her eyes were still trained on the new updates. After her initial failure, it seemed almost unlikely that things would be going so well now. But Eslar wasn't wrong; Takako and Wayne had managed to get Samson's machine into the hands of the right people. Now all they needed to do was wait for it to pick up the inevitable seismic activity, and then the regions would be evacuated.

It seemed so simple. So *possible*.

But because of that, it also seemed very, very hard to believe.

"I'm going to go give Snow an update," Jo heard herself say before she'd even properly made the decision to do so. Surely Snow had already heard, possibly even had his own way of keeping up-to-date. But suddenly she found herself almost eager to tell him the news.

She'd helped set things right. They'd managed to set the ball rolling. And somehow, her time with Nico had made something feel far more level inside of her. *Hope*, that's what this feeling would be called. It was the calm assurance that everything was going to be okay.

Eslar didn't say anything when she left, but she didn't miss the way his eyes followed her out of the common room. She tried to pretend there wasn't judgment in them.

This time, when she found herself in front of the solid, white door, there was no hesitation before her knuckles were rapping insistently against the wood.

She had a reason to be here this time; she knew exactly what she wanted to say.

Or at least, she thought she did, until the door inched its way open to reveal the man himself.

All thoughts of the team, the updates, her redemption, the serenity Nico had given her, seemed to flutter out of her mind like a butterfly escaping an outstretched hand. She tried to grasp for it, that reason for being there that had seemed so clear only seconds ago, but all she could think was that he was right there, within her reach. And looking really, *really* good. A flowing white tunic hung perfectly over the stretch of his shoulders, his toned chest standing out beneath the low-cut 'v' of the loose collar. A sinfully tight pair of black slacks wrapped around his legs and thighs like a second set of skin. Jo felt her mouth go dry.

How was it she had no control over herself when it came to this man?

When her traveling gaze finally found its way back to Snow's face, it was to find an expression of poorly contained amusement and an eyebrow raised accusingly. It wasn't until then that Jo realized she'd been staring. And not just normal staring, but shameless admiring, possibly even leering. Damn, she might as well have been drooling too.

She felt her face go hot, and she had to force herself not to look away in embarrassment. She cleared her throat, looking over Snow's shoulder in blatant request. Snow's face softened a bit, but the amusement still lingered at the corner of his eyes.

Without a word, he stepped to the side, motioning

for her to come in.

His room looked just as outlandishly regal as last time, not that she spent much time looking at it after her initial assessment. The moment Snow closed the door and walked back into her line of sight, he once again managed to take up every ounce of her attention. This time, when he looked at her, Jo felt a distinct energy to the gaze, like the prickling in the air of lightning about to strike.

She wanted to touch him, wanted it more than anything. She realized with a heady sort of clarity that it was something she'd been wanting for a long time, possibly even from that very first moment, surrounded by blood on the dirty floor of a backwoods barn in nowhere Texas. Quite possibly, it was something she'd wanted all her life, however impossible that was. Ever since his ethereal presence had slotted so irrevocably into her life, she'd wanted it. She just hadn't realized how much.

Something on Jo's face must have given her intentions away, because without preamble or permission (though it would have been easily granted), Snow covered the distance between them and inched himself into her personal space.

Though centimeters still remained between them, Jo could feel the heat of his body as though they were already touching. Eyes never leaving Jo's face, Snow raised his hands, let his fingers trailed up her arms, keeping just enough space between that she could feel the fabric of her hoodie shift but could not yet feel the press of his touch beneath.

"Do you know what you're doing here. . . this time?" Snow asked, and his voice seemed impossibly low, rumbling with a velvety warmth that she could feel deep into her chest.

She knew what she'd intended on being here for, initially, but that was as far from her mind as possible when she said, "Yes."

That centimeter of space between them suddenly felt like a mile-wide chasm, one that Jo was nearly vibrating with desperation to cross.

Snow's wandering, barely-there touch finally made it to her face; his palm gently, much too gently, rested against her cheek. She leaned into it without thought or care, shuddering against the feel of his thumb stroking an almost tender line across her cheekbone.

"I can never seem to muster reason when you are around. You make me reckless," he whispered, and she wasn't sure if she was meant to have heard it, but it settled like a comforting weight around her heart regardless. She knew all too well how he felt.

It took much too long for Jo's brain to send word for her own hand to rise, to touch back, but when it did, it found a secure place at the nape of Snow's neck. She could feel his hair brushing against her fingers, felt the slight shift beneath them with each breath he took. If she closed her eyes, she swore she could feel his heartbeat somewhere deep underneath.

She wondered if he could feel hers too. As erratically as it was beating, a heavy thud of rhythm against her ribcage, she wouldn't have been surprised.

It wasn't until their noses were practically touching

that Jo realized they'd been leaning in, gravitating towards each other like being pulled out of orbit. His lips were so close, all she'd have to do was—

There was no way of knowing who finally covered that last bit of distance, not that it mattered. All that mattered, the only thing in the whole of eternity, was the feel of Snow's lips finally, *finally* pressed against her own.

It was like an electrical current arcing across the ether to strike in an impossible way. Like a conduit finally slotting into place.

Finally, finally, *finally*.

Jo kissed back with a hungry desperation, a whine clawing up the back of her throat as she pressed herself against him. She would probably be embarrassed about that later, but she couldn't find it in herself to care. And with the way Snow's arm wrapped tight around her waist, pulling her flush against him, she figured the desperation was mutual anyway.

When they broke apart, panting and staring deep into each other's eyes, it wasn't in panic and regret, worry and shame. As they held each other's gaze, Jo's cheeks flushing at the sight of his kiss-swollen lips, it was to the feel of something wholly unexpected. Something infinitely *better*.

His arms wrapped tightly around her waist; steely eyes stared back at her in something she didn't dare hope was fondness that ran deeper than mere lust. On his lips, a soft smile just for her.

When Jo leaned back in for another kiss, heart soaring and giddiness bubbling up in silent laughter,

Snow followed.

22. A MOMENT OF PEACE

WANTS SHIFTED IN her faster than Jo could think, or even breathe.

She wanted him. She had him.

She wanted his lips. She had them.

She wanted his skin under her hands—well, that was still a work in progress.

From one moment to the next, she simultaneously wanted everything now and wanted to wait for it in blissful agony just as she had waited for this singular moment for what now felt like a millennium.

Her eyes slitted open, revealing a brief glimpse of his face. Long lashes covered the curve of his cheek, taking up most of her vision. In her periphery she could see his mouth moving to meet hers in a new and entirely delightful way.

His fingers buried themselves in her hair, pulling with need but tempered with a gentleness that she wasn't entirely sure she wanted. Again, shifting wants. She was somewhere between "perfectly sated" with mere kisses and "rip off my panties." Snow seemed to make the decision for her when he pulled away.

Snow's usually red lips had deepened in color to bright cherry, his usually ghostly cheeks flushed with color. Jo was certain she looked much the same. For several long moments, they just breathed, and stared.

Without warning he practically dove for her. His hands on her hips, pulling them to him. Jo felt his entire length from toe to chest and she swelled with a startled breath to close any remaining gaps.

Jo wasn't exactly sure when they'd made it onto the bed, but she knew now that it was possibly the most comfortable thing in the known or unknown universe. A veritable eternity of hours slept on it had worn it in a way that was simply perfect—not lumpy or awkwardly dipping, but the sort of cloud you sunk into to find support below.

Then again, the bed could've been a piece of plywood, all splinters and rough edges, and Jo still would've found it comfortable due entirely to the man who stared down at her—hands on either side of her head, one knee between her thighs digging pleasantly into their apex with every shift.

She trailed her fingers over his face, trying to commit every curve to memory.

"You're not going to kick me out now, are you?" Jo was glad her whisper still had strength to it, even if her knees didn't. Good thing she was lying down.

"I think we're past that."

"Glad you can finally see sense."

"As if that were ever a question?" He arched an eyebrow.

"You had me wondering."

The words broke the spell they'd fallen under, but they did not erase its effects. Snow eased away, shifting onto his back at her side. They were still flush against each other and he did not object when she shifted to place one of his arms behind her head.

For several long moments, neither said anything further, the daze of the kiss seeping into them like oil to a wick that would burn for hours to come.

"I want you to know that since the Society's founding I haven't—"

"I know." Jo cut him off. She didn't need to hear him say that he didn't usually take people to bed. He was very obviously not the type, so her question trended in the opposite direction. "Why now? Why me?"

She felt the pillow that was his arm shift as he turned his head, so Jo turned hers as well, studying his face.

"That's a difficult question."

"That's not an answer."

He chuckled. "Why you?" he repeated, more thoughtful. Jo hung on his words, her chest tightening oddly in suspense. "I've been alive. . . for more years than it's possible to count—especially with shifting time and jumping realities. In all that time, I was waiting, searching. So when I found what it was I'd been waiting for, there was—is—no question."

The idea was almost profound, and gave her pause.

Was she the same? She'd never felt so instantly head-over-heels with anyone else. Even if she wouldn't dare call it love so quickly (lust did not equal love), there was a connection there—how did Nico phrase it? *A foundation*, unlike one she'd ever known.

He was an enigma that felt like everything she'd ever wanted.

"You flatter me." She half shrugged and looked back at the mural on the ceiling to take off some of the pressure of being the sole focus. Stars dotted a canvas of swirling blues with ethereal god-like figures dancing among them. Jo tilted her head, slightly; it was almost as if she could remember a story that these very images depicted. Like a vague childhood tale. . .

Snow said nothing else, and Jo was inclined to leave it be. It didn't matter why he wanted her. It just mattered that he did.

"I don't want this to change anything." Damn Wayne for getting in her head now of all times. It was Snow's turn to look at her first. Jo took her eyes off the ceiling and its hidden story to give him a long, hard stare. "With the team, with wishes. I don't want this—whatever happens, whatever comes of it—to affect anyone but us."

Clarity dawned on him and Snow gave a small hum that she took to be affirmation. "It *is* only about us."

"Good." A smile stretched between her cheeks. She could have her cake and eat it too. Things dared to look like they were improving for her.

"But to that end. . . you should likely return to them."

She'd just said she didn't want things to change,

and her whole heart screamed in protest of leaving his bed. Still, once work was planted in her mind, it was hard to fall back into the bliss she'd lost herself in earlier.

"The wish, it's looking positive." There. Now she'd fulfilled what she said she'd come there for. So it wouldn't be a lie if Eslar asked later.

Snow sat, his expression distant. Jo followed suit, swinging her feet over the edge of the bed. It was weird to talk about work when they were lying side by side.

"Is it?" he asked softly.

"I think the evacuation will be successful, after all." Jo grabbed his hand. His head turned to her and Snow listened intently as she filled him in on the steps that Wayne and Takako had taken to see the evacuation substantiated. "We'll reduce the Severity of Exchange, I know it."

Pain.

That was a weird thing to flash through Snow's eyes and it struck Jo right in the gut, leaving her dazed and breathless.

"You don't think we can?" she dared to ask.

"I hope we can. For all of us." Snow squeezed her hand tightly.

"What happens if we don't?" The infamous question—one Jo couldn't seem to get an answer to no matter how hard she tried—returned to her. It didn't matter who she asked, or when, or how. Every time, it was dodged or passed off as a great unknown. And this time was no different. Jo was no fool; there was no way Snow out of all of them didn't know what would happen.

"It won't be good." There was a deathly weight, as cold as the grave, to his voice.

"What happens?" Jo repeated, insisted, pushed.

"Jo—" More pain on his face. "—please, trust me, some things are better left unexplained. But know that I want nothing more than to defend this team—to defend *you*. It's all I've ever worked for."

It wasn't an answer. But it was the truth, that much she could tell. Still, Jo sighed heavily at being put off again. Snow's hand rose to her cheek, cupping it thoughtfully.

"Pray you don't find out."

"That's easy for you to say when you have all the answers." Even frustrated and in the dark, she still leaned into his touch. It was sturdy and comforting; it was a lifeline to the truth she so desperately needed.

"Nothing is easy for me."

"Then let me help you."

"Careful," Snow whispered, "or I just may."

Despite herself, a smile cracked through the confusion and disappointment of being thwarted yet again. No matter what Snow said, she'd find out the truth eventually. She could be patient for now, especially if she had his touches to tide her over.

"You're right, I should go back to the group," she said, rephrasing his earlier sentiment. Jo eased herself out of the plush bed and stood, her mind gradually returning to the wish.

"You should." Snow made no motion from the bed, and Jo could not ignore the way his eyes lingered on her body from heel to head.

"Should I also. . ." She wasn't trying to be seductive, which made her feel all the better about herself when pure sex oozed into her voice, spilling over the well of want he'd tapped into with his kisses. "Come back later?" Jo leaned over, both hands on the bedspread, halfway to the man who regarded her somewhere between art and a feast for famine.

"I should say you shouldn't."

"But you won't." Jo loved the way his eyes were glued to her lips as she spoke.

"But I won't," he repeated, enthralled by a hypnotic spell she didn't know she'd cast.

"Later, then."

He sealed the vow with a kiss.

The world was under her feet as Jo all but sauntered back to the Four-Way. The wish was going well, she was settling into the Society, *and* she'd finally cracked the tension with Snow in the best of ways. Jo was already looking forward to the next stretch of time between wishes. With nothing else to do. . . she wondered how much time she could spend in his room before someone noticed.

Jo was so preoccupied with the lingering blissful dizziness, the pleasant heat that had bubbled from her stomach and into her head, that it took until she had a mug in hand and coffee pot tipped for her to notice the tone of the room.

Everyone was gathered, huddled on the couches, glued to the television. Jo stared at the news and felt her own jaw go slack right before hot coffee overflowed onto her fingers and her mug shattered against the tile floor.

23. PLAN C

"**W**E GAVE THEM everything they needed," Wayne repeated for what felt like at least the fifth time in the last ten minutes. This time, however, he punctuated it with a harsh kick to the edge of the couch.

"Wayne," Eslar chastised, but even the normal tone of his scolding was off, dulled by the somber atmosphere and the second run of playbacks still flashing across the television screen. The banner at the bottom of the screen read,

Prime Minister Nakamura Denies Scientists' Claims

Takako grabbed for the remote, pointing it at the TV and clicking furiously. A nearly identical broadcast popped up; the only difference was the talking head delivering the message.

"The prime minister has called into question the organization in charge of bringing forward the speculations that what has been deemed by the Japanese government as a cyber-attack on sovereign soil is, in actuality, founded. As of right now, the government's official stance is that—"

CLICK.

"We should not be made to feel afraid by these terrorists. In fact, I have little doubt that they've penetrated this so-called 'lab' and—"

CLICK. It didn't seem to matter how many news channels Takako flipped through, they were all the same.

". . . reiterate that the Japanese government does not give heed to influence from any forces beyond our borders." The prime minister was on, front and center. Takako's hand lowered slowly. *"It is my most sacred duty to keep safe our people and our land and I will not give in to baseless claims grounded in fear and terror."*

"Wh-why is he doing this?" Jo whispered, getting no answer, and not expecting one to begin with.

Takako cursed loudly and held up the remote again. CLICK. A new talking head appeared, a new timestamp in the lower corner of the screen. Were they watching re-runs? Or was time slipping away from them like sand in an hourglass, persistently flowing toward their ultimate failure?

". . . minister remains tough on terrorism in advance of next month's election," the newscaster said, matter-of-factly. *"His stance has earned him four points in the polls almost overnight."*

"An election." It was all so bloody clear now. The vague memory of a newscaster mentioning polls and points stuck out in her mind. It had always been about a stupid election.

"A damned election." Wayne growled, running a hand through his hair until the slicked-back quaff was completely disheveled. All manner of the man's usual bravado and affectations from his forgotten era had vanished, replaced instead with timeless frustration and rage. "Is there no end to the greed of politicians?"

"He's. . . he's risking everyone dying, so he can win an election?" It was phrased as a question, but Jo already knew the answer. Wayne had said it himself: there was no end to the greed.

"And to save face," Takako spoke without even turning. Jo didn't even think they'd known she was there until that moment. "If he backs down now, he'll have to admit he was wrong, and that he wasted precious time, which could mean the lives of his people."

"That's because he did!" Jo couldn't help herself. "What more does he want? We gave them proof that the evacuation wasn't wrong." *That I wasn't wrong*, her mind betrayed her, finishing. Yes, this *was* personal. This was her redemption slipping by for the sake of a man's pride.

"Well what more are we supposed to do?" Wayne asked.

Jo wasn't the only one who winced at those words. Wayne was right. They'd put all of their cards on the table with Samson's upgraded seismograph. What were they supposed to do now?

Eslar took the remote from Takako with surprising delicacy, muted the TV, and leaned back in his chair. For a long moment, the only sounds in the room were Wayne's footsteps pacing across the tile.

Samson was staring off into space, shaking hands fidgeting almost desperately. As usual, he held a small trinket that Jo couldn't identify, though she could suddenly see with new ease how to break it, if she wanted. At the look of pain on Samson's face, however, it felt as though *she* was the one breaking.

Nico sat next to Takako on the couch, an arm wrapped around her shoulders—not that the woman seemed to notice. Her head was buried in her hands, whole body hunched over and trembling as if trying to hold back a sob of emotion that could have been frustration or sorrow.

And Jo. . . continued to stand where the sickening realizations had left her, a puddle of coffee and shards of ceramic beneath her sneakers. She could barely think, let alone move, but regardless, her mind screamed to do something, do something, *do something*—

"I'm sorry." Samson's voice, barely above a whisper, sounded like a gunshot for the way everyone's attention jerked in his direction. The craftsman's hands had stilled, though they clutched at his trinket so fiercely that his knuckles looked all but seconds away from bursting out of his skin. "I'm. . . I'm sorry, I. . . I. . . I should have triple checked the specs or I should have. . . Or I should have—"

Samson's breathing picked up, and instantly Jo was reminded of Yuusuke, of how occasionally the stress would get to him, manifesting in ways beyond his control. It usually had to do with his family, or a job gone wrong, but it always ended the same. Jo could see the same symptoms of a panic attack rearing its ugly head in Samson, and, much like she would have with Yuu, she was across the room in a flash.

"Hey, hey." Jo winced internally at how her voice shook, hoping it wouldn't diminish the comfort she was trying to give. Not that it would be enough. The tense line of Wayne's shoulders and Eslar's closed off expression said as much. Takako's crumbling demeanor, beyond any comfort at all—despite the way Nico continued to rub soothing circles into her back. So Jo focused on the only thing she could do, because if she didn't do *something*, the weight of her own hopelessness would crush her too.

"Your machine did exactly what it was supposed to. This is just a stupid politician's fault for thinking that he knows better—his *pride* knows better—than actual science, not yours," Jo said, placing both of her hands over Samson's and doing her best to keep her voice steady. Confidence was beyond her at this point, but she could at least get the words out and make sure Samson knew that this wasn't his fault. If anything, this was the prime minister's.

Or hers.

"I failed, I. . . I could have. . . I could have done better, I—" Samson stammered, hands shaking beneath hers. Somewhere behind her, Jo heard a sound of frustration, probably from Wayne.

"We'll think of something else. We'll find a different

way to convince everyone. We'll come up with a Plan C or—"

"Plan C? Are you joshing with us, dollface?" Wayne bit out, and the coldness in his tone made Jo cringe. For the first time since her first few days in the Society, the sound of his nickname for her left a bitter taste on the back of her tongue.

"We only have two weeks left," Nico said into the tense quiet that followed. Jo's heart ached at the sound of defeat in his voice, but she couldn't deny the claim. When Jo looked over at the Italian, his eyes were shining, lost. Takako had stopped shaking, but she still hadn't lifted her head from her hands.

"So then we have time," Jo tried, but Eslar just shook his head. "It's something."

"That's two weeks until the incident itself. If we plan to get everyone evacuated in time, that barely gives us—"

"From our initial assessments, forty-eight hours." Takako's voice was muffled from behind her hands, but even so, Jo could hear the scratch in it. It was the sound of someone desperately trying not to scream, or cry, or most likely some mix of both.

Forty-eight hours. They only had two days left.

What sort of Plan C could they come up with in that time? Despite how Jo's mind raced, it already felt like a losing battle. Like pushing a boulder uphill just waiting for the eventuality of her foot slipping, her strength crumbling, and the boulder crushing her beneath its inevitable roll back down.

"We'll think of something," Jo eventually whispered,

but even she could hear the lack of conviction in her own words. *We have no choice.*

"Takako, wait!" Nico was suddenly on his feet, startling everyone out of their thoughts. By the time Jo followed Nico's stare to the Four-Way, Takako had already stormed off in the direction of the briefing room in an almost exact mirror to how the whole wish had begun.

Jo was torn, instinct telling her to stay with her team (with Samson, specifically), but when she caught the craftsman's eyes, he seemed to have found his resolve. He didn't say anything, just motioned towards the hall with his chin.

Jo was on her feet and following Takako at once.

Before anyone could object, Jo glanced back over her shoulder. "Start thinking up a plan," she called, already half-turned back around. "I'll be back with Takako as soon as I can."

24. TARGET PRACTICE

JO SKIDDED TO a stop, pin wheeling her arms and struggling to keep her balance as she bounded through the doors to the briefing room behind Takako.

Awkwardly, she gripped a chair for balance, panting softly. How Takako had managed to cross the mansion without so much as breathing heavy, Jo did not know. But there she stood, poised and still, right in front of the Door. Her dark eyes searched Jo, the only thing that betrayed any sort of emotion in her otherwise rigid pose.

"Takako. . ." Jo's words failed her. What was she really going to say to her? What could she say? "Where are you headed?"

"Trying to stop me again?" Takako looked back to the Door, as if contemplating making a run for it.

"No, not this time," Jo said softly. Her voice was

223

barely more than a whisper and her resolve just as thin and fragile "Why would I be?" She folded her arms over the top of the chair, sinking into the back. Jo rested her chin on her forearms and stared listlessly at the room.

"Trying to get me to go back and help with the wish then?"

"I probably should," Jo admitted. "But I don't have any ideas, do you?"

Takako shook her head.

"Then, let's go wherever you were headed," Jo suggested. It was pointless, but perhaps they both needed some pointless right about now. Perhaps she'd headed after Takako because she, too, was looking for a momentary escape. It was all she seemed to do these days—slave over the wish, or run as fast as she could away from it.

"You're sure?"

"Look, the way I figure, it's not like you're leaving forever because you *can't*. Neither can I. Snow isn't here to stop you this time, either. What's an hour?"

"One forty-eighth of what we have left?"

Well, that was a grim way of looking at it.

"Perhaps it'll be an hour well spent, gaining inspiration from the outside world. Nico and I went out earlier and it actually did me a surprising amount of good. People aren't meant to be cooped up in one place for so long." Jo paused, following Takako's line of sight to the double doors behind her. "Unless you'd actually rather head back to the common room?"

Takako's fingers flew over the keypad faster than Jo could blink.

Jo quickly crossed to her side with a few large steps, barely making it in time to be yanked by her navel through the Door and out into the real world.

The first thing she noticed was the nothingness. And not "nothing" like small town nothing. But "nothing" as in she would not be surprised to discover that they had somehow accidentally landed on Mars. As far as she could see were red rocks, rusty colored rocks, and more dark-brownish rocks. Jo turned, trying to get her bearing.

The land sloped upward, cresting at an edge with a sky bluer than she'd ever seen above. In the distance, she could make out the outline of some kind of rudimentary structure erected on the apex of a ledge. But there was little else.

The second thing Jo noticed was the wind. It howled around her, giving her skin a phantom chill. Even without being clocked into time, Jo knew that she was somewhere very, very cold.

"Where are we?" she asked.

Takako could hear her fine; the muted sensations in their ghost-like state assisted with communication in the barren landscape. "The summit of Mt. Fuji."

Jo did another quick 360, taking it all in. Tell-tale porous rocks sloped like some kind of bowl. An uninhabited and very high place. Everything that had confused her suddenly made a load of sense.

"So this is it, huh?" Jo shoved her hands into her pockets. "Kind of anticlimactic." Her words were bitter, angry. "Too bad we can't just kill it here and now. Take it out like a mobster gone rogue."

"Funny you should say that." Takako pulled out her phone, tapping the screen. Jo watched as time flowed for her. The wind whipped her hair and clothing, stretching it over her narrow, muscular frame. She shivered, but it looked more like shaking off the expectation of warmth and hardening herself against the cold than really feeling the chill.

Takako reached into her jacket, producing a handgun. It was the same weapon that Jo had seen her pull on Snow before they'd even begun the wish. Jo wouldn't exactly be surprised to learn that it was something she kept on her at all times.

"What're you doing?" Jo crossed over to her.

"I'm going to shoot it."

"Shoot what?" Jo grabbed her wrist. "The mountain?"

"Yes," Takako said it as though the fact should've been obvious. It had not been obvious.

"What do you hope that will accomplish?"

"You said it yourself, let's see if we can just take it out."

"But—"

"Has not shooting it worked?"

Jo's grip went slack. Why was she trying to stop her? The likelihood of shooting at the caldera doing anything (good or bad) was almost nonexistent. So why did it matter?

"No, it hasn't." Jo shrugged, finally taking a step back.

Takako's arms outstretched with laser-like precision and her finger squeezed the trigger.

The gunshot echoed across the entire summit, piercingly loud. It was quickly followed by another, and another, and another, until a shout rose to meet the final bullet.

The clip empty, she put the gun back into her jacket, tapped her phone, and sank to the ground. Jo eased herself down slowly next to her, as if trying not to startle a wild animal. Takako panted softly, eyes red and glossy.

"Maybe it is as simple as shooting something," Takako murmured.

"I don't know, the mountain doesn't look very dead to me." Jo didn't quite hear the severity in Takako's voice.

"No. . . I could kill him," she whispered.

"Who?"

"The prime minister." Takako looked to her, horror creeping onto her face. For a woman who'd given up her entire world for the sake of her country, Jo couldn't imagine what such a suggestion took to make. Jo couldn't even fathom what it felt like to be loyal like that to a country; she'd always been work-for-hire to the highest bidder.

"That isn't a solution." She decided to save Takako from that line of thinking. "It's a power squabble. Kill one and two more will rise up to fight over the scraps. Plus, the assassination would likely widen the Severity of Exchange, not lower it by throwing the country into sudden chaos. Everyone would focus on the death of their leader rather than keeping the discussion on the evacuations."

"You're right," Takako admitted, her breath growing regular once more. "I just. I wish I could do something. It's my family, my home. All I'm good for is pointing and shooting."

The confession, said almost offhandedly, startled her. It was such a similar feeling to what Jo had experienced during her first wish in the Society that she instantly felt a kinship with the woman that she hadn't before. Jo linked their arms, locking elbows.

"Let us take care of you, this time," she said, trying to will as much comfort and confidence into the words as she had to spare. But really, beyond all else, she just silently hoped they could.

"I'll leave it to you." Takako didn't make any motion away from her.

"But I'll grant you, it'd be nice to see if a bullet could even penetrate the PM's thick skull," Jo muttered.

Takako laughed, a sound as brief as it was soft. She looked back over the caldera, sighing, the levity unable to stick in the circumstances. "Do you really think we can do it?"

"We have to." Jo followed her gaze. "I don't think any of us are ready to accept failure."

25. TWELVE HOURS

EVENTUALLY, THEY PULLED themselves back to their feet and through the autonomous, free-standing steel Door that led to the briefing room. It shouldn't have been much of a surprise to find everyone seated around the table, presumably waiting for them to return, but it still made Jo bristle nonetheless.

Before Snow or anyone else could say anything about them wasting time, Jo dropped into her seat with an overly dramatic huff.

"I know we didn't clear it with team mom first." Jo shot a glance to Eslar. "But I didn't use any time and Takako barely used two minutes, so there's nothing to worry about, *all right*?"

Snow wasn't the only one who seemed surprised by her outburst, but he was the only one she locked eyes with, willing him to argue, to fight. But mostly she was just hoping to see a crack in his otherwise carefully constructed facade.

It hadn't even been hours since she'd been lying in his bed, reveling in the feel of his arms around her, his lips against hers. How had everything gone to shit so quickly? When a momentary stare-off provided barely more than a flicker of recognition from the man, Jo looked away, feeling something cold and heavy drop into the pit of her stomach.

Maybe this was what Wayne had been trying to warn her about? Pursuing the possibility of romance with any member of the Society was only going to complicate things, and Snow? It was an infinitely trickier balance. She couldn't hold onto him now with the same emotional grip she'd clutched him with in bed. She had to pull herself together and draw some demarcation lines in her mind and heart or things would go from merely complex to ugly, fast.

"Even if your moments beyond the Door were without lost time—" Snow eventually picked up the pre-derailed conversation and put them back on track. "I assume it was also without purpose. What we need more than tantrums is a course of action."

Jo opened her mouth to defend their spontaneous field trip, but one look from Takako kept her silent. She didn't look chastised, nor regretful, but rather accepting of her decision. Swallowing back her argument, Jo nodded, trying her best to accept the fact herself: Takako was truly a mature and admirable individual to be composed, even when hurting so completely and being chastised for merely letting out some of that pain.

"Fine, fine, okay," Jo said, sitting up straight and looking at each member of her team in turn. They hadn't failed yet; there could still be a missing piece to the jigsaw puzzle hidden beneath the great, despair-shaped couch cushions. . . or something. They just couldn't give up hope, couldn't stop searching. "So what have we done so far? And what can we do different in forty-eight hours?"

"Both very good questions."

When all eyes followed the interjection to the double doors of the briefing room, it was to find Pan leaning against the frame, fingers linked behind her head and feet crossed lazily at the ankles.

"Time's a ticking, you know," she said, using one of her knuckles to tap a rhythm against the wood that seemed eerily accurate to the width of a precise second. "What exactly *are* you going to do?"

Pan let her hands drop then, turning towards the room with a flutter of long, obnoxiously bright pink fabrics. And the dress wasn't the only thing bright and obnoxious about her ensemble today. Beneath the dress were blue- and purple-striped hose cut off at the knee by white gogo boots, and atop her head, her hair sat in two elaborately curled pigtails dyed an unnaturally iridescent gold.

The contrast of such bright colors intermingling with such a somber conversation left Jo feeling almost disjointed, off-kilter, and particularly annoyed. Not just for the unwelcome presence, but for the teasing lilt of Pan's voice, the obvious smirk on her lips. How she'd managed to put herself together in such a way eluded

Jo. What made it all worse, was that she didn't exactly look like someone trying to update them on their time; she looked like someone eager to gloat over just how little they had left.

Or, gloat over that she'd known what had been coming all along, a tiny and very suspicious voice whispered in the back of Jo's mind. But such a thing was impossible. . . at least, Jo thought it was impossible.

"So?" Pan raised an eyebrow at the room, though her gaze seemed to settle lazily on Jo for a moment. Maybe she just imagined it, but either way, it left Jo's pulse racing.

"Just because the prime minister shed doubt on the findings doesn't make them any less true." Wayne picked them back up before Pan could rile them further. Though Jo didn't miss the way the woman-child's smirk morphed into a rather uncomfortable looking grin as the conversation resumed. "The populace, and more importantly the scientists, still have their proof. Can't just brush that under the rug, right? The news pundits are already picking up on the fact, calling out the PM for what he's doing."

"In essence, we're not dealing with scientific findings anymore," Jo chimed in, following his train of thought and trying desperately to ignore the way Pan settled herself elegantly into her seat, watching them all with an intrigue bordering on sly amusement. "We're dealing with public knowledge?"

"We already tried convincing the country," Samson added, voice small and unsure, but trying. Everyone was trying. "But that didn't work out so well. . . Plus, they're on our side, right? Because of that proof?" He seemed to need to talk himself in a circle in order to spiral towards a conclusion. "So, so, maybe we don't need to convince them anymore. Maybe we only need to focus on one person now."

"Samson's right." Eslar nodded in agreement. "This isn't about the populace at all anymore; it's about the prime minister. No matter the proof, no matter the number of citizens who believe, if he continues to deny scientific claims, we have no evacuation."

"I can convince him." Nico punctuated the claim by instantly rising to his feet. He looked around the room, even locking eyes momentarily with Pan, but his gaze eventually settled on Snow. His expression was determined, a confidence in his eyes that Jo had never seen before, though she found she wasn't surprised by it.

While the two men had their mental discussion, the rest of the table focused on Nico.

"Are you sure?" Eslar asked hesitantly.

"I am," Nico answered with more strength to his voice than Jo had ever heard.

"You're nuts. . ." Wayne trailed off in disbelief with a shake of his head. "You'll have, what? Fifteen hours to finish with enough time to get it to him?"

"I'd recommend no more than twelve," Pan said, lazily investigating her nails.

"I can do it." Nico continued to speak right to Snow, as though he had been the one asking the question.

Snow returned the Italian's gaze for a long moment before motioning towards the doors with his chin.

"Then go."

Just as quickly as the claim had been made, Nico nodded and left. "Will twelve hours really be enough?" Jo murmured to no one in particular. And yet her focus drifted from the doors to their leader. She caught a glimpse of sadness, of something like worry etching Snow's face. But when he caught her staring, he didn't look away—simply held her gaze, face open and the makings of a tired smile forming before his mask fell back into place once more.

"If anyone can do it, it's Nico," Snow said in a surprisingly overt display of confidence.

"He's got to," Takako said. As confident as her statement should have been, the lingering quiver beneath gave away the woman's nervousness.

As if picking up on a cue, Pan chose those words to hop back to her feet, dusting nonexistent wrinkles out of her dress. "Well, we most certainly have faith in our Italian romantic, don't we?" she said, this time not bothering to look at anyone but Snow. With a twirl of one of her golden pigtails, she cocked her head. This time, there was no way to describe her grin other than "devious." Maybe even twisted. "Let's just hope that faith is well-founded. For all your sakes."

With that, Pan spun on her heel and sauntered out the door. When Jo looked at Snow, hoping desperately for an answer, all she got was his usual blank expression.

"Dismissed," he said, a simple if not painful demand.

But without question or complaint, they listened, mutually ignoring all things left lingering and unspoken.

26. TOGETHER

J O HAD NEVER experienced a more agonizing hour of her life than the first hour in the common room following Nico's announcement.

That was, until she experienced the second hour.

And the third.

She sat, white-knuckled and buzzing with an inexplicable energy that eventually gave way to bouncing knees and tapping fingers. Jo tried to keep her eyes on the television, or focus on the sturdiness of Wayne's very welcome touch on her knee after the first hour. But it was impossible to do anything other than obsess.

The room wasn't quiet, but her mind was, and it put her in a dangerous place. All sound stayed in the realm of the physical: the television, the forced friendly chatter of Wayne and Eslar at the couch where she sat,

Takako bumbling around the kitchen with Samson. It all blurred into white noise. Her mind had withdrawn to where none of it could reach.

It's my fault, a tiny voice betrayed once again.

She'd wasted so much time on her own arrogance, her own confidence that this wish would be so easy to maneuver around with a few lines of code. It had been her actions that had set them on this path; she'd rolled the dice of their fate from the onset. She had tried to thwart a natural disaster with man-made technologies; Jo could practically hear the cackle of Mother Nature grating against the back of her mind.

"Jo," Wayne's voice soothed. Firm but gentle, fingers closed around her wrist and pulled lightly.

The room returned to her as Jo lifted her head from her hands. She straightened her back, curling away from where she'd sunken in on herself. Jo didn't even remember her cheeks meeting her palms. How long had she been like that?

"It's going to work out," he encouraged.

Now say it like you mean it. Jo bit back the harsh words and forced a nod.

"What happens if it doesn't?" She braved the question that had been trailing behind her like a scrap of toilet paper since they'd first received this impossible wish. And, just like a trailing scrap, no one seemed to want to say anything about it.

No one said anything. But for the first time, it felt as if people were actually considering the question— rallying behind it, even. Eventually, one after the next, every eye in the room landed on Eslar.

"I honestly don't know." It sounded like a confession and an omission of guilt at the same time. He looked directly at Jo, referencing their conversation days ago. "I was not lying to you, then. Such a thing has never come to pass, and Snow has never elaborated to me."

Jo wondered if she could get Snow to tell her. But if he did, would that mean she'd used their closeness to her advantage? Would it be so wrong if she did? Why had she dared enter into some kind of relationship *now,* of all times?

"We won't fail though," Wayne reiterated. "We just won't."

None of them could seem to muster more than a nod of agreement.

"You're right." She wouldn't discount Nico. She'd felt the power of his magic first-hand, she knew how evocative his paintings could be. If anyone could do it, it would be him. Jo would give him all the faith in the world to see it happen.

"Would you like to bring this to him?" Samson's voice pulled Jo's attention back toward the kitchen.

"Huh?" It took a moment to register that Samson was holding a plate of food. "Oh, that?" Jo quickly rose to her feet, eager to have something to do other than sitting and worrying her hands into bone-popping tension. "Gladly."

Samson transferred the plate, and Jo eagerly left the room. It wasn't that being around the other members was hard; there was a solidarity there—bonding that could only be brought on by a terrible situation. But solidarity through terror wasn't the sort of team building she wanted.

Jo clung to the plate, her only lifeline to feeling useful, like she was still able to do something for their cause.

Instead of heading toward Nico's room, she turned left and headed up toward the recreation rooms. Nico had escaped there following the meeting, claiming that for such a work he needed the freedom of a completely new space. Jo wasn't sure if she quite understood it from an artistic perspective. But she understood it enough to see the merits from her own past work. Sometimes it took a new environment to see a problem with new light and find the right solution.

Please let Nico have found the right solution, she prayed silently.

Shifting the balance of the plate to one hand, Jo located the shelf holding Nico's timepiece and gave a few solid raps on the adjacent door. She waited a moment that ticked away into minutes. There was no response. Jo debated knocking again. They didn't *need* food; it wasn't possible for Nico to be truly hungry anymore. Certainly food wasn't a worthy-enough reason to throw any potential artistic groove he was in off-kilter—

The door opened, revealing a frazzled-looking, paint-splattered Nico. His eyes dropped from her face to the plate and his face relaxed into a tired smile. "Samson always knows just what I need."

He opened the door the rest of the way, motioning for Jo to enter.

The recreation room had molded itself into a

cramped little studio. Plaster had cracked and fallen away in most places, to reveal porous brick walls underneath. The spider-web fractures rose to meet sturdy-looking, but weathered, wooden beams that supported a squat roof. Fire burned low in a white stone hearth—the only source of light as the world beyond the iron grated window was dark.

"Is this. . ."

"My old atelier? Yes." Nico moved to an easel set up to the left of the hearth and across from the door so that the light would reflect off it without being obstructed by his shadow. "You can set that there." He pointed to a worktable to Jo's left, already picking up a paintbrush and dragging it across his palette.

Jo let the door close behind her and crossed over to the table. It was narrow and not an inch of its surface was visible through the clutter of artistic tools—some of which she now actually recognized from the store in Florence. She took the liberty of pushing some to the side, clearing just enough space for the plate.

Nico hadn't moved, already seeming lost in a world only he and the canvas shared. Jo watched as the two continued their discussion through paint, magic, and undeniable skill. He seemed to have already forgotten she was there.

"You can sit, if you'd like." Or he hadn't quite forgotten. Nico motioned toward a stool by the hearth.

"I don't want to disturb you," Jo said hesitantly.

"You won't," he assured her without looking. "Julia would sit there from time to time, and I'm used to working with you around now. Perhaps it will invoke her spirit and bring me some luck."

Jo took the sentiment at face-value, not peeling it apart to search for meaning she knew wasn't there. She knew neither she, nor any woman, could ever be a replacement for Julia de'Este in Nico's heart. If anything, he had just paid Jo the highest compliment he could by saying that, just maybe, she could offer the ghost of a replacement in body, a balm in the form of a personified memory.

She assumed the seat, leaning against the pleasantly warm stones of the hearth. By all logic, she should feel more restless here than in the living room. The wooden stool was far less comfortable than the plush of the couch. And she could see how much progress Nico had yet to make (unless he was going for something *very* abstract this time).

But some of the tension in her shoulders gave way. Not a lot, but enough. Just seeing progress being made with her own two eyes was reassuring.

"How is the rest of the group?" he asked after silence had made its pass.

"Restless," she answered honestly. She wouldn't insult Nico's intelligence or ability to handle the truth with an attempt at lying.

Nico nodded.

"But we all have faith in you."

He took his eyes away from the painting a moment to give a smile of appreciation. Jo almost wished he hadn't. The look was so distant; like the darkness beyond, the seemingly perpetual sunshine of Nico's face had finally set, and now he looked every one of his years.

Nico turned back to the painting. "I hope I do not let you down."

"I'm sure you won't." When did encouragement turn into unnecessary pressure? It was a line Jo didn't want to cross.

"I have a favor to ask of you, Jo."

"Anything."

"Come with me to deliver this painting."

Jo straightened away from the mantle, leaning forward as if the stone had somehow obstructed her hearing. "Me? Why? I mean, yes, of course, but why?"

"As I said, I believe that you are good luck for me." The scratch and swish of his brush was the only thing filling the silence between his words. "Having you around helped me recall details I'd long forgotten of my Julia. Her youth, our youth. . ." The man stilled for only half a breath; a dot of paint dropped from brush to floor. "It has truly been so long since I have been the man she courted."

Jo opened her mouth and closed it again, unsure how to respond. She had never intended to evoke painful memories for him with her presence. Until today, she'd had no idea Julia kept him company while he painted. Yet suddenly, things began to make a little more sense, such as his openness with her and his willingness to take her to Florence.

"In any case." Nico shook his head and his eyes regained clarity, brush strokes becoming more confident once again. "Your magic of breaking into places could prove useful."

"Then it's yours. We'll do this, together."

"Together," he repeated, like a vow. "The whole Society. We'll make this happen."

There was no alternative—no other reality Jo or any of them would accept.

27. BREAKING AND ENTERING

NICO WORKED RIGHT up until the end of his twelve-hour time allotment. His arms were coated up to his elbows with an array of colors and his shirt was splattered in odd places from his frantic desire to finish. All calmness Jo felt had begun to flee the moment she saw the man's shoulders starting to rise toward his ears in tension.

"That'll. . ." Nico pulled away, looking at the painting. "It'll work."

"Are you sure?" Jo hated herself the instant the question left her lips. Nico's head turned to her and the uncertainty—the panic—that filled his eyes made her heart sink to the bottom of her stomach like a lead weight.

"Only one way to find out, I suppose." He reached out toward the painting, running his hands over the small mountains and grooves in the paint.

The instant panic of him smearing the recently completed work disappeared when the picture held firm—magic, no doubt. Jo stood, pulling her arms above her head, trying to pop the tension that sitting on the stool for such a long, tense amount of time had left. It didn't work. Her body was as rigid as it had been the first moment she'd gotten to her feet.

"We should go, then?" She phrased it as a question, but what other option did they have?

"We should." Nico lifted the canvas, barely wider than his chest, and took it over to the worktable where most of Samson's food still remained untouched. Collecting some butcher paper and twine, he tied it in a sort of protective sling that could be worn over his shoulder.

"To the *Shushō Kantei*, then."

"The what?" Nico asked, as he followed her from the door. The man stopped in the hallway, pointing to the other recreation room. "Do you need to do any of your computer magic first?"

Jo paused as well. "Computer magic" had a nice ring to it. If she was back in the real world, perhaps she'd exchange "Shewolf" for a moniker of her own creation, like "The Wizard." Still, Jo shook her head at him. "This shouldn't be too difficult. We're evading guards and more simple security systems, not massive database firewalls. If I need anything, I have time enough to do it on the fly."

Nico nodded and caught up. The faith he had in her made Jo's chest swell. "How do you know where we're going?" His question reminded her of Takako and the *mugicha* they shared.

"Japan shares a border with the Lone Star Republic. It's pretty much standard education to learn about their government. Well, that, and I took a fairly recent interest when I realized how much more the Yakuza would pay for good work than other syndicates." Talking felt good, Jo realized. It kept them on task, and it kept her mind from winding around and around with worry. "The *Shushō Kantei* is across from the National Diet Building of Japan. It's where the Prime Minister lives and works."

"If we don't find him there?"

"Then he's likely in the Diet Building."

"And if—" Before Nico could finish what was no doubt an additional worry, he paused at the stop of the stairs.

Every other member of the Society (save Pan and Snow) sat in the Four-Way or right at the beginning of the hall that led to the common area. Eslar sat on a couch, reading, his air of calm unflappable. Samson was at his side, fiddling with some random object. Wayne lounged on the stairs across from them, flipping his nickel. And Takako stood by one of the tall windows. Jo wondered if she was looking at the mountains in the distance, filled with longing and concern for her home.

All heads turned when they appeared at the top of the stairs, and all eyes were on the canvas-shaped bundle slung over Nico's shoulder.

"It's done?" Eslar rose to his feet.

"It is." Nico sounded far more confident than he ever looked in the recreation room.

"We wanted to see you off," Wayne pointed out the obvious, rising as well and pocketing his nickel along with both hands. "Wish you luck."

"Jo is coming with me," Nico said quickly. "In case I need help getting in somewhere."

"Smart idea."

"Careful Eslar, or I'll think you value me as a member of this team." Jo took a shot at levity as she started down the stairs.

"Why, of course—"

"I'm kidding." She gave him a small smile that relaxed the elf's face as well. "We'll be back soon."

"Good luck," she heard Samson's small voice say after them, as they started toward the briefing room.

Jo folded her arms over her chest, then undid them. She put them on her hips, then let them sway at her sides. When had having arms become so awkward? *Everything would be fine.* Nico's power was impressive and they had the whole team behind them. *This would work.*

Yet Jo found herself wishing Snow could've been there to see them off as well. As if, somehow, the presence of the Wish Granter himself could bestow some sort of innate blessing onto their mission. At the very least, seeing his face would've given her a much-needed boost of courage.

Without fail, by her own magic or the magic of the Door itself, the alphanumeric keypad seemed to light up only in Jo's mind, pulling her fingers toward the numbers that would lead her to where she wanted to go. Eventually, Jo thought she might be compelled to figure out the pin system—how and why certain places had certain strings of numbers and how the other members knew them—but for the near future, she was content to let it remain a magical mystery.

Pulled through the portal to reality, the Texan and the Italian stepped onto Japanese soil.

Jo didn't want to fuss with anything more than they had to. The more variables that were introduced on a project, the more room there was for error. This was fairly simple: get in, show the painting, leave.

"The Door could've put us right in his office." Jo sighed heavily.

"It's not an exact science."

"It's not science at all," she said in exasperated agreement.

They found themselves in a clean if dated lobby. A receptionist busily answered phones, looking no doubt frazzled due to the extra commotion the panic had brought on. Jo felt some sympathy for the woman; it wasn't her fault that her boss was being pig-headed.

"We could try again," Jo suggested. "See if we can get closer to the office now that we're here."

"The Door has never worked that way." Nico shook his head. "I'd rather not risk it, not when we're already this close."

Jo bit her tongue a moment, chewing over the fact that the Door had, indeed, worked that way for her on more than one occasion—notably their first wish. But she didn't want to give any cause for Nico to panic or stress. If he didn't want to make an attempt with the Door, they'd just go it on foot. "Come on, this way."

"Do you know where you're going?" Nico asked.

"Just a hunch. . ."

Jo followed the flow of people in the lobby toward a back elevator, walking undetected. She listened in on the chatter. Most of it was general government business; the cavalier attitude grated on her. If they didn't start evacuations in the next twenty-four hours, it would be too late.

They emerged on an upper floor and Jo trailed behind one of the men she'd decided to follow from the elevator around the hall and up a short side stair to yet another reception area. However, unlike the main lobby of the building, this was much smaller. A single couch sat opposite a small desk where a woman greeted the man. Jo looked down the hall to a lone door bearing the white and red Japanese flag proudly.

"That must be the office," she said, starting off in its direction.

The ease with which they'd managed to get this far astounded her. Because if there was one thing she'd learned early on, it was that no job ever went off "without a hitch."

So she shouldn't have been surprised, really, when she finally stood before the door and encountered a problem.

"Jo? What's the matter?" Nico whispered, despite the fact that neither of them had their watches on. He was standing at her side, shifting the painting on his shoulder.

It wasn't until then that Jo realized she'd been staring at the door, or more specifically the biometric security system attached to it, for a good couple of minutes, frozen under the weight of the unexpected lack of magical sensation. There wasn't that same unraveling she usually felt. The lock didn't transform into a deeper understanding before her eyes. It did. . . nothing.

She closed her eyes, trying to remember anything she'd seen or heard about the technology before her. *Nada.* Eyes still closed and mind whirring like an overheating, old, moving hard-drive, she tried to imagine what the tech on the inside might be like. There had to be a weakness somewhere she could exploit. *Still nothing.* No magical spark buzzing beneath her skin, no sense of the door's secrets laying themselves bare at her feet.

With a huff, Jo let her eyes flutter back open.

"I've never seen a lock like this before," she finally managed to mumble, brow furrowed in concentration as if she might be able to will her magic to work anyway.

"I see. . ." Nico said, even though his tone betrayed that he clearly did not understand.

A new thought had a spike of terror running down Jo's spine. "Usually, that shouldn't be an issue. But my magic isn't working. It's not—I can't decipher anything." She dug deep, trying to see if she felt any hint of it at all. Nothing, nothing, *nothing.* In fact, it almost felt like an absence of magic entirely; that part of herself that was now distinctly "other" felt almost empty, hollow, the more she stared at the lock. Her stomach dropped. Not now; her magic could fail any time but *now.* "It's not helping me work out a way to break in like it normally does. I—"

"What do you mean?" Nico asked, voice equally panicked. "I don't understand."

Frantically, Jo peeled her eyes away from the biometric scanner, looking about the mostly empty hallway before landing on a wall-mounted thermostat.

Without a word to Nico, Jo rushed over to it, analyzing the make and model and recognizing it as one she'd seen installed in many of her higher-paying clients' offices. It was based on a semi-artificial intelligence unit set to recognize the average heat signatures of the bodies within the building. It pinpointed algorithmic consistencies through the sensors in the smart bands everyone wore on their wrists, adjusting each floor to benefit the widest demographic.

Hardly a look was all it took for Jo to know exactly how she would be able to access those commands and issue a building-wide freeze or meltdown. She could feel the certainty of it in her veins, hear the echoing thrum of something ethereal yet distinctly *her* buzzing about between her ears.

The relief behind the realization was so potent she could taste it. Her magic was still working, after all. *If she knew what she was dealing with.* Nico's earlier comments, before the start of the wish, returned to her.

"It's my restriction." The admission left a sour taste on her tongue.

"What is?"

"I can't crack something apart unless I sort of know how it's put together—at least the basics, I think. I have to see something of its guts. . . Without that fundamental knowledge, I'm useless." She looked back at him, panic rising in her. He'd brought her to help him get where he needed to go and now she was going to fail him. Just like she'd already failed all of them. . . again.

"Everyone has their restrictions." Nico put on a brave face, brave enough to dare a smile. "I'm sure it's nothing we can't work around." *Bless him.*

"You're right." Jo leeched off his certainty. She'd been in tougher spots. Restrictions be damned, she could do this. "If I can't break the lock, we just have to find another way in," Jo said once she was back at Nico's side.

"Likely for the best, really." He looked back down the hall. "Even if you could break into it, you'd have to have your watch active. If we clocked into time now, we'd surely be noticed."

Jo nodded in agreement. Simply unlocking the prime minister's door and strolling in was out of the question. They had to find another way to get the door open without causing a scene.

"Okay, okay." Jo ran both hands through her hair before clapping them hard on Nico's shoulders. He jumped, but otherwise made no motion to shake off the touch. "We need someone else with access. Someone else he'd trust with entry to his personal office. Maybe like, a cabinet member? Or the deputy prime minister? Something?" But where were they supposed to find someone who prime minister Nakamura would answer his door for? Especially in a crisis like this one? And with what *time*?

251

"Maybe we don't need somebody that high up." Nico's voice pulled her away from the spiraling "what ifs" and back to their present situation. He, too, seemed to be lost in thought, looking off in another direction, focus unwavering and expression set with fierce determination. It was the same resolve she'd seen when he took up the torch the rest of them had all but extinguished.

She followed that gaze back to the desk situated at the front of the hall like a guard post. A woman, likely the prime minister's secretary, sat, chatting with the man they had followed up to this floor to begin with. All at once, Nico's plan of action solidified amidst the growing details of her own.

"You're a genius, Nico!" She nearly laughed, her hands finally falling from Nico's shoulders as she began another quick search of the other offices on this floor. All she needed now was an open door and an active third-party computer, and they'd be golden. "Wait here. This won't take long!"

Jo sprinted back down the hall to one of the larger main areas. A door several yards ahead swung open, and Jo doubled her pace as she b-lined for entry. A distracted businessman exited, more focused on his phone than anything else—especially not a phantom outside of time sprinting toward the room.

Please don't shut the door. Jo prayed silently. *Please,* please *don't shut the door.*

Popping out of time to let herself into the man's office surely wouldn't go unnoticed. Discovery would force them to abort, pull out of time again, and wait until the chaos their presence caused died down. The prime minister would perhaps leave for a more secure area, and they'd have to figure out a way to follow. All of which wasted time they barely had.

Luckily, the distracted businessman remained exactly that, rushing out of his office without bothering to close his door, leaving it wide open for any lucky wish granter to take advantage of. From there, it was simply a matter of jumping back into time, hacking into the computer's communications systems, and accessing the right connection.

"Let's get into your email. . ." Jo crouched down behind the desk, peering up at the oversized monitor she hoped would hide her from any wandering eyes. "Dear miss secretary. . . looks like your boss needs you," Jo paraphrased as her fingers typed with a magical command of the Japanese language.

Jo had no doubt that it wouldn't do them any good if the secretary called the prime minister; the man was probably too busy dooming his country to deal with any of her problems beyond a curt reply over the phone. But if *he* were to request *her* presence—

Letting a combination of magic and skill flow down from eyes to fingertips, Jo sent the email from the prime minister's personal line to the secretary's desk. Even from around the corner and a few doors down, she heard the *beep beep* of a message received almost instantly. Jo clicked her way out of the various windows she'd opened, made a hasty cleanup of her work, turned off her watch, and hurried back to Nico.

He was practically bouncing on the balls of his

feet as she sprinted down the hall, half watching her approach, half watching the secretary get to her feet. The woman crossed swiftly to the prime minister's door, leaving the man she'd been speaking to waiting on the couch.

They'd have seconds, if that, to get past her once she opened the door, but it was their only chance. And they were going to take it.

The secretary placed her hand over the biometric lock and Jo watched carefully: still, no magical understanding. But the lock opened, and that was all that mattered. When she cracked the door open with zero room for them to get past, Jo's heart somehow managing to plummet into her stomach and jump into her throat simultaneously. The sudden look of anxious fear on Nico's face said he felt the same way. What would they do now? There wasn't enough room for them to squeeze through.

But as if the gods of ironic fate had decided to share with her the gift of convenient memory, Jo found herself thinking back to the Rangers compound.

Snow and she had walked at a casual pace down the hallways, never once diverging from their path. All the while, they remained unnoticed, and despite the many occasions that Ranger personnel could have collided with them unknowingly, they'd somehow (subconsciously, magically, or otherwise) chosen to go around them. The elevator had been the same—cramped, yet none of the other businessmen and politicians there had decided to even try to occupy the little bit of space in the corner where Jo and Nico had stood invisible. It was just a hunch, but Jo ran with it, stepping in front of Nico and inching towards the secretary's right side.

The woman was in the process of inquiring as to the prime minister's concerns when Jo managed to get a foot between the Japanese woman and the door. There was no movement, and Jo felt her chest clench in steadily rising panic. Still, she tried to inch her hip into the smallest amount of open space the woman's leaning frame provided; to maintain her balance, she pressed her hands ever-so-slightly against the secretary's right hip.

The barely-there touch might as well have been Jo asking the secretary to step aside, what with the way she abruptly pulled back from the door to bow in apology at the prime minister's confusion and annoyance. The polite motion gave them ample room to get not just Jo, but Nico and the painting inside without issue.

By the time the secretary ushered herself out with one final, profuse apology for bothering him unnecessarily, they were situated in front of the prime minister's desk. For a breath or two, Nico and Jo just stood there, watching the face of the man standing between them and the deaths of hundreds of thousands of his citizens—content, it would seem, to pour over what looked to be poll numbers instead. It was surreal, knowing that so many lives rested on this moment, this *second*, of precious, borrowed time.

"You ready?" Jo asked, even though it didn't matter. Nico nodded, but his trembling hands said otherwise; he understood, too. Whether they were ready or not, this was happening in "Three, two, one."

Nico jumped back into time and held up the painting in the same fluid motion.

Jo held her breath.

28. FINAL HOPE

"WHAT THE—" THE Prime Minister of Japan froze mid-sentence. His jaw went slack and his eyes grew glossy as he stared at the painting, seemingly no longer concerned that it had somehow magically materialized before him.

Jo shifted her weight from foot to foot. Time ticked on Nico's watch, though he barely seemed to breathe as the minutes passed. The only thing about him that betrayed life was the slight tremble in his forearms as he continued to hold out the painting.

"Is it working?" Jo finally whispered by letting out a breath she could no longer hold. Her eyes ping-ponged between the painting and the man still enthralled by it.

"I. . . I think so," Nico whispered in reply. Even though he was in time, the prime minister didn't even move or react to the voice. "I can feel the magic."

Jo closed her eyes. She blocked out the stately office and wall of windows that let in a midday sun, already setting on the last of their time. She tried to feel the magic, too, tried to sense it like she could her own.

There was a tickle on the edge of her mind, a growing sensation the more she focused on it. Nico's magic, and then hers, side by side. She stared at the painting, at the aura of power that radiated from it. Jo probed further, curious. She couldn't just leave it be. Her magic curled around Nico's magic, trying to pick it apart and understand just what she was sensing.

Something fractured against the force of her magical exploration. In her mind was the echo of something that resembled a lake in winter, ice cracking under the pressure of a weight it was not yet ready to bear. Jo opened her eyes, instinctively retreating from the odd and unwelcome sensation. She didn't need to know how his magic worked. She had already put all her faith in Nico.

He glanced over at her, as if sensing what she'd done, but said nothing.

Nakamura was still frozen, but his expression was slowly beginning to change. It morphed from a blank slate to a look of abject horror. Jo turned to look at the canvas, trying to see what he saw (without magic, this time).

Mt. Fuji rose from a haze over a land cast in shadow. What looked like the first smoldering rays of sunrise reflected off high gray clouds and put the peak in silhouette. It was almost. . . tranquil.

But when she looked back to the man in power,

his brow had furrowed and his mouth was gaping, as if locked in a soundless scream. *Yes*, Jo's heart pleaded with each beat, *yes, yes, yes!*

"What should he be seeing?" she asked; conversation clearly had not broken the trance.

"Pain, destruction, loss." Generic words that could be assumed, but Nico needed to say no more. If the prime minister was witnessing even half of what the Society had seen over the past months, it would be enough.

Slowly, the man's eyes regained clarity. The glossy sheen of magic began to lift, its remnants blinked away by the most powerful man in Japan. He leaned back in his chair and stared at the ceiling.

Jo gripped Nico's wrist; the trance was clearly broken. But the Italian stayed in time. He held out the painting as if all his muscles had locked into place.

She looked back to the prime minister, who was now blinking away rogue tears spilling over onto his cheeks. "It worked," Jo whispered in relief.

"An evacuation," Nakamura whispered to himself. He turned to his computer. It was as if Nico had become a fixture in his office, a statue and a painting, nothing to be alarmed by.

Nakamura stroked in a few commands on the computer. Jo sprinted around, looking at the screen, hovering invisibly over him, a hand he couldn't feel grasping for stability on his shoulder. A document was open: standard, official-looking letterhead. The date was already typed in—

"Nico, it's a press release!" The rush of joy was going

to tear her apart. The sheer relief was overwhelming. "We did it!"

As if hearing her (which was impossible since she was out of time), and as if determined to prove that everything that *could* go wrong with this wish would, Nakamura's fingers stopped mid-sentence. He hung his head, magic continuing to evaporate off his immobile shoulders like the last frayed threads that had held together the Society's hopes.

The man slowly shook his head and deleted the draft—an omen of doom. "I can't. . ." he said, as if speaking to them both.

Nico's fingers uncurled and the painting dropped like dead weight, a curtain falling upon their last hope and revealing its maker's horror. Jo watched it happen, as if in slow motion. She didn't hear the canvas striking the floor. She heard, instead, the sharp intake of breath from Nakamura. She saw the man's brow furrow and his lips part as his head snapped upward, all traces of magic gone.

"We have to go!" Jo practically leapt over the desk, bounding to Nico in a few wide steps. She grabbed the frozen Italian, shaking him. "Get out of time."

"Who the hell are you?" The prime minister was on his feet. His hand slipped under the desk, no doubt to push a panic button. "How did you get in here?"

Jo rummaged through Nico's pockets, pulling on the chain of his watch to free it. She wondered how it looked to Nakamura, if the watch was merely floating in space or perhaps didn't exist to him at all. It didn't matter; they were about to be ghosts anyway. She tried to push on the watch, turn the dials, open the face, but Jo couldn't affect it. She recalled what Takako had said when she'd first used the recreation room: *No one could activate another person's watch.*

Clinging to the chain, Jo pushed it toward Nico, dangling it in front of his face. "We have to go, Nico, *now*, push it now!"

A commotion was rising outside the door. Jo practically punched the man in the face trying to get his attention. Numbly, a hand rose, tapping on the watch.

Jo heard the prime minister's shock from behind her, no doubt coming from the fact that the strange man had just disappeared in thin air. She turned, glaring at him, and in the same moment stooped to scoop up Nico's painting. She pulled them toward the door of the room before it could be thrust open by whatever responders were fast on the way to the office.

It wasn't so much belief that made the Door appear this time, but a magical demand. Jo silently shouted across every possible universe. *Appear or feel my wrath.* And appear it did.

She wrenched it open with the energy of all her anger and sorrow, feeling like she could rip the thing off its hinges if she so chose. All at once, she allowed herself to be pulled through, painting under one arm, the other linked tightly with the now-trembling shell of a man who had been their final hope.

29. WE WAIT

NICO WAS STILL in shock when they stumbled back into the briefing room, but by the slight tremor in his fingertips, it wouldn't be long before that shock wore off. Jo didn't want to know what would happen to the poor man then, almost as much as she didn't want to see the reactions on the team's faces when they found out. And they would, any second now.

Because, as expected, the briefing room was already full, brimming with tension so thick, Jo had been able to feel it even before stepping fully through the Door. Arm still looped around Nico's, helping him a wobbling step at a time towards his seat, Jo looked from face to face around the table.

Pan and Snow were missing. *The hell were they doing?* an angry little voice in her wanted to scream.

Everyone had gotten to their feet upon Jo and

Nico's arrival, and after helping Nico sit down, Jo took Wayne's usual chair so as not to remove her steady presence from the Italian's side. She could feel the trembling of his fingers stretch up into an outright shaking along his arms. Any second now, he would fracture, crumble into pieces, and Jo didn't think she'd be able to put him back together. But she would damn well try. It was better than focusing on her own rising guilt, her growing panic, her pain and misery at the loss, so much loss, and they'd tried *everything,* so why had at all still turned out so, so—

"So?" Takako's voice caught Jo off-guard, wrenching her back to the briefing room. The woman was smart; she should've been able to see the creeping mental devastation all over their faces. Maybe she had. Because even though Takako had bothered to ask the question on everyone's mind anyway, it was already obvious she knew the answer. "How'd it go?"

That was all it took for Nico to lose it.

A broken sob tore its way up his throat, a sound that held as much emotional anguish as physical. Nico had worked for hours, poured everything he and his magic had into the painting that now leaned, forgotten, by the Door. There was no doubt in Jo's mind he'd been exhausted and broken down even before watching that final blossom of hope wither and die in the prime minister's eyes.

Now, he was beyond broken, inconsolable. If they could manage to ease his suffering at all after this, it would be a miracle. And after today, after every one of her own failures, believing in miracles seemed incredibly naive. They were the ones who were supposed to be the miracle workers, and they'd failed.

The group probably didn't need her to explain, but Jo couldn't handle the idea of Nico's sobs being the only sound in the room.

"He wouldn't change his mind. *Couldn't* apparently. Not even with Nico's influence." She hated the way Nico's back seized beneath her hand, whole body tense and shaking in what was more than likely guilt. She wanted to tell him it wasn't his fault, that he'd done all he could (which was true, of *course* it was true), but she knew he wouldn't hear it; Jo felt guilty too, had ever since that first botched evacuation hack. So instead, she just kept talking, raising her voice a little to drown out some of Nico's softer whimpers and cries. "Twelve hours just. . . wasn't enough time. The magic wore off too quickly and it. . . it just wasn't enough."

"No. . ." That simple word, whispered past Takako's lips, felt like having the breath ripped from her lungs. With the hand that wasn't rubbing comfortless circles into Nico's back, Jo gripped ruthlessly at her own knee. She shook her head.

"I'm sorry, Takako."

A whimper this time, Nico's hands falling from his face.

"So that's it then?" Samson whispered, and when Jo turned her head in his direction, he was staring at her with sad, scared eyes.

In fact, everyone looked worn out and filled with a hopelessness that overtook each of their usual features. The bags under Samson's eyes were prominent, his fingernails chewed down to the nubs. Takako looked like she was facing down the barrel of a gun, her hands tangled in the short hair on either side of her head. Wayne paced the room, the usual slicked-back perfection of his hair in complete disarray, his bottom lip bruised from being chewed on. Eslar's complexion was pale, the usually rich darkness of his skin almost resembling the lighter brown of Jo's own, and his face held more heavy emotion than she'd ever seen in him.

It took Nico rising slowly, shakily to his feet, for Jo to realize he'd stopped crying. Though how long ago, she had no idea. For all she knew, they could have simply been staring at each other, staring off into the panicked black holes of their own minds, for hours since their return. But now? Now everyone's eyes were on Nico.

His hands, splayed out on the briefing room table, still trembled. His eyes, staring down Eslar with a fierce attempt at an even fiercer determination, were still red-rimmed and wet. But when he opened his mouth to speak, his words were steady, steadier than any of them should have had any possibility of being in that moment.

"I'll do it again," he said. Plain and simple.

Jo's heart ached. "Nico, your restriction—"

"I'll find someone else. There must be, right? Another diplomat. Perhaps the leader of an allied power? There has to be someone else to try."

"There's not enough time," Eslar replied, brow furrowing in obvious frustration.

Nico looked down at the space between his hands,

head falling between his shoulders. "I'll do it. Again."

"Nico—"

"I'll do it again!" He cried, ripping himself away from Jo and turning to face Eslar fully. "I can do it, Eslar, I can! Just let me try one more time!"

He was screaming now, Eslar looking from Nico to the rest of the room and back before walking around to their side of the table. Samson buried his head in his hands. Wayne kept pacing. Takako finally let her fingers fall from the stranglehold she had on the strands of her hair, knuckles of one hand hitting the briefing room table on its way down to her lap; she didn't seem to notice.

"Nico, enough," Eslar said, tone bordering on an order, but Nico just let his head hang again, shaking it back in forth. Jo watched, her own eyes burning, as fresh tears made new tracks down Nico's cheeks. Eslar placed a hand on Nico's shoulder, but Nico shrugged him off.

"If we have even an hour left, a *minute,* then I have to keep trying," he whispered, words beaten and battered beneath the weight of his own guilt, beneath the cruelty of their own hopelessness. "I have to try. I'll show a painting to every individual citizen if I have to. Please let me keep trying."

For a long moment, there was silence. Everyone looking at Nico and Eslar in turn. Even Wayne had stopped his pacing, though he chose to look down the hall instead, away from the room. In the hand that wasn't buried deep into his pocket, Jo could see Wayne's thumb rubbing circles into the face of his nickel.

"Eslar, I can fix this. I can do better. Please let me—" Nico started again, but Eslar just sighed, the unexpected sound cutting him off. He didn't bother with words, a nod of his head and gesture of his chin towards the door the only indication of his acquiescence.

Nico wasted no time, grabbing the painting and sprinting off towards his chosen recreation room.

There wasn't enough time. Eslar *knew* there wasn't enough time the same way they all knew. And even if there was, who else could they show that would be as effective as the Prime Minister? It was like a visceral thing writhing inside their bellies, their chests, weighing them down and keeping them from moving.

But Nico had asked anyway. Eslar had let him go anyway. Because what else could they do at this point but pretend, and wait?

Jo looked around the room; no one returned her gaze, each too caught up in the suffocation of unknown consequences to do more than stare off into space. When Jo let her stare finally fall to her lap, the shift in line of sight helped a tear slip beyond its hold. It fell in a silent lament down her cheek, off her chin, and onto the white-gripped knuckles of the hand still clutching her knee.

"What do we do now?" She asked, though the words were purely selfish, her own spiraling mind throwing a plea out into the universe. It wouldn't have mattered if no one had responded, but it was Eslar who did.

"We wait." He sat down next to her, and it took all she had to lift her head enough to look him in the eye. She'd never seen his face filled with so much emotion;

she just wished it was a better emotion than grief. "Other than that. . . I don't know."

30. PLEASE

IT WAS PROBABLY only a few minutes later that Jo found herself in front of Snow's door, but her time in the briefing room felt like hours and weighed on her like years. She'd offered to break the news to their leader, refusing to feel self-conscious when nobody was surprised. What was the point in that, after everything that had happened? Everything that was *going* to happen?

She wanted to see Snow. Even if just to tell him of their failure, she wanted to *see* him. She wanted to find solace in his presence and comfort in his arms. She wanted to hear words of hope spill from his lips and swallow them up with her own. So for the first time, led purely by that need, that fragile and terrified desire, Jo knocked on his door without hesitation.

And for the first time, as if knowing she would come, Snow opened the door at once.

As much as she wanted to look at him, touch him, fall into him until nothing of her was left, all Jo seemed able to do was stare at her own feet. They'd failed him. *She'd* failed him. Surely he was disappointed, maybe even angry. Why would he want to see her? Why would he want to see any of them now?

The sting of tears from earlier returned, Jo's throat tightening enough that she had to clear it twice before she felt brave enough to speak.

"I'm sorry," she said to her feet. "I. . . we tried."

She closed her eyes for a moment, willing that burn to go away, for the pathetic grip this whole situation had on her throat to loosen. It took a moment, the pain still fresh (if not overwhelming), but eventually she felt confident enough that tears wouldn't fall if she opened her eyes.

When she did, it was to find a pair of crisp, white dress shoes standing centimeters away from her own. She glanced up, breath hitching at the sight of Snow's face, not looking down on her in shame or disgust, but in something soft and open and otherwise indescribable. Much like at the Rangers' compound (a moment that now felt like it belonged to another lifetime), Snow raised a hand to her cheek, thumb dragging lightly across her cheekbone to catch the remnants of a stray tear.

"You did everything you could," he affirmed, and his voice settled over her shoulders, into her chest, its own kind of comfort. A warm blanket to keep out the cold, a deep cave to wait out the storm. When he motioned for her to step inside, she did so with lighter steps than the ones that had brought her to his room only seconds ago. Or perhaps more accurately, steps heavier in a different way.

Snow closed the door behind her and stayed, waiting for her to come back to him, reclaim that space between them. So she did, nearly pressing against him from thigh to chest, arms wrapping around his waist to pull him even closer still. Her head fit perfectly beneath his chin, and as his arms returned the embrace, his breath brushing her hair, she let her ear rest against his chest. For a long moment, she did nothing more than listen to his heartbeat.

Suddenly, it was all she could do not to focus on the fragility of their situation, the creeping sensation that was quick to replace the timeless warmth of his comfort with a cold and pressing desperation not to lose this, not to lose *him*. It became clear—through some kind of evidence she wouldn't have been able to provide, but nevertheless knew existed—that if they didn't do this now, they never would. If they didn't do something, say something, right now, neither of them would get another chance.

Something terrible was coming. Jo could feel it like a shadow, looming closer and closer as the sun split apart the sky. And when that something finally got here, who knew what it would mean?

For the Society. For the team. For them.

"Snow," Jo whispered, pulling her ear away from his chest to look at him again, raising a hand to his face. Her fingers brushed lightly against his cheek before traveling to the back of his head, settling along the fine, silver hairs at the nape of his neck. Ever so slightly, she tugged him down. "Kiss me."

He bowed easily to her will, arms tightening around her waist as he brushed a chaste kiss against her lips, then deepened it into something not chaste at all.

His tongue traced her bottom lip and she opened her mouth for him in obvious invitation. She wanted every inch of him, wanted to melt into him until they were one person, close enough as to be indeterminable from each other, unrecognizable to the world beyond. Then maybe, just maybe, she could forget for a little while. After all, working and running was all she could do now. And there was no more work left to be done.

As Jo moaned into the kiss, fingers tightening in the fabric of his shirt, she felt something slotting into place, a familiar yet wholly new sensation. Her chest ached and her eyes burned, but her heart sang with the feeling of rightness, of finally, finally being where she was supposed to be.

It felt like home, like love, something she'd never known but somehow instantly recognized.

"Please," Jo gasped into his mouth, hearing her own voice on half-second delay. They hadn't even done anything yet and she already sounded wrecked, *felt* wrecked. Snow pulled back just enough to see her face, though he remained as close as possible, as if desperate not to put any unnecessary space between them. It wasn't until she saw the flush to his cheeks, the plush wetness of his lips, that she even realized how heavily she was breathing. Panting breaths whispered humid air between them; she felt dizzy from the lack of oxygen.

He looked beautiful, she decided then. More beautiful than she'd ever seen him, and more beautiful than he had any right to be. His eyes were heavily lidded but still shining like moonlight beneath the fringe of his silver hair. And the way he looked at her. . . it did things to her heart that, were she not already outside of time and reality, would have probably left her worried for her health.

Snow raised a hand and ran gentle fingers through her hair when she didn't answer right away. "Please what, my love?"

Ah. So he felt it too. Jo wasn't sure if she felt more like laughing or crying. Both probably. But later. There were more important things that needed taking care of right now.

"Please take me to bed." Jo tried for sultry, confident, but the heaviness of the day had left her emotionally exhausted, barely hanging on by a thread. The crack beneath her words, the undeniable shakiness to her tone, had her burying her face in Snow's chest, face heating.

She was no stranger to sex, even Wayne could attest to that, but *this*? This cliff they were both standing on the edge of? This wasn't sex. This was so, so much more than sex. This was something she couldn't put a name to, something she wasn't even sure she *wanted* to put a name to. All she knew was that it was important. And incredibly fragile.

"You have always had a place in my bed," Snow said. "Then, now, and for as long as you want it."

"Have I?" Jo whispered back, something about the words seeming odd, though unimportant in comparison to the meaning behind them. "I'll always want it. I'll always want you. You should know that by now."

In lieu of a response, Snow leaned forward to recapture her lips, a deep and searing kiss that seemed to instantly return her to breathlessness. He sucked her bottom lip between his teeth and she gasped, arching reflexively against him. As close as that left their bodies, there was no denying the already hard line of his arousal pressed between them. The realization of his own desire alone was enough to have her all but drowning in her own desperate need.

There were suddenly too many layers between them, her hands wandering the planes of his chest, the wiry muscle of his arms, his shoulders. Every spot of skin felt like it singed her fingertips, sparks of electricity running up her arms at the contact. As he walked her back towards the bed, never once breaking his fierce and persistent kiss, Jo tugged just as fiercely on his shirt.

When simply tugging the fabric up wasn't enough for him to get the hint, Jo groaned, reluctantly pulling away. "Off," she huffed, lifting the bottom of his shirt enough to afford herself a delicious view of his toned abs. He chuckled in response, though whether at her shameless staring or her eager demand, she wasn't sure. Either way, he followed her order, which was all that mattered. Because within a handful of breaths, Snow was standing bare chested in front of her, a sight to behold.

Jo felt her mouth go dry, reaching out to place her hand against his chest, simply because she could. Snow's heart beat quick and firm beneath her hand, and Jo couldn't help but shudder at the rush of connection she felt—an unexpected intimacy when they hadn't even been properly *intimate* yet. So, as not to get off track, Jo ran the tips of her fingers across one dusky, pink nipple, then the other, secretly thrilled when Snow took in a quiet breath as they hardened in response.

His hands were suddenly at her back, slowly inching the fabric of her hoodie up until his fingers could rub circles into the revealed stretch of skin. Just that simple touch alone had her eyes fluttering shut, her heart stuttering into a faster rhythm.

"May I?" Snow asked, lightly tugging on the material. Jo nodded, lifting her arms when he pulled both her hoodie and the shirt beneath up and over her head. A fresh heat crawled up her neck to settle in her cheeks as Snow's gaze drifted lazily over her half-naked body. When he licked his lips, a seemingly unconscious motion, Jo felt the pang of her own arousal like a burst of adrenaline.

She took a step forward and placed her hand on the waistband of his trousers, only barely touching despite the obviousness of her intention. "May *I*?" she asked, a breathless request. She waited just long enough to see his head tilt forward in a nod before lowering herself to her knees.

When she looked up, it was to find Snow gazing down at her in equal parts surprise and dark, hungry desire. It was an expression Jo planned to memorize and treasure, her confidence bolstered and the heat between her legs growing at the sight.

She wanted to taste him, feel him heavy on her tongue. She wanted to make him moan around the syllables of her name and crumble beneath his own pleasure. In that moment, Jo couldn't remember ever wanting something more.

Once his trousers were pooled around his feet, the thrill of what she was about to do took over, a fresh wave of need leading her almost involuntarily forward. She mouthed briefly at the obvious bulge beneath his boxers, dampening the fabric, before sliding her fingers beneath the waistband and pulling down.

There was the sound of her name, rough and desperate as it escaped past his lips, and then she was taking him in, swallowing him down as far as she could. Snow hissed, already breathing heavy, and when Jo looked up, cheeks hollowed and eyes dark with her own lust, she swore she felt the length of him twitch between her lips.

He looked sinful like this, coming apart at the seams yet still ethereal; even with his own lips bitten and parted in pleasure, he seemed otherworldly in his beauty. Jo couldn't help the swell of pride at being the one who got to see him like this, got to be responsible for the hungry look in his eyes and the fingers tightening in the long, knotted strands of her hair.

Snow's hips stuttered, not thrusting so much as desperately trying to hold himself back, and the need to watch him come, to swallow him down and milk every ounce of pleasure she could from him, was only outweighed by one thing.

She needed him inside of her. Now.

With a lewd sounding *pop*, Jo pulled away, panting softly against the spit-shiny head of him and admiring her job well done. When she got to her feet again, it wasn't without a few good strokes along his now-throbbing length.

"I want you," she confessed, leaning in to whisper the words as her teeth grazed the shell of his ear; she hoped he could hear every layer of those words, every facet of what she meant but didn't say. *I want you near me, I want you inside me, I want everything you're willing to give me. I want you, I want you, I want you.*

As if the words had spurned him on, Snow chased down her lips in another fierce kiss, tongue delving strong and wet against her own. They breathed each other's heavy breaths, swallowed down each other's desperate moans, and before Jo even really registered it, her knees were hitting the back of the bed.

When she settled back into the plush comforter, Snow followed, barely willing to leave an inch of space or single moment between them untouched. He kissed her until she was dizzy and begging, soft words strung together in a barely coherent jumble. All she knew was that she wanted him, so much, more than anyone she'd ever wanted before.

Somewhere in their passionate blur, Snow must have helped her remove the rest of her clothes, because the next moment of clarity was the feel of their naked bodies pressed flush. She could feel his erection between her thighs, not yet pushing in, but grinding against her wetness in subconscious impatience.

Well. She was impatient too.

So when he didn't make the first move, she reached between them, captured his gaze, and guided him in. His eyes fluttering shut as he sheathed himself fully inside her was another expression she planned to commit to memory.

Not that her mental functions had any hope of continuing properly once he started to move. His first thrust had her gasping out his name, back arching off the bed as he filled her completely. She wrapped her arms around the back of his neck, locked her ankles at the small of his back. And when he picked up a rhythm, not fast and rough, but slow and deep and intimate, she swore she could feel every inch of him, sparks of pleasure building into a heat that would eventually set them both aflame.

This was so, so much more than scratching an itch.

Eventually his pace wasn't enough, her whole body teetering on the edge of something mind-blowing without knowing how to topple over.

"Faster, Snow, please. . ." She half-moaned, half-whined, into his neck, lips brushing against his pulse. He obliged, making her cry out and cling harder, so close it was like riding a constant wave of pleasure that refused to crash.

But somehow, Snow seemed to know what to do, navigating that rising tide with a hand between them, fingers rubbing a quick rhythm between her thighs that had her whole body quaking. It was a rush of pleasure so profound, she swore she blipped out of existence for a second, her brain shutting off and rebooting under the pounding burst of pure ecstasy.

She might have screamed his name.

Even as she came down from her high, that same pleasure thrummed like a second skin beneath every inch of her, made only more prominent as she felt Snow's thrusts lose rhythm, his hips stuttering in the aftermath of his own release.

He whispered something into her neck as he came, something she didn't catch over the ringing her ears, but by the way he continued to hold her tight, she figured it was something good.

The echo of his climax rang through her ears as he breathed, his weight on top of her heavy as his breath. She trailed her fingers up his spine, to his shoulders, and back down to just above the firm curve of his rear. He seemed in no haste to move and she was in even less to push him away.

His fingers were the first to find life, tangling in her hair, catching the side of her face in gentle caresses. They unwound, releasing her as he pulled away. The fullness was quickly disappearing as he went soft within her. But they shared an unspoken agreement to savor every last moment of that connection, every tingling, shivering sensation that there was to be felt until the very last second.

When Snow finally lay beside her, Jo could feel the floaty high of post-orgasmic bliss starting to fade. But she didn't want it to. She wasn't ready for it to end, for any of it to end. So she curled up against Snow's chest and closed her eyes, holding him just as tightly as he seemed determined to do to her. She felt his heart slow and listened to him catch his breath, and she pressed kisses against his collarbone, his shoulder, his jaw.

Neither of them spoke, too afraid of popping the bubble they'd managed to temporarily hide themselves inside. And when they eventually managed to drift off to sleep, it was to nothing more than the sound of each other's breathing, and the millions of things neither of them could bring themselves to say.

31. THEIR LAST MEAL

MORNING CAME TOO soon.

Though perhaps it wasn't the morning—merely the aftermath. It was the calm not before, or after, but between the storms.

Jo rested in that eye, clinging to the stability she'd found in the man who was still curled naked next to her. She pressed her forehead into the center of his chest, her nose crushed against his breastbone, and she breathed him in as if to absorb his essence, commit it to memory, and store it for whatever was to come.

She could've asked him then, what awaited them all the moment the clocks ran out. But Jo couldn't find the words. She would wait, and tolerate the unknown, if it meant the preservation of the space that they had collapsed into together and made their own.

Eventually, the tension in his arms increased and

then lessened. Whether he had been asleep until now or just mindlessly drifting in a similar twilight haze, Jo didn't know. But he shifted now, alerting to his consciousness, accepting—however reluctantly—the passage of time. The deadline of some unforeseen consequence loomed overhead like a guillotine. Wordlessly, he pulled away, enough to look at her and enough for Jo to breathe. She searched his face, waiting for whatever he had to say next.

"We should return to them," Snow whispered, punctuating it with a long press of his lips to her temple. "They need you now."

"They need you as well," Jo insisted. "They need their leader, Snow."

"I'm not one for support. . ." He wavered, tipping his head to nuzzle her cheek with his nose. "I've always kept my distance, I've had to."

"Not with me."

"You're different."

"Why?" The question flew from her lips like an arrow from the bow. Pointed, poignant, fired to kill. It struck true; Snow stiffened a moment.

"You just are." He sighed softly and curled into her once more.

Jo wanted to tell him it wasn't good enough. She needed more from him. She needed a better explanation. She needed answers to something, *anything*.

But there were no more arrows in her quiver. Jo merely closed her eyes and leaned into him as well, savoring the last moments before Snow pulled away; she'd seen it coming, felt the rift before it had even begun to grow, but awareness made it hurt no less. He shifted to the edge of the bed, his agonizingly perfect, chiseled back to her, his head hung.

She sat as well, then was the first to stand and start scooping up her clothes. Jo was completely dressed and Snow still hadn't moved. She held a brief debate with his back, before saying, "Come with me."

It wasn't a command but not quite a request either. A strong suggestion, perhaps, one that had Snow rising to full height. Jo kept her eyes locked on his face, chin set.

"Come with me, Snow," she repeated. And then, far more lightly, "Samson makes a great breakfast, you know."

"I do know." Snow looked around his room and Jo wondered if he saw a safe-haven or a tomb. "And it has been far too long since I've enjoyed it."

Jo felt her face relax into a smile, her shoulders sink toward the floor as relief tugged happily on her palms. Snow finally stood, strolling over to a wide wardrobe, carefully picking out an outfit. His selection process gave Jo an opportunity to wander the room, her curiosity nothing more than an excuse to hide her shameless glances at him. That was, until something caught her eye.

Jo paused at a low table just beneath a window, one she'd overlooked on her first assessment of the room. It was obsidian, the only bit of furniture that wasn't made of wood. At its center stood a small box, crafted of gold and silver. The ornate designs, patterns of no particular logic, glinted in the sunlight. The whole of her attention was on it and, as if in a trance, Jo reached out a hand.

Snow's fingers wrapped around hers, stopping her before her skin could make contact with the box. Jo's gaze flew to his and they locked eyes for several long moments. His face was passive, void of expression.

"Do you know what it is?" he asked softly.

She shouldn't. "I recognize it." *Why?*

"From where?" His voice was little more than a husky whisper. But it was not sensuality that put the gravel under his words. It was. . . fear? Had she read that flash of emotion correctly?

Jo looked back at the box, trying to place it. "The room you took me to." She remembered suddenly. "Where you grant the wishes. You had it there. Inside is the magic you use to destroy worlds."

His fingers tensed on hers, drawing Jo's eyes back to him. Snow's brow furrowed. His lips pursed. Whatever internal battle was raging, he wasn't about to give it voice.

"Yes." His tone had changed again to something gentler, more tender. He brought her hand, still encapsulated in his, to his lips and planted a soft kiss on her fingertips. "Do not touch it, Josephina."

"Why?" It should be obvious: the power to destroy worlds was inside. But something in the way he said it—

"That is a great power, Destruction. One that should not meet with you." And with that, Snow walked away, fussing with a cufflink.

Jo took one more look at the box, turned to stare

back at him, then followed. She would allow him this secret without a fight. She was too tired for fighting and, even if she wasn't, this was his secret to keep. It was his magic, after all.

"Should we stagger ourselves?" she asked, thinking of Wayne's warning.

"No point. I've no doubt they already have surmised the situation." He adjusted the collar of his shirt, looking positively regal. *Well, he was a royal demigod at one point, after all.* For as much as she wasn't exactly surprised, it was still a realization that floored her.

"I guess you're right," she admitted to herself as much as him, and led the way toward the common room.

Most of the rest of the team was there. Samson stood in the middle of the kitchen, looking at the oven as if willing it to cook something for him so that he would not have to put forth the effort. Eslar sat at the chess table with a book, though it didn't seem he was reading or playing. Wayne and Takako were at the couch, silently staring at the blank screen of the television.

Nico was nowhere to be found; his watch was still sitting on the recreation room shelf, Jo had noticed as they'd passed, so it was safe to say he hadn't yet left.

"What's for breakfast?" Jo asked softly to Samson.

He seemed to startle at her voice, then startle again when he saw Snow. "I-I haven't decided yet. . ."

"You made sweet cinnamon toast once and it was divine. . . if I may make a suggestion," Snow said in a soothing tone. For a long moment, Samson didn't seem to know how to respond, unblinking eyes locked on Snow and set wide. But before it could get awkward, Samson shook his head and let out a soft breath of laughter.

"You remember that, huh?" He was suddenly moving, picking out a skillet and gathering ingredients. "When was that?"

"Not long after the fall of the Age of Magic."

The little discussion had drawn the attention of the others in the room. Eslar was the first to come over, sitting on Snow's other side.

"That morning was a while ago, just the three of us." Eslar folded his hands, still looking at nothing and no one in particular. "How many breakfasts have we shared since? How many wishes granted?"

"Both are numbers too great to count." Snow shared a small smile of camaraderie with the elf, one that was quickly abandoned.

Wayne and Takako eventually came over as well, though Jo couldn't remember when or why. They didn't say anything, just sort of appeared. Samson cooked, the skillet sizzled, and the room was heavy with silence.

But for the first time, she didn't want the weight alleviated, because if—when—it was, there would be no turning back.

The food was delicious, as expected of Samson's incredible skill, but that didn't diminish the looming sensation that they were consuming a "last meal." Regardless, they shared it in quiet solidarity, no small talk brave enough or bold enough to fill the gap of wordlessness.

Jo pushed herself away from the counter, dismounting from her stool. There was someone missing, she realized. Someone else who needed to share this last, silent display of unity. She turned toward the hall, ready to hunt the missing teammate down, and nearly jumped from her skin.

"Well, isn't this somber?" Pan lounged in the doorframe. For the first time since Jo had met the mysterious not-quite-woman, Pan appeared muted. Her hair was done in a natural blonde, strands stick straight and hanging just past her shoulders. Also unlike her usually eccentric appearance, she wore nothing more than a simple, tailored suit, cloth sitting snug around her petite frame. A thin, red ribbon accompanied the high-collared button-up, shockingly bright against the black layers of fabric.

"When did you get here?" Jo asked, the memory of Pan appearing out of nowhere right before the wish jolting back to the forefront of her mind.

Pan merely shrugged. "We should get started."

"Pan—" Snow began to say.

"It's time, Snow." *Time for what?* Jo wanted to scream. But she could barely find air enough to breathe. "They've run out of hours on the clock and the gap is still too wide. Call the meeting."

All eyes pivoted back to Snow. He stared at Pan, and Pan only, as if waging silent war against the woman herself. Through gritted teeth, Snow finally spoke: "Everyone. To the briefing room."

Everyone stood silently, obediently, pulled along

by an unknown thread.

"I'll go get Nico," Jo offered, sprinting ahead of the rest. She slowed just long enough to give a long, hard look at Pan. But the other woman just smiled on, turning to saunter ahead of the pack toward the briefing room.

Jo got to Nico's recreation room and had a long debate with the door. She waited for courage to find her, and when none came, she pretended just long enough to give a solid knock.

The door cracked open, revealing a sliver of face and a bright red eye.

"Jo. . ." Nico said softly, pulling open the door the rest of the way. The man disappeared behind the door itself, leaving that as her only invitation to walk in. She took it with painfully hesitant steps.

A canvas stood on the easel. Paint was smeared and splattered on it in a pattern Jo needed no magic to interpret. Rage, pain, hurt—it was all there, plain as day. If she could see it, then it didn't bode well for anything else working on any sort of deeper level.

Nico leaned against the wall behind the door, staring at her listlessly.

"There's a meeting."

That was all it took. He crumpled, burying his eyes in the heels of his hands and resting his elbows on his knees as he sank to the floor. She heard the tears before she saw them and was instantly at his side, holding him once more.

"I tried, I tried!" he repeated, over and over with agonizing repetition.

"I know. . ." she whispered, smoothing her hands over his shoulders and back. "No one blames you."

"How can they not? I was the last line of defense, our last hope, and I—"

"I failed from the start." She'd put a stop to that line of thinking then and there. "We all failed. This is our collective failure, and we'll all stand together for whatever comes next."

Nico's hands reached for her, clinging to her in a way even Snow hadn't. Jo hoped no one would ever cling to her in this way ever again.

"I'll be there," she whispered, as if that meant anything, as if it could solve anything.

"Promise?"

"I promise. No matter what."

Nico found the strength to pull himself together and face the world. Or at least enough to pretend. They stood together, arms linked and breaths shuddering in time. Together they walked toward the briefing room, and to whatever fate awaited them all.

32. DRAW STRAWS

A T ONCE UPON arrival in the briefing room, the atmosphere felt different. If not because of the nearly palpable concern spreading like dust over every corner, then because Pan, for the first time, was seated at the head of the table. Jo looked at her in confusion, locating Snow at once as if doing so might make sense of the anomaly. But he was in an unusual seat, pushed just slightly away from the table, at Pan's right. He refused to look at anyone or anything, eyes glazed over and staring down the hall as if he could see past the Four-Way, into the common area, and to the mountains beyond.

"Kind of you two to finally join us," Pan purred, hands coming into graceful contact with the table as she leaned forward. Her eyes shone a bright red to match the ribbon at her neck, and the pupils shifted between thin, cat-like lines, and blown-wide circles. Jo couldn't help but shudder under the eerie woman's gaze.

Jo opened her mouth to argue, possibly even question her position at the helm of their sinking ship, but the feel of Nico's hand tightening around her wrist kept her silent. When she looked over at him, Nico looked near to shattering, eyes not on her but touch desperately clinging. She figured it wasn't worth the unnecessary fighting, not after all they'd already lost, so she bit her tongue and followed Nico the rest of the way to the table.

Wayne saw them approach and, without even needing to be asked, removed himself from his chair, settling into Jo's so she could stay at Nico's side. She hoped her soft smile in his direction conveyed as much gratitude as she felt.

"So!" Pan got started without preamble, clapping her hands loud enough that at least half the room couldn't help but jump, the other half wincing in sympathy. "Where should we begin?" She tapped red-tipped fingernails against the polished table and the whole area exploded in swirling colors and shapes. When it settled, a glitching image of Mt. Fuji stood before them; one second the volcano was inactive, the next frozen in mid-eruption, and back. Beneath the grotesque visual reminder of their oncoming failure was a ring of various timestamps.

As Jo watched the rest of the team glance first at the numbers, then at their own respective watches, she realized what Pan was trying to display. Jo ran a finger over her own wristband, a number illuminating that perfectly matched one of the six beneath the volcano's magical visage.

"None of you have enough time left," Pan continued once it seemed as though everyone had begun to catch on. "And even if you did, the window of opportunity is closing and Snow has already reset time by destroying the world of possibility and expending that allotted amount of magic. He can contribute no more to this wish." The usual lilt to her voice, mischievous and playful, had given way to something heavy and serious, something clearly meant to be intimidating. "We need to make this wish happen *now*, so what is there to do, *hmm*? What option do we have left?"

Nico flinched at the words, the hand still linked loosely with Jo's suddenly tightening, his shoulders tensing in guilt. Anger ambushed Jo's nerves, her head snapping in Pan's direction as she momentarily forgot about the undefined threat looming on the horizon. All she saw was a pompous member of their team that hadn't done *shit* since day one. They'd exhausted themselves and dragged every ounce of their magic and determination and skill out into the open for the sake of the wish. What had she done? What right did she have?

"So why don't *you* actually do something for once?" Jo hissed before she could stop herself. She'd gotten to her feet without realizing, though thankfully she'd had the wherewithal not to drop Nico's hand. By the way he clutched ruthlessly at her fingers, she may as well have been the only thing anchoring him to the present. She squeezed back, but her eyes never left Pan's impassive face, the casual arch of her eyebrows and quirk of her lips. Jo could have punched her.

"I'm about to." Pan pulled her hands from the table and crossed her arms over her chest. When the stare-off seemed to grow boring for her, however, Pan glanced in Snow's direction and grinned, an ugly and devious thing. "So how would you like to do this, Snow? Draw straws? They pick? Or should we let them fight it out? A battle royale might get messy, but I can't say I wouldn't enjoy the show."

"Quiet, Pan." Snow refused to meet Pan's gaze, and even though it was subtle, Jo saw his shoulders tense, the tendons in his neck sticking out against his attempt to stay still. But Jo wasn't going to let him shove this under the rug just like everything else. She needed answers, *deserved* answers. They all did.

"What does she mean?" Jo asked him directly, stomach churning when he refused to meet her eyes. Distantly, Jo could feel Nico squeezing her hand again, but she was too distracted by a sense of steadily rising panic to process anything more than the look of defeat on Snow's face. "Snow?" Jo tried once more, voice softer this time, and he flinched, eyes closing as if to block her out.

That sick feeling in her stomach doubled.

"Don't worry, pet," Pan cooed. She straightened, twirling elegant fingers through her hair. "I can fix this. I can make the magic we need to close the Severity of Exchange and grant the wish." She cracked her neck, hand resting at the base of her skull. When she dropped her arm to stare back at Jo, it was with a different demeanor, an indescribable essence that seemed to throb in ripples from her center and out to every corner of the briefing room. Something in Jo pushed back in response, as if her very existence both knew and revolted against the woman.

"How? Snow already converted the world of possibility of the wisher to magical essence." Someone asked from the other side of the table, but Jo could barely hear it, eyes trapped beneath Pan's crippling stare.

She had seen those eyes before. And not just in the Society. But when? Or more importantly, how? Had she unknowingly encountered Pan before joining the Society when the woman-child was clocked into time on a wish?

Jo rubbed her eyes, blinking, and the world clicked back into focus. The stress of it all was getting to her, making her brain do odd things.

"Oh, but there are more worlds of possibility, of a sort." Pan grinned, letting the oppressive waves of her magic finally abate. For the first time in what felt like hours, Jo could breathe. Just in time for Pan to send her an infuriating wink. "Snow requires a wisher's sacrifice. I require a sacrifice of a different sort to convert essence."

Jo opened her mouth to demand more information, but she couldn't seem to find her words, throat tight and body heavy beneath the wave of whatever power Pan had held over the room only seconds ago. Thankfully, Wayne didn't seem to be nearly as affected.

"What the hell does that mean?" he snapped in Jo's stead, completely ignoring the way Eslar reached for his arm, holding him back, though only just. Pan seemed more amused than anything, leaning casually against Snow's chair. When Snow didn't bother to move, Jo felt the distinct feeling that there was no coming back from this.

Whatever happened next, he wouldn't be helping them. Maybe even wasn't allowed to.

Just who was in control here?

Pan rested a hand on Snow's shoulder, perfectly manicured nails drumming another light rhythm against his collarbone. Jo swore she saw red at the uninvited contact. But then, at Pan's words, she saw nothing at all.

"I get to kill one of you."

A second of shock, of incomprehensible void, and then reality snapped back into painful focus. Unfortunately, Jo was a good couple of seconds behind everyone else.

"Snow?" Samson begged weakly as Wayne pushed a chair out of his way so hard it toppled. He didn't even seem willing to barter for information, already spiraling into a confused and panicked rage.

"What in every circle of hell is *that* supposed to mean?" he yelled, slamming a hand down on the table. Jo felt her knees buckle, her body falling heavily back into her chair.

What was going on?

"Wayne, stop." Eslar was obviously out of his depth, eyes frozen on the empty space in front of him, disbelieving. Chiding on autopilot. When Jo finally managed to drag her eyes away from where they'd fallen in anxious devastation into her own lap, it was first to the sight of Nico, silent and gradually shattering at her side. Then secondly, to Pan, her gaze seemingly already waiting to capture Jo's stare.

If Jo didn't know better, it looked like a challenge. Or maybe a dark and eager promise. Either way, the look made Jo feel sick with anger. And fear. It was like she'd known what was coming all along, and willingly stayed on the tracks.

"You've got one day to decide," Pan said, lazy and indifferent as ever, as if her unspoken but obvious amusement had already long since passed. There was no time to process, no time to argue or beg or scream or cry, before she was waving over her shoulder at the room at large. "Let me know what you lovely lot come up with."

Just as quickly as she'd doomed one of them to death, she vanished back into the halls of the mansion.

33. FAVORITISM

"**T**HIS IS NOT happening."

Jo wasn't entirely sure if she said the words very softly, or thought them very loudly. Either way, in the commotion of the room, they were lost.

"Get back here you rainbow haired bi—"

"Wayne, stop." Eslar all but shouted, lunging for the man. "There's an explanation here, I'm sure."

"What possible explanation can there be?" Wayne roared in reply. "She didn't seem to me like she was just having a good ol' joshin' at our expense." His voice had gone thick with his usual accent, but different. . . rougher. The airs he usually put on had vanished into something more serious, and now it had come full circle into an accent that was far more authentic, a tonal quality that was more a reversion back to his roots than an homage to them.

"Kill one of our own?" Takako's face alternated between composed, confused, and about to tear someone apart. "What is the meaning of this, *leader*?" The way she spat out the moniker might as well have been an insult or a challenge. Probably both.

"It's my fault," Nico sobbed, but Jo was the only one who heard.

"What do we do?" Samson's small voice asked from opposite the table.

Eventually, in the whirlwind of everyone else's slow and steady breakdowns, Jo found her feet again, still clutching Nico's hand. "Snow!" She waited until his head jerked in her direction at the sudden shout of his name. "*Say something.*"

It was the verbal slap he needed. The man blinked, stunned, and then swallowed. His mouth hardened into a line and his eyes gained clarity. As Snow stood, assuming control of the now-quiet room, Jo sat.

"Pan—" He paused, clearing his throat before continuing. "Is not lying to you."

"You're going to let her kill one of us?" Takako asked, void of emotion.

"All this time. Were we just sheep awaiting slaughter?" Wayne snapped.

"You know that's not the case," Eslar replied, still clearly giving Snow the benefit of the doubt.

"Do I? What do we really know?" Wayne pushed his chair from the table, folding his arms as if to keep him from lunging at the elf. "What do *you* know? You seem awfully cool. Have you been keeping this from us to?"

"Eslar didn't know anything," Samson interjected.

"Of course you'd say that, you always take his side," Wayne sneered; Samson sunk in on himself.

"Wayne, stop," Jo chided. Wayne was about to object, but one look at Jo's face had him closing his mouth and looking away.

"She's right, there is no other option at this point. The Severity of Exchange is too wide." Snow struggled to keep some semblance of control over the situation.

"Surely, there's another way to convert the magic?" Eslar asked, pleaded. "Why not a ritual, like Springtide, or—"

"All relics were lost with the Age of Magic, you know that as well as I," Snow said sadly.

"Or, I have an idea." Jo could feel the venom of her own words dripping in sickly tendrils down her throat "How about we just say 'Screw it we tried'?" She looked around the room, registering the surprise that appeared on every face, and felt only overwhelming frustration. Really, how had they not thought about this before? "We put forward a good effort, we did all we could. What's our wish success rate until now? One hundred percent? Who's going to come after us for failure, anyway? We exist outside of time and space."

"But—" Takako began to say.

"I'm sorry." Jo knew exactly where the Japanese woman's mind was. "Really, I am. And we can try to just get your family to safety. That should be do-able. We don't have enough time to meet the parameters of the wish—to save *everyone*. But saving at least them shouldn't be a problem."

"You'd really condemn all those people to die?" Eslar asked. Jo wasn't sure if he sounded surprised or impressed.

Either way, she answered him levelly and honestly. "Yes." Jo shook her head, cursing under her breath. "Look, I'm not pleased about this. I'm not suggesting this lightly. But isn't this what you taught me from the first wish, that we can't save everyone? Haven't you all watched thousands of people die horrible deaths? Why is this any different? Good, evil, failure, or triumph, the world keeps on turning."

"We can't," Snow stopped her before a seed of hope could even be planted.

"Why?" Jo challenged.

"Because if we fail to grant a wish, we all die."

Stillness across the table. A collective inhale. Than an almost unanimous, "What?"

"The Society exists because of the wishes we grant." Snow placed his hands on the table as if inspecting it for the first time. "I destroy worlds of possibility to fulfill wishes and, in doing so, some of that energy goes to continuing to keep this pocket of existence outside of time. Without the energy and magic of the wishes we grant, we cannot exist. It is part of what binds us to this place—our duty. And part of what, in return, binds us. . . to this life itself." The sound of Snow's voice cracking on the last words had Jo's heart stuttering, tipping to the floor, shattering. Even when Snow lifted his head, a mask of faux composure back on his face, she couldn't unhear it as he tried to explain further.

"Every time we grant a wish, every time the world

is redesigned, I am able to siphon a little from the world of possibility that I destroy and we are gifted enough magic in return to sustain ourselves. But my capabilities on channeling that destructive power aren't perfect, and we can sustain only for a little while longer. This magic, the magic that keeps us alive, it needs constant replenishment. So if we stop granting wishes, or if we fail to grant an accepted wish within the allotted time frame, that magic runs out. I don't have the power to break the cycle, even if I wanted to."

Snow's mask crumbled then, not enough to catch everyone else's attention, but enough that Jo could feel the weight of his pain like a dagger through her own heart.

"The magic runs out, we all die."

Jo sank into her chair, his words circling around her head like so many taunting birds. It was truly a rock and a hard place. No way out. She couldn't breathe.

So instead, she distracted herself by looking around the room; surely, the rest of them had known this. But everyone's faces displayed matching looks of shock and horror, even Eslar's. How had no one known this before? What other fundamental secrets to their existence had been kept from them?

"So that's it, then," Wayne murmured bitterly. "One of us dies to grant the wish, or we all die."

Silence was his only reply. Jo's eyes had fallen to her lap, so she could only assume that Snow had nodded. It didn't matter. There was no simple solution or crafty work-around to get them out of this. It was exactly as Wayne said.

"Now what?" she whispered.

"I'll do it." Takako's voice was clear and strong. Level. Takako knew what she was offering, sacrificing. Probably more than any of them. "It's my country. My family. Let it be me."

"No," Jo's voice quivered and she wished she could be as strong as the other woman in what she was about to do. An icy fear ran through her veins, but still her mouth formed words. "If anyone should—" Her throat tightened and she swallowed twice to clear it. "*Go*. . . it should be me. I was the one who was arrogant from the start. My hack job was shoddy and I was overconfident. I wasted our time and set us on the path that put us in this spot. Plus, I'm the newest here, so—"

"Just stop." Wayne slapped his hand on the table, startling Jo into a silence. "We all know that I'm the king of screw-ups. You said it, doll. You're the new kid, so I'm not letting you take the title."

Nico opened his mouth, no doubt about to offer to martyr himself with the rest of them when Eslar interrupted.

"Snow should decide."

All eyes drifted back toward their leader. To his credit, Snow did not shake or waver. He met their attention with rigid posture and the same careful regard that he always had at the head of the table. It was as if every ounce of tension he had ever carried himself with was in preparation for this moment.

"So be it, then," Snow said softly. "I will decide within the day."

Jo pressed her eyes closed. It was an impossible

decision for him to make. They were clearly all willing to make the ultimate sacrifice for the sake of their team. How would he choose?

The sensation of Nico's hand finally uncurling from hers barely registered, and despite Jo's underlying guilt, evoked no response in her. She couldn't muster the strength to comfort him when she was beginning to unravel herself; hopefully, one day, he'd be able to forgive her for it.

"I'm going to the recreation room. . . Maybe I can still do something," he said hopelessly.

No one stopped him. Not even Jo. Her mind was too far from that room to think of anything other than the phantom fingers that ghosted over her cheeks, as if wiping away rogue tears that had yet to fall.

It would not be her.

It was a horrifying truth, and one Jo knew deep in her bones. She could feel Snow's mouth on hers, their hungry kisses, his promises to protect her. If it was left to him, right or wrong, deserved or not, Snow would not choose her to die.

34. SNOW'S CHOICE

A S JO SAT, staring at nothing, Takako's measured steps blazed a trail for the rest of them. Samson and Eslar left together. At the edge of Jo's hearing, she could make out softly spoken words between them, diminishing like a trembling note until nothing more could be heard.

A palm on her shoulder startled her back to reality. Wayne hovered, looking down with heartbreaking sadness. He opened his mouth, but only a sigh escaped. What more was there to say? What could be said?

They were all waiting for the verdict of their fate.

He left as well, head bowed, exposing the nape of his neck for the guillotine of Snow's decision that hung invisible over them all. Jo looked at the chairs, ears buzzing. Her eyes drifted toward the Door and the instinct to run in the opposite direction, go as far as she could anywhere else in the world, had her standing.

She fantasized over the idea of opening the Door for the last time, finding the pin code that would lead to their freedom.

Her hand pressed against the cool steel, dropping to the pin pad. It hovered, quivering like a hummingbird in suspension.

With an animalistic noise of anger she punched her hand right into the steel. The skin over her knuckles split instantly and her bones vibrated into her jaw. Jo hovered, panting, leaving crimson streaks as she slumped away.

It was useless. There was nowhere she could run. She existed nowhere else. She and everyone else in the Society were chained to their mission. Perhaps it would be better to take the out of death.

Jo shook her head violently and turned away from the door.

No.

She might dream of escape. She might be the sort to nest under covers until frustration and pain subsided. She might let anger get the better of logic at times. But she would not run in that way—never in that way.

Alone, Jo made her solemn march towards the Four-Way. *Snow*. She had to tell him before his thoughts got too far. She had to make sure that his decision, whatever it was, was not influenced in any way by *them*, whatever they were. If she was chosen or spared, it had to be because of more than their affections.

Voices slowed her steps halfway between the stairs and recreation rooms: Nico's honeyed tones and Snow's icy words. Jo slowed to a stop. Vaguely, she remembered Nico leaving the briefing room while muttering about the painting, though it seemed like a far-away dream now.

Jo didn't know why she crept; she had nothing to hide from these men. She had no anger for Nico, and whatever frustrations she held toward Snow for his secrets would keep. There would be a time and place to fight for answers. But the eve of an impossible decision was neither.

Undetected, Jo shifted along the wall, leaning a few feet from the door, close enough to hear the quiet words within.

"It must be someone," Nico said tiredly. She could envision the man she'd watched work the night before, eyes grown distant and sad by the weight of the world. "Let it be me."

"Your magic—"

"Is far more limited than the rest of them."

Jo would disagree with Nico here, but she kept her mouth shut for the sake of listening to the rest of the conversation. Expectedly, Snow spoke for her. "Your magic. . . is critical. Changing the hearts and minds of people is something not easily accomplished."

"And is useless if it doesn't work every time." Jo's heart ached at the sorrow in his words. The man's guilt was apparent. "I'm tired, Snow. I've been at this a long time, surely you understand."

Silence.

"I didn't quite understand until I had her here. She sat there, in that stool, just as my Julia had." Jo's heart clenched, unprepared for Nico's mention of her. It felt wrong somehow, listening to his words while knowing full well he was unaware of her audience. Still, she stayed, transfixed and curious. "My muse is gone, and her legacy is beginning to wane. Every time I return to her place of rest, I see it a little more weathered, her expression a little further worn away. With it, my inspiration, my will. . . and my magic itself."

Jo leaned back, looking up at the ceiling. To love someone so much that your very essence, your magic, was tied to them. She glanced back toward the door, imagining Snow within. Would she, they, someday be so entwined? For all it sounded thrilling, it was also a terrifying notion, and one that seemed almost impossible to envision.

"Your magic is lessened?" Snow asked, his voice bringing her back to the present. It was Nico's, however, that kept her there.

"I have no other explanation for my failure. It was as if everything I had painted cracked under the weight of the Prime Minister's will."

"Lack of time?" Snow suggested, seemingly reaching. The iciness of his voice had lifted some, as if the warmth of Nico's words had melted it.

Another silence left Jo wondering what body cues Nico was offering. A nod? A shrug? She inched closer to the door. If she couldn't see them, she didn't want to miss a single word.

"You're sure?" Snow asked, finally, and Jo's pulse picked up.

"I am," Nico said with conviction. "I owe it to them, for my failure."

"The failure belongs to the team, not one individual."
Snow's egalitarianism should've been heartwarming,
but Jo just found her heart in knots. The failure was
the team's, but one person must bear the consequences
alone. Surely some cruel god was sitting and cackling
at their fate. How else were they meant to explain such
undeserved tragedy?

Nico laughed softly. "Accept this, will you? As a
professional favor, if nothing else. We've had a good
run."

"We have." A genuine sorrow, the ache of it
seemingly splintering his composure, finally leached
into Snow's words. Jo felt a similar ache blooming
across her chest, spiraling like sticky tendrils down
into her heart.

"There is someone waiting for me in heaven, you
know." Nico's claim was honest and pure, a belief there
that Jo had neither expected, nor could even begin to
understand. In any other situation, Jo was certain it
would have been comforting. "I have been away from
her for far too long. . . and while she may not recognize
me, I will have much to tell her. Surely, you must know
how I feel." There was an agonizingly long silence. "I
knew you would."

What had she missed? What non-verbal exchange
had just happened? Jo's heart could still somehow
flutter, even among knots.

"Very well." As if she could block out the
condemnation of Snow's words, Jo pressed her eyes
closed, desperately biting back a sob. If she thought
she felt guilty listening in on this conversation before,

it was infinitesimal to how deeply she regretted it now. She did not want to hear what could be Nico's final moments; it didn't seem fair. "It shall be you."

"I have one request," Nico added hastily.

"Yes?"

"I have a time I want it to be done."

Another delay, long enough for Snow to comprehend something Jo could not, judging from his tone. "Of course."

Despite herself, tears broke through Jo's emotional dam and streamed down her face. It wasn't fair. None of it was. She wanted to take action, she wanted to do something. But what could be done at a moment like this? She knew too little of magic to hack a solution for the very fabric of reality that surrounded the Society. If anyone did, it was Snow. And something in Jo assured her that if there was a way for him to redesign their fate, he would. He'd said it himself: he didn't have the power to do so. The pain in his voice proved the truth of it.

Which meant he was a prisoner, just like the rest of them. A chess piece in a greater game. A powerful piece, certainly, but a piece nonetheless. Jo turned her head toward the black door adjacent to Snow's.

There was one other person seemingly as old as the Society itself and with a magic as terrifying as Snow's.

Even as her eyes blurred with fresh tears, Jo stared the door down as if willing it to give up its occupant's secrets. Pan, their executioner. If there was one person who would see their circumstance as a game, it would be *her*.

35. UNTIL THE END

J O'S EYES WERE still pinned on the ominous black door when the recreation room Nico had taken residence in finally opened wide. She turned towards the sound on reflex, the motion causing unfallen tears to give way, her already wet cheeks glistening with new streaks of pain and sadness.

It wasn't Nico who greeted her startled attention, though she shouldn't have expected him to be willing to leave the sanctity of his room so soon after being sentenced. Instead it was Snow, his own eyes red-rimmed and holding far more exhaustion than she'd ever seen in a person.

When he captured her gaze, it was beyond Jo's capabilities to hold back her fresh wave of tears. She felt whipped about in a hurricane of her own emotions, torn apart by the need to scream and the need to beg. She wanted Snow to hold her, to comfort her, but she also didn't want to be comforted. She didn't deserve it, not when Nico was the one damned by the brutal reality of sacrifice. She wanted Snow to fix this, to tell her he was mistaken and that everything would be okay. She wanted him to promise her that Nico would live, that they *all* would live. But she also knew he wouldn't, was painfully aware that he *couldn't*. So she also wanted him to say nothing at all.

She wanted to go back to before they'd failed, when the promise of success had led Jo to Snow's room, to his bed, reveling not in physical intimacy, but an intimacy nonetheless. She wanted to feel his closeness, his touch, and not have it tainted by the fear of what was to come. Jo knew that if Snow couldn't save Nico's life, there was no way he had enough magic to turn back time (at least not for them; for a wish, maybe, but not for them), but Jo couldn't help silently praying for a miracle regardless.

It seemed greedy to wish for more time when she'd been given an endless supply of it. But Nico's was being unexpectedly cut short, which made the Society feel less like the blessing of eternity and more like the eventuality of a slaughterhouse.

In the end, Snow chose silence, his eyes the only thing betraying his own swirling typhoon of barely-contained emotions. She could see him hurting, could practically feel it emanating off of him in waves of self-loathing. It was impossible to miss; Snow wanted to be the executioner no more than any of them wanted to bear witness to the execution.

But it wouldn't be Snow in the end, would it? He'd

been forced to choose the head that would fall in the basket, but it was Pan who'd be swinging the ax.

Amid the ever-present grief, Jo felt a spike of pure rage dig deep into the center of her chest, the tears filling her eyes almost hot with anger. It was an anger that must have shown on her face, because Snow's own expression shifted at the sight. She caught a brief glimpse of pity, of immeasurable heartache, and then, once again, he schooled his features back into place, all traces of that previous openness gone.

The change in demeanor caught Jo off guard, her rage snuffed out. But before she could put any of her own emotions into words, Snow walked past her, leaving her alone with her silent tears in front of Nico's doorway.

For a brief moment, Jo considered following him, but there was nothing she could think to say, no amount of comfort she felt able to give. Not to Snow at least. But when Jo glanced at the still slightly cracked door of Nico's room, she realized where her comfort might still be of use.

It was probably selfish, forcing herself into Nico's personal space when he might wish to spend his last hours alone, but Jo needed his presence as much as she hoped he might need hers. Even if it meant overstepping, she needed to be there for him—needed as much time left with him as he was willing to give.

When Jo let herself in, it was to find Nico standing by the window, staring out at the impossible view of a Florence sunset. The buttery glow painted Nico's silhouette in hues of orange and pink, the last rays of the sun catching at his cheeks in a telling shimmer. That was all it took, the sight of Nico's own tears causing a new wave of grief to settle into Jo's bones. She tried to swallow down the lump in her throat, but a soft sob still escaped.

Nico turned to look at her then, a flash of surprise giving way to a soft smile. The crinkle at the corner of his eyes caused another tear to fall, and Jo was wrapping the man up in an embrace before she even registered the decision to do so. Nico settled into her arms easily, pulling her close with his own wordless thanks. It felt like the comfort she'd been needing; even though Nico was the one knocking on death's door, he was still the one doing the comforting. Jo would have laughed if the very thought hadn't filled her chest with another blossom of devastation.

There was no way of knowing how long they simply held each other, sometimes crying and sometimes just finding comfort in each other's silent presence. Eventually, Nico pulled away, raising both hands to gently cup Jo's face as his thumbs wiped away the remnants of tears. He leaned in, chastely kissing one cheek, then the other, before letting his hands fall.

"You know." It wasn't a question, and Jo wondered how long he'd been aware of her presence lurking outside the door.

"I do." She wiped her nose with the back of her hand, stifling a loud sniffle.

"It has been an honor working alongside you, Josephina Espinosa," he said, grabbing her hand and giving it a squeeze. "And it has been nothing short of a blessing to get to know you." Nico's smile held every ounce of the sunshine she'd come to expect of the man, even if his eyes were mostly clouded.

"I'll stay with you," she found herself saying, knowing instantly that the words were right. "Until the end, to the very last minute." For a breath, Nico simply held her gaze, but then the clouds in his eyes parted some, his face filling with matching warmth. When he hugged her once more, it was as true and heartfelt a "thank you" as she'd ever received.

She watched him paint for hours, curled up in a blanket on the stool by the fireplace. It was another portrait of his Julia, Jo realized, around the time her eyelids began to get heavy. She watched him carefully shade in the curves of her face, add highlights to the flowing waves of her hair.

It was sometime between the streaks of yellow being added to the background and Nico signing his name that a deep and dreamless sleep overtook Jo.

35. ONE-SEVENTEEN A.M.

J O BLINKED, DROWSY. She'd fallen asleep. When was the last time that had happened?

Everything was hazy as her mind began to work once more. This didn't feel like waking, it felt like suddenly *existing* again.

The beginning of the wish—that was the last time she'd actually slept since becoming a full member of the Society. She'd been woken the night Snow had come to her after he'd rewound time.

Jo searched her memories further, willing her mind to work, slotting things back into place. The details of the past day were suspended just out of her reach like the tiny motes of dust drifting past Nico's easel. Jo blinked, her eyes dry and aching; she'd shed more tears in the last few days than she ever remembered shedding in her life. The room was filled with a serene stillness—a stillness that came from being the only

321

breathing presence within.

With the stone of the wall now more warmed from her back than the smoldering remnants of the fire, Jo rubbed at her eyes and straightened. She looked around the room. Everything was as she remembered—the cluttered work table, the easel perched with the (now mostly finished) painting of Julia, the other various shelves and half-finished canvases. Everything was in its place.

Everything but the painter himself.

Jo stood with a stretch and a yawn. Everything seemed like a distant dream.

No. It all came rushing back, right as she was about to leave. Something struck her as odd: this wasn't a distant dream she could shrug off alongside the shroud of sleep, but a vivid waking nightmare that she couldn't escape even if she tried.

At the foot of the easel, surrounded by splotches of dried paint, Nico's favored brush rested. She tilted her head, looking at the object in confusion; something about it rankled her so, but she couldn't seem to pinpoint what it might be. The hair on her neck stood on edge. She stared at that mauve splotch on the floor where the paintbrush had landed; there was a splatter, and a streak where the brush had rolled before coming to its final resting place.

Final resting place.

Jo spun in place. "Nico?" she called out to the empty room, as if he would step out of thin air and surprise her. "Nico?" Her voice was a little more strained when he didn't.

She took several long steps into the hallway; it was completely empty in the early dawn. "Nico?" she called again. There was still silence, still a creeping sense of foreboding waiting to swallow her up. She wouldn't let it; she'd find him before it could.

He's gone to his room, she told herself, lied to herself. That was it. He'd needed. . . a new tube of paint, or canvas, or something. He'd gotten tired. He'd worked hard enough to want somewhere to rest his weary hands, and in all his infinite manners he hadn't wanted to disturb her.

Story after story ran through her mind, every possible reason concocted for where the painter might be.

Jo paused at the Four-Way, looking down the hallway to the common area and listening. There was no sound, yet her feet carried her in that direction anyway. In a surreal daze, Jo stopped at the entryway. It appeared empty, until she saw a foot hanging over the edge of the couch.

Half-jumping, half-running, Jo dashed over to the couch, her hands on the back, leaning over, and— her heart sank. Samson lay curled up, one of Eslar's elegantly designed, elvish blankets draped over him. His red-orange hair frizzed from his tight braids and matted where it was free. Even in sleep, he looked exhausted.

Jo reached for his shoulder, shaking it some. "Samson?"

The man woke with a start. "Wh-what?" He practically fell off the couch, shrinking away from the contact, until the sleep lifted from his eyes, his mind, and vanished. "Oh, I must have fallen asleep. How odd. I think the last time that happened was. . . But good morning, Jo."

"Have you seen Nico?" She didn't have time to feel guilty for the way she'd woken the man. Not when there was something else far more pressing, something that demanded all of her attention.

"Nico?" Samson squinted in confusion. "He's with you, right?"

That wasn't the answer Jo was looking for. She looked around the room, as if something could've changed without her noticing, wishing something had. It was that same foreboding stillness from the moment she'd first woken. Now, the hair on her arms was on-end as well.

"What's going on, Jo?" Samson asked.

"Nico?" she called, rushing out onto the wide patio, hoping he'd be waiting for her in their usual chairs, tablet in hand. She sprinted around, as if he could be hiding behind the outdoor grill or randomly swimming beneath the surface of the pool.

"Jo?" Samson was standing now. "What's happening, Jo?"

She ignored him. Even on her own, Jo could barely come to terms with the truth in front of her; there was no way she could break it down for someone else, too.

"He must be in his room," Jo mumbled to no one, her eyes glued to the bloody sunrise. "His room."

On the last word, she turned and began to run; her heart was already racing before she took her first step.

It was already in her throat, suffocating her.

Jo tripped, scrambling up the stairs to the hallway. How long had it been since she'd come back here? Everything blurred together into an agonizing slurry, sloshing between her ears where her brain once used to be.

"Are you all right?" Samson held out a hand, offering it to her.

She stared at the step before her; had she not caught herself, she would have split her skull open on it. The knuckles on the back of her hand were still bloody from punching the Door, and the way her knees ached suggested that it may not be the only split skin she was presently sporting.

"We have to get to his room," she panted. Her voice sounded alien even to her own ears, rough and determined but also bordering on hysterical. "We have to get to his room, Samson."

Ignoring the outstretched hand, Jo continued on. The hallway was a million miles long at the start, but only a few short steps at the end. They stopped before Nico's door.

They stopped before what *had been* Nico's door.

Jo raised a hand to the wood, running it over where his nameplate had been. The surface was smooth, unblemished. There was no scarring from where Nico's painted bird had been scrubbed away. There was no discoloration from where the man's name had been protecting the wood underneath for hundreds of years. It was perfect, pristine—a blank slate.

There was nothing, as if the man who'd occupied

the space had never even existed.

In a disconnected sort of awareness, Jo heard Samson's soft murmur of denial. A denial that stretched and contorted, cracked inch by inch until it shattered into equal parts disbelief, gnawing fear, and undeniable pain.

His wail barely registered though. It was a sort of guttural cry, an agony that she'd never heard the likes of in any of her lives, but still, it came from far, far away. Her hand rested on the door handle.

Open it, a voice goaded, and she listened; she had to see what was inside. She had to see it or it wouldn't be real.

"What's going on?" Wayne's voice appeared from the end of the hall. Another door opened, another voice.

But the only thing Jo saw was the handle turning. The only thing she heard was the smooth whisper of well-greased metal on metal as the latch released. The hinges sighed softly and she pulled open the door.

Nothing.

It was a blank slate: white walls, white floor, a white roof that seemed to glow with its own unnatural light. She dared to take a step into that void, as if she'd somehow be able to find Nico and retrieve him from it.

But there was nothing there. The warm light of Florence, the messy, clean look—everything that had been the heart of the artist's studio had vanished.

"What the hell?" She heard Wayne curse, the words almost managing to bring her out of the haze of her own encroaching breakdown. "I actually fell asleep for an hour and. . ."

"What is this?" Takako was behind her now too. "I was asleep too."

"Let me through—" Eslar's voice stopped short.

With renewed desperation, Jo turned, looking at the elf. "What does it mean?" Her voice was barely a quivering whisper.

"I—" Eslar blinked furiously, though not from the light of the void. She'd never seen so much emotion on his face, yet she couldn't find it in herself to care.

"What does it mean?" she repeated. "You're the oldest. You've been here the longest. You know magic the best, don't you?"

Eslar looked over her head, transfixed by the nothingness. The look of fear and heartache creeping into his eyes left Jo mentally reaching out for a lifesaver no one had thrown. Still, she treaded water, refused to drown. Surely he had answers, surely *somebody* had answers.

"What does it mean?" she demanded, grabbing the elf's shoulders and shaking him back to reality. "Eslar, what does it—"

"He's gone!" The man wrenched himself from her grasp. A long moment passed, Eslar reaching out towards Nico's door frame with shaking hands, as if he needed it to hold himself up. At first, long, dark fingers barely touched it, but then he curled in on himself, dark green fingernails scratching harsh lines into the wood. "He's. . . He's really gone."

No one seemed able to say anything for a while. They all stood paralyzed in that ominous glow of nothingness, a glow that suddenly seemed to cast new light on the hopelessness of their situation.

And yet.

"No, he can't be." Jo refused to believe it. It seemed too inconceivably horrible to fathom. "He can't be, because, because the recreation room still had his watch on the shelf." They all stared as if she'd spoken in a language that no magic could enable them to understand. It was the tether she'd been looking for, something she could cling to with a desperation she'd never felt in her life. Not even when she'd sacrificed herself for the sake of Yuusuke. "I'll show you. I'll show you!"

In an all-out sprint, she was flying across the mansion once more. There were hurried footfalls behind her, as hasty as hers, but Jo didn't look to see who was following. She leapt down the stairs, clearing half, stumbling the rest, before scrambling up the other set. Jo didn't trip this time.

"There it is!" she shouted, finally looking over her shoulder. She could hear the unnatural crack to her voice, a pitch so many decibels away from calm that it was almost pathetic. But still, she kept her arm steady. Still, she pointed to the rec room shelf. "See, I told you." Everyone was in tow. "His watch is still here." Jo flung wide the door. It was the same studio she remembered waking up in. Even with his actual room wiped clean, surely this meant something. Surely he was still here. *Somewhere.* "Nico!" she called.

The rest of them caught up, Wayne huffing and puffing. Eslar hardly seemed winded, so it was the elf who first inspected the watch. Jo made to take a desperate step into the room, but what he said next froze her stride.

"It's broken," he whispered.

Everyone stilled, hanging on his next words, but there were none. There was nothing more to be said, only to be inspected.

Jo backpedaled, stepped over to the shelf. Sure enough, the watch was there, but its glass front was fractured. The second-hand no longer moved; the clock face that counted his time was frozen at 1:17, matching the time that had always been mirrored on the second dial.

"Julia," Samson whispered, his understanding full of aching intimacy. They'd spent hundreds of years together, after all.

1:17, the time Julia had died. It made so much sense now, gave meaning to Nico's request. He'd asked Snow for a specific time, wished for a last connection to his love, and someone had obliged.

"He's really, g-gone, isn't he?" Samson forced through tears. No one seemed willing to capture anyone else's gaze; everyone kept their eyes pinned on the last remaining fragments of the man they'd all come to care for.

No one could answer, and that was answer enough.

Takako leaned against the far wall, unwilling to touch anyone. Eslar wrapped an arm around Samson, pulling him close. Wayne just stared at the watch, lips parted, and eyes glossy. The hurt in everyone's expressions was obvious; the exhaustion even more so. The pain Jo felt slowly began to molt into hatred.

"It's her fault," Jo whispered.

In her periphery, Jo could see Eslar shake his head. "It's all of our faults, we didn't close the Severity of—"

"Don't give me that!" The words were out before she could stop them. Jo didn't want to scream at Eslar, but she also didn't want Nico to be dead. She wanted revenge but she also wanted to curl up into a ball and pretend none of this had happened. Everything felt beyond her control, and she couldn't stand it. "Don't you even dare give me that! We didn't know."

"If we'd known, would that have changed anything?" Eslar shouted back. Samson cringed in his arms.

Jo opened her mouth and closed it, angry. She searched for facts, for arguments, digging deep for some explanation for all this, but in the end could do no more than fold her arms over her chest and try to stop the shaking. They'd done all they could; that was the hardest part. They'd done all they could and now, this.

"She could've let us say goodbye, at least," Wayne whispered, staring into the room.

It has been an honor working alongside you, Josephina Espinosa.

Jo spun in place. That was it. That was the thing causing the creeping dread since the first moment Jo had woken.

She hadn't even gotten to say goodbye.

Jo pulled away from the group at once, her fist meeting Pan's door and banging frantically. "I know you're in there," she shouted at the unwavering expanse of black. She heard the rest of her team come up behind her, but she ignored them, slamming wounded knuckles against wood.

"Jo, stop!" Wayne called.

"Open up. Open up and own up to what you did!" Jo banged harder. Her voice was beginning to waver and crack yet again. The anger was threatening to give way to the bottomless sadness that had hollowed out the cavity of her chest. "How could you? How *could* you? You knew it was coming, didn't you?"

The white door at Jo's right opened suddenly; Snow stood in its frame. He looked no better than the rest of them. A long shirt hung rumpled from his shoulders, falling over tight-fitting trousers.

"What's going on?" His voice echoed through the hall with an air of authority. Jo ignored that too.

"We were just going back," Eslar began to say. But Jo cut him off before any other weak explanation could be given. She wasn't going to sweep this under the rug.

"We want answers!"

Snow's gaze turned to her.

"We want answers from *her*." Jo punctuated the statement with a pound on Pan's door. She turned towards Snow, seething, snarling. "But she's too much of a damned coward to give us any."

"That's enough, Jo," Snow scolded, and Jo couldn't help but bristle.

"Don't say that!" she screamed back. "Don't act like you're not hurting at the fact that one of us was murdered under your roof, under your care. I see it Snow, I see it!"

She called him out with a certainty she hadn't possessed until that moment. Because, until then, she hadn't quite grasped it. But as their "leader" stood there, helpless and hurting, he was no better than the rest of them. Jo turned back to the door.

"Open up and face us, you coward! Face your actions!" Jo screamed at nothing, her voice echoing sharply down the hall.

"Jo, please. That's enough," Wayne tried to console, taking a step forward.

"I don't want to hear it from you," she lashed out. If no one would help her, then everyone was her enemy.

"Jo, let's—" Takako didn't get to finish her statement.

Jo's stomach shot into her pelvis at the brief experience of weightlessness, returning when a shoulder pressed unexpectedly into her gut. Snow's arms wrapped around her as he carried her, over his shoulder, to his room; the familiar smell of cloves threatened to soothe her anger just enough that the sorrow would win.

She couldn't have that—wouldn't be able to handle that. She'd break.

"Don't you dare, Snow!" Jo cried out instead. "I deserve vindication, an explanation, *something*. She didn't even let us say goodbye, Snow. She didn't—she didn't even let us say goodbye!"

Jo could feel the rage slowly unraveling beneath the rough demands of her voice, the dam of her own resolve slowly crumbling to dust. She could see the rest of her team watching her be carried away, their eyes wet, their teeth gritted, their fists clenched in anger. But no words were spoken in retaliation. Their lack of fight eroded hers.

She could feel her cries shredding themselves beneath the sharp claws of unrelenting devastation, the pounding of her fists against Snow's back quickly losing strength and purpose as her tears regained their own.

The slamming of Snow's door punctuated her sobs, cutting their echo short to the remaining four members of the Society.

Pan's door never budged.

36. GOODBYE

JO DIDN'T KNOW how long she cried, curled up in Snow's bed like a child. It could have been hours, could have been days, but it didn't matter. Once the dam had been broken, there was no stopping the tears from flowing even if she tried.

And what use was there in trying?

She had vague recollections of Snow trying to talk to her, of his hand on her back and his lips against her temple, of soft attempts at comfort, reassurances that at least the wish had been granted and they were safe, even softer admittances of understanding. But she could find none of her own sympathies, every verbal grasp of Snow's falling on deaf and unaccepting ears.

She wasn't ready to hear any of it, not when it all ended with the same brutal and unforgivable truth.

Nico was gone. Pan had taken him from them, and he wasn't coming back.

She thought, during one of the times she'd cried herself into a daze, in and out of sleep with her chest aching and eyes sore (sleep was something Jo never wanted to do again), that Snow tried to apologize. But even with anger boiling her blood, and distress gripping tight at her heart, she couldn't find it in her heart to blame him. Not when he'd looked at her with such shame, seemingly sharing every ounce of their heartache.

No. This wasn't about forgiving Snow; a pawn needed no forgiving for the whims of his queen. This was about mourning Nico, about maybe one day soon, avenging him.

So it was after an indistinguishable amount of time that Jo sat herself up, leaning into Snow's touch when he instantly responded to her presence. She wasn't sure how long he'd been waiting at her side, coming and going to check on her, but she was eternally grateful. Even if she couldn't find it in herself to say so.

"She did this," Jo muttered first in blatant repetition, clutching tight to Snow's arms as he wrapped them around her waist and held her close to his chest. It almost made her want to start crying all over again, but she did her best to hold herself back.

"I know," he said, whispering the agreement into her neck. Jo swallowed back the whimper of renewed regret that the words threatened to pull from the center of her chest. Instead, she distracted herself with the feel of his forehead pressing firm into the juncture of her shoulder.

Without meaning to, Jo exhaled a shaky, "It's not

fair." When Snow said nothing in reply, Jo turned herself as best she could into his embrace and hugged him closer. "It's okay," she said once she could feel her lips pressed loosely against the shell of his ear. She felt him shiver, heard him choke back the first broken sob of his own. "I know it's not your fault."

Snow stiffened in her arms, obviously surprised, but then settled, hugging her like he might fall apart without her body there to keep him together. He stayed silent, but somehow Jo could tell he was grateful; it was clear in the huff of his breaths against her skin and the dig of his fingers into her waist.

Eventually, no matter how much she wanted to ride out the rest of her mourning in his grasp, she couldn't deny the immense desire she had to get back to her team. It didn't seem right that she got comfort from their leader when everyone else was forced to handle their grief on their on.

But as much as she wanted to be strong, she was only human.

"Will you come with me?" she heard herself ask, surprised internally at her own forwardness. She did her best to school her expression into something more confident than she felt. The words, however, were more hopeful and real than any she ever remembered speaking. "I don't know if I can go back out there alone."

Another brief pause, another quiet breath against her neck, and then—

"Whatever you need."

It took a while for Jo to work up the courage.

Sitting up and voicing her concerns was one thing, but actually pulling herself away from the safety of Snow's bed was another. Eventually, however, she managed to drag herself back out into the hall, Snow not far behind.

The group was all there once more, making Jo's mind whirl with just how much time she'd spent grieving. At first, no one seemed to notice her approach, too consumed by whatever it was they were doing. Which was all well and good, considering Jo had no clue what to do or say to them yet. But the closer she got, the quicker she realized she couldn't stay silent on the matter.

"Wait," Jo spoke up the moment she was within earshot. Eslar had one hand on Nico's watch, pulling futily, and Wayne was digging the edge of his nickel beneath it and the shelf. "Wait!"

Everyone turned in her direction, Takako and Samson startling at her sudden presence as Eslar and Wayne backed away from the recreation room shelf on reflex. They couldn't touch another's watch; no amount of physical force could remove it from its last spot.

And maybe no force ever should.

"Leave it," Jo said, pushing her way through the group until she could place a hand on Nico's watch, looking first at the broken clock face and then at each of them in turn. "Just leave it."

At first, no one seemed to know how to respond, but eventually, Eslar caved, taking a step towards the shelf. "Jo, we need to—"

"No!" She shouted, cringing at the sound of her own voice, especially when Eslar recoiled at the unexpected volume. She felt her grip on the stationary timepiece tighten, fresh tears threatening to spill as she closed her eyes. How was it possible she had any tears left to cry? "This. . ." She swallowed, willing herself to straighten before she said anything further. It was important; this was something she needed to do. Not just for Nico, but for all of them.

"This is all we have left of him," she eventually found the strength to say. Some part of her was right back in the graveyard in Florence. That courtyard, seemingly forgotten by all but one. Nico had been its lone mourner for years; now, he needed someone to mourn him. "We can't just erase that too. We can't. . . We can't just—"

Jo choked on the rest of the phrase, trying desperately to swallow the lump in her throat.

"A memorial." Takako put into words what she was trying to say, the girl walking up to Jo's side and placing a hand over hers. When Jo looked over at her, hoping her face showed every ounce of gratitude she felt, Takako didn't smile. She did, however, give Jo's hand a squeeze. "He deserves that much."

Jo nodded before pulling her hand away from the shelf. As if sensing her unspoken need, Takako let her fingers slip between Jo's, to hang intertwined at their sides, offering the strength of her presence. Maybe someday, Takako could teach her how to stand so tall.

Jo clutched at Takako with one hand and the edge of her own hoodie with the other. "If we don't do our best to remember Nico, then who will?"

Wayne was the first to respond. Not with words

but with the silent removal of his nickel from the shelf. He clutched it tight in his palm for a second before pocketing it. After that, there seemed to be an unspoken agreement.

One by one, everyone went into the recreation room, slow and silent, as if walking up to a grave. And it was. The only grave Nico would ever receive. It seemed appropriate that the portrait of Julia lay eternally inside the man's proverbial tomb.

Until the bitter end and after, they deserved to be together.

It took Snow's touch, a gentle pressure against her shoulder, for Jo to realize everyone was looking at her. Waiting.

She looked at each member of her team, her family, and offered what she hoped was a look of deep understanding. They were all going to miss Nico; they all recognized that he'd deserved far better. So, with steady steps and steadier hands, Jo walked up to his final painting, a perfect likeness of his Julia, his love. Jo knelt before it and picked up the forgotten paintbrush. Dipping it in an open tube of paint, she drew a small star on the corner of the easel before returning it to its rightful place. And where it would stay.

Jo wanted to tell herself that there was nothing more that they could have done. Perhaps one of them had always been doomed to this fate. But, she was discovering that the actions of so-called "fate" left a bitter aftertaste. It was something she'd never quietly swallow again. She would rip the very notion of destiny to pieces if she must to protect her friends.

Yes, Jo would destroy everything, if that's what it took to free them from the Society itself.

The story continues in. . .

WISH QUARTET BOOK THREE

JOSEPHINA IS UNRAVELING. A new wish is pushing the weary members of the Society to their breaking points. But as Jo's complex relationship with their leader reveals dangerous truths about who she truly is, and was, her priorities quickly change. Now, she seeks to expose the enemy lurking in their midst, but it may already be too late to thwart an ancient goddess bent on stealing Jo's power and destroying everything she loves.

ELISE'S ACKNOWLEDGMENTS

MY EDITOR, REBECCA—I do not think a manuscript will go by where I do not thank you. Your patience, professionalism, and pushing me to always do better is critical to the creation of my stories.

LYNN—Thank you for all of your hard work on this project. I believe so much in this world we're building and have had such a great time building it with you.

ROBERT—I can never seem to find enough words for you, my dear. But I'll keep writing books until I get close.

CAITLIN, MELISA, and MI-MI—Thank you for continuin to work with us on beta reading. Having your eyes on this project early has been so helpful.

AMANDA—You're an absolute gem. Thank you for all your support. I can't wait for the next signing I have in Austin so I can catch a ride with you again.

EMILY, HETAL, LINDA, and MEGAN—When the call went out, you each stepped up to help me re-tool book one and give me new insights on what needed to happen to make book two even better. Thank you for your support and friendship.

THE TOWER GUARD—I can't say enough how much you all help me and shape my work. Your never-ending support is the foundation of my survival as an author. It's dramatic, but I do not think I would be anywhere close to where I am now without having you there as readers, as feedback, and as friends.

DANIELLE—My books would each have the worst synopsis in the world were it not for you. Thank you for always being such a good friend, whether it's professional advice or just rambling away on Twitter.

MOM and DAD—Thank you for your never-ending support and interest in my work. I so appreciate the "CT" and the proofreading around the world. Love you both.

MER—Thanks for helping make my new office, and the home around it, amazing. I'm so much more productive because of it.

LYNN'S ACKNOWLEDGMENTS

ROBERT—For always being there when I need someone to lean on, for playing checkers with me when I feel like running away, and for being totally and completely awesome.

BLAINE—For being so supportive of my ventures in another field, for housing us at our first book signing, and for being the literal best boss a person could ask for.

THE WILLARD'S BEER COMMUNITY—For being the most kind and supportive group of people a debut author could hope to surround herself with. To everyone who showed up at my first signing, to everyone who bought a book, and to everyone who left a review, you have all of my thanks and more.

ELISE—For continuing to put up with my shit.

ABOUT THE AUTHOR

ELISE KOVA has always had a profound love of fantastical worlds. Somehow, she managed to focus on the real world long enough to graduate with a Master's in Business Administration before crawling back under her favorite writing blanket to conceptualize her next magic system. She currently lives in St. Petersburg, Florida, and when she is not writing can be found playing video games, watching anime, or talking with readers on social media.

She invites readers to get first looks, giveaways, and more by subscribing to her newsletter at: http://elisekova.com/subscribe

Visit her on the web at:
http://elisekova.com/
https://twitter.com/EliseKova
https://www.facebook.com/AuthorEliseKova/
https://www.instagram.com/elise.kova/

ABOUT THE AUTHOR

LYNN LARSH considers herself to be a serial hobby-dabbler. She got a bachelors degree in music (which she used for all of four months), studied aerial acrobatics and classical piano for many years, worked briefly as a stunt woman in a Wild West stunt show (it's a long story), and eventually settled down into the bar tending business in St. Petersberg, FL. When she's not acting as a purveyor of fine libations, you can find her diving head first into her newest venture as a New Adult author, or simply writing Voltron fan fiction on Archive of Our Own.

Visit her on the web at: https://www.lynnlarsh.com/

Also from Elise Kova
A young adult, high-fantasy filled with romance and elemental magic.

A library apprentice, a sorcerer prince, and an unbreakable magic bond. . .

The Solaris Empire is one conquest away from uniting the continent, and the rare elemental magic sleeping in seventeen-year-old library apprentice Vhalla Yarl could shift the tides of war.

Vhalla has always been taught to fear the Tower of Sorcerers, a mysterious magic society, and has been happy in her quiet world of books. But after she unknowingly saves the life of one of the most powerful sorcerers of them all--the Crown Prince Aldrik--she finds herself enticed into his world. Now she must decide her future: Embrace her sorcery and leave the life she's known, or eradicate her magic and remain as she's always been. And with powerful forces lurking in the shadows, Vhalla's indecision could cost her more than she ever imagined.

Praise for Elise Kova's AIR AWAKENS

"DEAR BOOK GODS, THANK YOU. THANK YOU FOR THIS MASTERPIECE." – *Rachel E. Carter, USA Today bestselling author of the Black Mage Series*

"Avatar the Last Airbender meets The Grisha Trilogy in Air Awakens." – *RHPL Teen Book Reviews*

". . .THE book for people that love the Throne of Glass series" – *IrisjeXx*

"Phantom of the Opera meets Cinderella in a wonderfully crafted world." – *Michelle Madow, USA Today bestselling author of ELEMENTALS*

Loom with the best person to get him where he wants to go.

He offers her the one thing Ari can't refuse: A wish of her greatest desire, if she brings him to the Alchemists of Loom.

Praise for Elise Kova's THE ALCHEMISTS OF LOOM

"Kova (the Air Awakens series) crafts a fascinating divided world" – *Publishers Weekly*

"Prepare to have your mind blown. THE ALCHEMISTS OF LOOM is the perfect mashup of genres, with a killer heroine, fiery romance, and friendships that run as deep as blood." – *Lindsay Cummings, #1 New York Times bestselling author of ZENITH*

"Reading THE ALCHEMISTS OF LOOM was like curling up with a favorite fantasy classic. Yet what truly transported me was the brilliant twists and layers that make this story totally unique, totally fresh." – *Susan Dennard, New York Times bestselling author of TRUTHWITCH*

Made in the USA
San Bernardino, CA
24 April 2018